Grinning wolfishly, Fang thought he had caught sight of Landry and the horse once; then for certain he heard the metallic crunch of iron on rock. Landry and the girl were approaching. He readied his rifle and aimed. But the chestnut did not appear. Did Landry suspect something? He thought of pumping bullets into the area where the horse waited, but he knew that could prove fatal.

Against his better judgment, he rose and advanced, pushing the branches quietly apart. He paused cautiously. Then he saw the chestnut, riderless. His toothy grin froze. Apprehensive, he looked around expectantly. When he saw no one, he turned his attention to the chestnut. He raised his rifle for the kill.

"Looking for me?" Landry growled. Fang swung around to see the marshal at his backside and slightly below him, and the two black-eyed barrels of the shotgun. The double cannonade echoed and reechoed.

Also by Kenn Sherwood Roe:

MOONBLOOD
DUST DEVIL*

Published by Fawcett Books

DEATHSTALK

Kenn Sherwood Roe

FAWCETT GOLD MEDAL • NEW YORK

A Fawcett Gold Medal Book
Published by Ballantine Books
Copyright © 1993 by Kenn Sherwood Roe

Library of Congress Catalog Card Number: 92-97067

ISBN 0-449-14863-7

Manufactured in the United States of America

First Edition: March 1993

To

daughter, Lorraine, and sons, Kevin & Brian

(1)

The squeal of a fiddle blended with a tinny piano and a wheezy concertina, to flow sadly from the Glacier Palace into the desert night. A steady summer wind gusted from the far mountains, bringing the scent of sage and of dry grass withering in the burned earth. The revelry drifted around wood and brick buildings and down the side streets to the miners' shacks on the east meadow, and on up to the foremen's homes at the foot of the bluff, and west toward the holding pens where white-faced cattle lowed indifferently; the sound worked its way beyond, even to Chinese town, the stone hovels barely perceptible on the horizon. Horses, a few conveyances, and high-booted men raised dust through the crisscross of streets between the saloons and the gambling dens. A number of visitors and locals found entertainment in the several call houses. The girls upstairs in the Glacier were not as select or as experienced as those at Lilli's down the street, who were considered some of the best in the territory. The Glacier girls, however, were younger and less hardened. Mostly they entertained as dance partners, but many were not above giving favors if the price was right.

The whirl of roulette, the clink of glass, the movement, the throaty roar of liquored males continued along the main street as the hours ticked by. Broken Bluffs had the shaky aura of a town past its prime, one that had produced a respectable tonnage in gold and silver, but one that had never

1

been a center of trade nor had ever basked in the light of national or even regional recognition.

In a back room upstairs in the Glacier, a girl turned up an oil lantern, its golden glow flushing upward, distorting her plain features; a mane of auburn hair frizzed about her face and shoulders. She cinched a robe around her ample waist, picked up a washbasin from a small unpainted table, and stepped behind a dressing curtain. She did not speak to or look at the man buttoning his clothes before the dresser mirror. The man, tall and slender, adjusted a vest, then draped a thick shawl up around his jaw and mouth so that only his intense eyes showed from beneath the slouch-brimmed hat pulled low. He watched her in the mirror, his faded eyes burning an inward amber. He saw the woman move behind the curtain, heard her sponge the water and vinegar against her body, intimately cleansing. He saw her head tilted, the red curls parting around the white of neck. His eyes had a faraway, vacant look, absorbing something beyond, hardening; he winced then, his lips trembling. A purple of pain came into the flaming eyes as he stared; he straightened woodenly, pivoted slowly away from the mirrored image and toward her. From his coat pocket he slipped loose a strand of hemp; his slender hands rolled it around his palms and tugged it taut.

"You can leave now," she said firmly without looking back. The man advanced, the rope vibrating between his extended hands. The low light played across the narrow room, across the yellowed sheets, across the tarnished dresser, across the thin of his face; the eyes dilated, frozen, engrossed, but strangely detached. "There is another customer waiting. You've taken more than your time." She shook her head and pushed her coiling hair back over her shoulders, hesitating then, intuitively sensing his closeness. Defensively she spun about, gasped, her eyes going wide; but before her open mouth could emit a cry, his garrote was about her neck, one loop, two loops, the thongs sinking cruelly into the white flesh. She struggled, her short fingers groping at the rope, clawing at his arms.

He left her on the bed, staring lifelessly at the dingy gray ceiling, but not before he ripped her bodice to reveal the sagging breasts, or before he severed the lobe of her left ear with a small knife he kept on a metal ring along his wide belt. He then stretched her on the bed, tucked her feet together and folded her hands primly across her stomach. Methodically, he turned off the lamp, opened the door. He saw a woman and a man sway drunkenly toward a crib room on the far end of the hall, their voices raucous with mirth. They did not see him. He emerged, walked down the hall to the outside entrance. A girl suddenly came out of the door nearest the exit. She was young, lovely, blond—a refreshingly pleasant temptress, seemingly out of place. He hesitated, saw her fully as their eyes met and held momentarily until she looked away. Hurriedly, his footsteps heavy, he moved down the side stairs and into the night.

An evening breeze showered a stinging dust against the battered wood structures in Broken Bluffs as U.S. Marshal Dirk Landry drew rein in front of the combined jail and law office. Weary from a pressured ride out of Limbo, to the west, he regarded the town through heavy-lidded eyes, red-streaked from sun glare. He sat his horse high, a big man with broad shoulders and a lanky frame, well-proportioned in the blue shirt and the black vest. His face was narrow, with a broad forehead and a generous mouth tight with determination. His strong-angled nose had been broken, revealing his brawling youth—memorable features, as if chiseled from granite. There was purpose in his every move, an overbearing presence that made strangers aware of him and a little uneasy, for they sensed he could be dangerous if provoked.

Town Marshal Hal Sundon, watching Landry arrive, stepped onto the boardwalk, thumbs hitched in his gun belt.

Rawboned and slightly hunched, his straight blond hair plunged thickly over his ears to frame a lean, scrutinizing face. A dedicated lawman, he had built a solid reputation among his constituents, although his awkward stance, constant frown, and much blinking eyes gave those who didn't know him a different impression. "Glad you got here, Dirk. Didn't expect you this early," he said, addressing Landry. "Me and my deputy, we got as much information as we could. We packed the body in ice for you to see. We'll have to bury her shortly. Summer, you know."

Landry climbed stiffly from the saddle and wrapped the reins around a hitching post. "Any suspects?"

"None whatsoever, except one of the girls apparently saw that killer close up; but she ain't talking much. Scared spitless, I guess. Figure it must be a drifter, same one who got them others. Strangled just like them other two. And in all three cases an earlobe was sliced off."

Landry nodded seriously. "Would seem that we got one hardened culprit leaving his sign—somebody who doesn't like soiled doves. Of course, word of this thing has spread, and there could be others out there, somebody deranged enough to copy the killings. A whore doesn't often attract the best of company in the fittingest of conditions; you know that." Landry moved into the office—a spare room adjoining some cells. Sundon shuffled in after him to watch the marshal sprawl wearily on a wooden bench. "Territory is getting too many people; too much going on."

This was the third girl in less than two weeks—all prostitutes, all free-lancers with their cozy niches on the second floor of a saloon or in some back room. The first had been a popular Mexican girl in a nearby way station, discovered dead in her room, strangled and lying daintily across a bed, her bulging brown eyes staring sightlessly at the ceiling, her throat bruised from a thin rope twisted tightly into the soft flesh. The second had been from the back street of a camp called Bullion, out in the hinterland, found strangled and neatly arranged on the bed, an earlobe severed. All had their clothes torn.

Landry tipped his hat back. "Have to get me a room and shake this trail dust, but first it's best I see the body and that we talk to some of the ladies," he said, rising stiffly. "I want to talk to this girl who saw the killer."

"I told you, she wasn't cooperative at all. Came to town a couple weeks ago. Damn pretty, as whores go. Popular all of a sudden, too, which don't make her close friends amongst the other females. They call her Eve. That's all I could learn about her."

"Well, there's ways to find out. Let's go."

That evening a Willard Dragmire sat cleaning revolvers at his table near a window overlooking a back alley. From his upstairs room over the Cheveny Gun Shoppe, he could see into the rear of the Wrangler Saloon, a popular hangout that offered relaxation and pleasure twenty-four hours a day. In his loneliness, he enjoyed the revelry and the tinny refrains from a worn piano. Often he saw the painted ladies and their patrons steal away toward the Glacier or to Lilli's. Sometimes he saw drunken fistfights over some argument commenced inside; sometimes he saw gunfights at close quarters, which often left both participants sprawled and bloody, hopefully wiser if they survived. Through the half-open window he listened to the music, to the hum of roulette wheels, to the clink of glass—pleasant sounds in the cool sage-scented air.

Dragmire, a shy, sallow-faced young man with an angular body, long arms, and sensitive fingers, had retired from much of life. Sickly as a child, he had found health in the West, but he had never felt comfortable among the crude and boisterous types that inhabited much of the land. Although he was finding his niche as a gunsmith and as a traveling salesman, he preferred his own company in the sanctuary of his room. Except for business contacts, he had no friends and few acquaintances other than his boss, Noah Cheveny, and Cheveny's wife, Henrietta, a shrewish woman who dominated her husband, except when he was drunk.

Dragmire did not care for his boss. A dwarfish man, Cheveny had a pink, egg-shaped head completely devoid of hair. His owlish eyes blazed through wire-rim glasses when he ranted about late arms shipments or slack orders. He liked to sit behind a worktable piled with miscellaneous papers, which gave him an image of importance, although his shrunken frame made it appear as if his head were reposing on the table. Dragmire sometimes fantasized about crushing the head, but because the job made him pretty much his own boss—he had just returned from a ten-day circuit—some time ago he decided that he could tolerate any vented abuse.

He yawned sleepily; Cheveny and his wife had gone to a new theatrical play for the evening. Dragmire liked the quiet, for when the Chevenys were home, they often quarreled or she banged on her piano in anger, the sounds pulsing through the thin flooring until her husband slammed into his back room to lose himself amongst his gun collection. He had built an impressive assortment, ranging from Spanish matchlocks to dueling pistols reportedly owned by Aaron Burr and a breech-loading pistol etched with Napoléon Bonaparte's initials. His specialty, martial pistols and turret rifles, had been collected over many years. Cheveny was conservative with his money except when it came to his guns.

The soft breeze billowed the curtain. Dragmire oiled the cylinder of a Colt that he'd disassembled and spread before him. The voices of a man and a woman drifted loudly from the back of the Wrangler. The woman was protesting something; the man warbled his words drunkenly. Dragmire thought of closing his window. Fool whores brought such things on themselves, he told himself. Then he heard the man swear gruffly, heard the woman cry out. The gunsmith turned the lantern out and peered into the purple dark, not wanting to be involved, but recalling bitterly the pain of a year before: a stage robbery, the passengers forced to stand outside, forced to give up their money and valuables while the six highwaymen blew open a strongbox. Dragmire would never forget them; masked and confident, they had moved quickly and efficiently under the direction of a stocky man whose voice crackled with impatience and whose piercing dark eyes had bored through them. A youngish bandit had made suggestive remarks before ripping earrings from Dragmire's bride of a month; as his wife swooned, he tried to catch her, only to be clubbed senseless.

"Bitch," he heard the man hiss. The sharp smack of a hand on flesh resounded above the music and revelry. He saw the man push the woman, tear at her clothes and grasp her as she attempted to pull away. Dragmire stood up, his knees weak, his stomach churning. A damned whore—why was he letting her affect him this way? he thought. But he knew. He walked to a gun cabinet, removed a rifle and hurriedly inserted bullets, pumping one into the chamber. The memory of that night nearly a year earlier flooded over him; his returning to their room in Midas, a boomtown to the north, his finding his door ajar, the tables and chairs overturned, pictures askew, lamps broken, his wife arranged neatly on the bed, her face open-eyed and bloated with the twisted garrote around her throat. He had lost control of himself, and could not remember much about the days afterward except that authorities had locked him in a local jail for his own protection. His bride murdered. No suspects. No one ever arrested. No one ever paying for the crime. The anguish burned always with him now; forever, he thought. Shortly afterward he had come to Broken Bluffs, starting anew. Trying. But the pain and the hurt were always there, smoldering.

Dragmire climbed down some side stairs into the back alley. He saw the man lift the girl and slam her down. He heard her moan. Hunching over, the man struck at her, but

she writhed away, fighting him; he cursed her and reached
again.

Dragmire took sudden aim and fired. The impact straightened the man, wrenching his shoulders and head back, his
arms fluttering outward like a vulture taking flight. The man
swayed, dropped to his knees, and pitched headlong over the
stricken girl.

Dragmire froze. He clutched the rifle with such force that
he began shaking violently. Inside the Wrangler Saloon the
nightlife roared on. Apparently nobody had heard or cared.
Dragmire abruptly heaved the rifle aside, then staggered into
the shadows and retched. Afterward he wiped his face with
a handkerchief and steadied himself. The girl had disappeared, but the man lay unmoving in the dust. Dragmire
recovered the rifle, stole back to his room and carefully
cleaned the instrument, despite his trembling hands. For each
killing of late it was the same, but growing easier.

When finished, he replaced the rifle in the cabinet amongst
a number of arms that Cheveny kept in reserve. Then he
removed a bottle of whiskey from a bureau and poured an
ample drink, took it in one gulp and closed his eyes to let it
burn down. He took a second swallow and felt better. For a
time he relived the sight of the bullet searing home, of the
man rising in death; the quaking and nausea eased, and a
satisfying warmth came over him, a comforting sense of
power and of justice that blended headily with the whiskey—
a feeling he had never experienced so acutely before, better
than the last time. The gunsmith lay back on his cot, still
holding the bottle and glass, distorted flickerings from his
lantern making designs on the walls and on the ceiling.

Nobody admitted to knowing the murdered girl in the Glacier Palace; certainly not any patrons; not the bartenders,
except one who offered that she hadn't worked long at the
establishment; and not the girls of the house, although several claimed she was called Virginia Sue. The females grew

morose and withdrawn, obviously frightened. "Well, for your own protection, all of you better start remembering something," Landry told them.

From years of prowling the Basin country professionally, he and Sundon knew the types: hurdy-gurdy girls—a slang term in reference to a German musical instrument used to grind out tunes for street festivals. The hurdy-gurdies made their livelihood dancing with men. Many were prostitutes; some remained dancers only. Their purpose—to please men, and most important, to encourage them to buy drinks at inflated prices. After each dance, the man bought the girl some champagne or a liqueur, usually tea from a fancy bottle that the bartender kept under careful scrutiny. Although rouged and wearing gaudy clothes, most of them were gawky, raw boned country girls attracted to the life because they could support themselves; or because they were one of a passel of children and could no longer be of value to their family; or more likely because they could meet a lonely man, marry, and become respectable. Others were eastern professionals who had entertained and plied their trade on riverboats or in the cities and were now seeking excitement and money in the West. Perhaps less than one of the girls in twenty was beautiful or even attractive. The girl named Eve was that: long-limbed, slender of hand and neck, her golden hair piled massively about a Grecian face sculptured with narrow nose, strong jaw, and wide, deep-set eyes that observed one with a green intensity.

Landry hesitated, his eyes encompassing her totally. Painfully he said, "You saw the killer?" He waited. Sundon stood to the side, listening. The girl had ivory skin, a heart-shaped mouth, and dimples in her cheeks.

She did not or could not look at the marshal. "I saw someone."

"Meaning?"

"I didn't see his face. He had a floppy hat pulled low, and he wore a shawl."

"A shawl?"

"Yes, wrapped up around his ears and cheeks. The only thing I saw for certain were his eyes."

"What about them?"

"They were like ice—blue ice. They were wild and crazy eyes that went right through me."

"Anything else? Anything about his clothing, his boots? Was he tall? Heavyset? Anything?"

"He was medium tall, slender. It was hard to tell, Marshal. He wore a coat."

"Did he look familiar in any way? Could he have been a client before?"

"I don't know. But I'm sure I never saw him before."

"Did he say anything? Did you hear his voice?"

"No."

"I did," said a mousy little woman called Mime, who had been tearful for some time.

"Speak up."

She blew her nose, choked some, then said falteringly, "I was in the room next to where it happened." She hesitated.

Landry leaned forward. "Go on."

"The walls are so thin, you can hear people talking. I couldn't make out what they was saying, until . . ."

"Until what?"

"I heard her tell him it was time to leave."

"And then?"

"I thought I heard a struggle, but I'm not sure."

"Why didn't you check?"

"It wasn't my business. Sometimes we get drunks that start demanding. But we're expected to handle them—if we can't, we got a cowbell next to the bed, or at worst, we scream. That brings the bouncers."

"What else did you hear?"

"Nothing, except it got quiet. And I was frightened. Then I heard him talking to her or to someone."

"What did he say?"

"I couldn't make it out exactly, except one thing. He said something like, 'I'm sorry, Mary Lynn.' " The little woman had a concerned expression.

"Well, what about it?"

"But her name was Virginia Sue."

Landry rocked back slightly as one of Sundon's deputies entered the room. "Sheriff," he announced, "some men found a cowpoke out back of the Wrangler Saloon, backshot. Murdered."

(2)

With the bright of morning, a head drover named Halvern
rode in with one of his boys, looking for the gunned cowpoke. Camped outside of town, they had come in the night
before for a little relaxation. "We played some poker. Johnny
talked about a little whorin', so the rest of us headed back to
camp," he said to Landry and Sundon in the latter's office.
"That was the last I seen of him. Ordinarily I'd figure he got
drunk somewhere and is sleeping it off. But it ain't like him.
He's always pronto on the job. And he knew he was heading
out by dawn. That's why I decided to come in town."

"Was he wearing a checkered gray shirt and a brown
vest?" Sundon asked.

Halvern, a bulky man with a bloated red face, looked at
the young cowpoke who had accompanied him. They nodded in accord. "Yes. Is he in trouble?"

"Bad news for you. He's dead. Back-shot by somebody
last night," Landry interjected.

"Back-shot? Dead? The hell you say!" Halvern and the
cowpoke sat down.

"His body's down at the undertaker's. Best we go down
there now. You can identify him for me," Sundon added. "I
was hopin' to find out who he was before havin' to bury
him."

"But why? How?"

"Don't know." Led by the sheriff, the four men headed

up the main street. "We have no suspects so far. But we'll find whoever it was."

"How did it happen?"

"He was discovered late last night, back of the Wrangler Saloon. Apparently it wasn't a robbery. He had money intact."

"Did he quarrel with anyone last night?" Landry asked.

"Not that I know of."

"Did he have any enemies? Any in town here?"

Halvern looked at the young man. Both shook their heads negatively. "He was a damn good cowhand. Certainly no saint. But who in the hell is?"

"Explain," Landry pursued.

"He had a temper, especially if he was drinking. Liquored up, he had a mean streak."

"Did he drink much last night?"

"He'd had his share. But nothing more than usual."

"We found his horse hitched in front. It's at the livery stable," said Sundon.

"Good. I want to take Johnny with me. Give him a proper burial." Halvern stopped. "He said he was going to look for a woman. Did you follow that up?"

Landry said soberly: "We talked to the bartender. He remembered your friend with a girl named Holly, a dancer/entertainer out of the Glacier Palace. We already talked to her."

"What did she say?"

"That your friend got abusive over the price and place, I guess. She claims someone shot him out of the dark, that she panicked and fled. She never saw anyone, and, of course, she had never seen your friend before."

"Maybe she killed him. You can't take the word of a whore."

"No," said Landry. "The bullet blew a sizable hole in him. I'd say it was from a rifle a hundred, hundred and fifty feet away."

"But why?" said Halvern, shaking his massive head.

* * *

That same morning, a short day's ride west of Broken Bluffs, six men cantered boldly into the faded remains of Whiskey Springs, a bleak line of buildings that fronted a rutted road and a stretch of gray desert. The riders, a hard lot, approached indifferently, almost defiantly. Leander "Rattlesnake" Morton, their leader, had built a reputation that was becoming legendary in the Basin country: an ex-convict, stage and bank robber, he had killed several women as easily as the numberless men who had fallen before his gun. An expert horseman, tracker, knife fighter, and escape artist, he had proven a nearly impossible challenge for lawmen, especially since he was adept at living off the land.

Only Dirk Landry had ever brought him to justice, which resulted in a lengthy sentence in the state penitentiary, cut short when Morton pulled off a massive release of cutthroats, a near army, that made national headlines. Not known for his loyalty, Morton had headed several gangs since the break, losing men in daring plunders, but attracting others drawn by his success and seemingly invincible life. And although an impressive reward has been posted for him, no one so far had come close to ending his career as he struck guerrilla-like, pillaging the land.

Short, but powerfully built, Morton wore a slouch hat that clung tightly to the straight black hair, shielding a round, dish face and a flat nose accentuated by a droopy mustache. His deep-set eyes gleamed constantly like black diamonds as he ferreted out details and movements around him. He seemed a natural extension of the long-legged pinto that he flowed along with.

Behind him came Riles, young, handsome under several days' stubble. Riles had an eye for women, and they for him. Hot-tempered, prone to argument, he was good with a hand-gun and not afraid to stand up to any man. Perhaps, because of his youth, he was sometimes too quick to act.

Next rode Liddicoat, dark-clothed, a lean, angular chap in his mid-thirties, the patient, quiet member, a marksman of extraordinary ability with a rifle. He was the sniper, the eliminator, whose talents Morton had often used effectively.

The man called Fang had a wolfish face with snaggled teeth and glazed, hypnotic eyes set closely. He wore a high-peaked, sweat-stained hat that shadowed an expressionless face. Fang seldom showed pleasure, unless he observed or contributed to another's pain.

Jenson was a wisp of a man with a twisted mouth and nervous eyes. Because he lacked stature and was quite non-descript, Morton employed him as the gang's eyes and ears. He could pass freely among good citizens without drawing attention while listening and observing.

Last came Beatty, brutish, a grizzled bear of a man who hunched hugely over his horse. His pleasures were eating and drinking and fighting. Despite the weight of an over-hanging belly which forced him to move ponderously, he had enormous hands and powerful arms that could crush a skull or snap a back. His small red eyes could chill a man whom he regarded with hate.

Morton reined before the general store, the others pulling up beside him. A rising wind whipped dust and tumbled balls of sage down the nearly empty street. Two men sat whittling in front of a blacksmith shop, a rangy dog sprawled at their feet. They straightened up to watch curiously. Whiskey Springs had once been a watering hole for freighters carrying bullion and gear; but now, with the decline of nearby mines, the spot served only a few isolated farmers. "We get some grub and ammo here," said Morton, his eyes narrowing. They all dismounted. "An old man and his wife own the place. They won't be no trouble."

"Broken Bluffs tonight," said Liddicoat.

Morton grinned. "Just long enough to hit the gunsmith there. From my grapevine, I understand he owns a Laffite blunderbuss and an Aaron Burr duelin' pistol and more. People pay big for things like that.''

"Them must be big names," Fang said.

"I don't like it," Riles growled. "Foolish to take chances. It's getting the Kurt girl off that stage that's important. That's all we should be thinking about.''

"You leave the thinking to me," Morton said evenly. "On the way I ain't bypassing a chance for them pieces. I hear some of them have pearl handles, all carved with pretty sketches.'' He dropped the reins, settled his horse, and moved his coat behind the holstered gun.

"There's big money in that girl," Riles insisted. "That's what we should be concentratin' on.''

"You're not listening to me, son. I always hankered to be a gun collector, and this is my chance. You, Riles, you and Liddicoat take your horses out back and keep watch. Fang, you come with me.'' Fang chuckled with anticipation as he and Morton, both with saddlebags, stepped onto the rickety boardwalk and entered the store. The two observers and their dog slipped out of sight.

Inside, the place smelled musty of old leather and dust. A gray-haired man, slightly bowed, looked up apprehensively through thick glasses. When he saw Morton bolt the door, he reached clumsily under the counter. "I wouldn't, old man.''

Fang snapped his Colt out and pointed, his lips drawing back around the hooked teeth in a singsong braying laugh. The proprietor paled, lifted his hands shoulder high, and waited.

"We ain't going to hurt no one," said Morton, "long as we get what we come for. But first get your old lady out here.''

The proprietor hesitated. "There's just me.''

"You got an old lady in the back. I been through here before. I know.''

"Please!''

"I said, get her out here."

Fang brayed again and cocked his revolver.

"Maude," the old man called, without lowering his hands or removing his eyes from the gun. "Maude, come out here." A paunchy woman with large, frightened eyes emerged through a beaded doorway. She held her hands crossed at her throat and waited.

From a saddlebag, Morton removed a folded duffel bag with a choke string. First he ordered ammunition, boxes that he dumped into his and Fang's pouches. And then he handed the proprietor the sack and strolled about, pointing silently: salt pork, jerky, hardtack, sugar, coffee, salt, beans, a little flour and cornmeal, some dried fruit, plugs of tobacco, a few whiskey bottles, and finally a sombrero. Fang pointed glee-fully at some stick candy. When the old man selected a few pieces, the outlaw reached over and clutched a handful.

"Tell the boys we're heading out, we'll split up the goods outside town," Morton said to Fang. The man slunk to a back door to deliver the message, his eyes and gun still on the couple. "Now you two, I know there ain't a lawman within a half day's ride, so any ideas about fetching help ain't going to do you no good. Keep this place locked and closed for a half hour, do you understand?" The old man nodded. "Or if I learn different, next time through I might just fire up this fine store of yours."

Morton turned and strode out to replace his saddlebag and hook the duffel bag and sombrero over his pommel. Fang stood for a long moment grinning at the couple before clos-ing the door. The two outlaws kneed their horses to the rear, where the partners waited, and galloped into the desert a hundred yards before Morton pulled a halt. "Maybe we should let them know we mean business." He motioned to Liddicoat. Without replying, the slender rifleman removed his Winchester, took aim, and in rapid fire pumped five bul-lets through the back door and window.

* * *

In Broken Bluffs, Landry and Sundon watched the head drover and his man ride off, the stiffened body of the murdered cowpoke tied in a tarpaulin across his horse.

"No suspects, and nobody saw nothing except what that dance girl tells us," said Sundon. "As perplexin' as the whore murders. Proprietor of the Glacier Palace is going to give Virginia Sue a decent burial. All this didn't help the reputation of his place, which wasn't too good anyway."

Landry tipped his Stetson back and leaned against a post. "What concerns me is that girl, Eve."

"Damn pretty, ain't she? Don't see lookers like that out here. But I know what you're sayin'. If she did see the killer, he might just come back."

"Her room is on the end, near a balcony and an exit. I'm sure they keep it locked, but that won't stop somebody who really wants to get in."

"The girl belongs in a better place than the Glacier, that's for sure. Lilli—she owns the main cathouse here—would probably take the girl in if she saw her. Girl would draw good money for Lilli. And she'd sure get better protection and food there."

"Well, I'm way ahead of you," said Landry. "I already talked to Lilli and Eve. The girl should be moving out shortly, if she hasn't done so already."

"The hell you did. That's good."

"I tried to talk her into taking a boardinghouse, told her the government would pay for it until I can get her out of here, but she's bullheaded. Wants to make big money. So I guess Lilli's the best compromise."

"For now, yes."

"I'll be heading up there shortly to make sure she made it." The two lawmen sauntered back into the office. Sundon took a seat next to his hightop desk, and Landry slung his good leg over a chair, leaned on the back and faced the sheriff. "I'm going to need your help, Hal. You should know I'm here not only because of the murders, but because of Leander Morton.''

"Rattlesnake Morton? Morton here, in my town?''

"Not yet, but we got a good tip he's heading through here. He's up to something big, but we can't put a finger on it yet.''

"I know he's been playing hell with the territory again. Always has, I guess.''

"Our latest source was a bounty hunter tracking him, who walked into a trap. Morton left him staked out to die, but a trapper came across him. The hunter had gotten wind that Morton was coming here for some reason and then swinging east to Midas and the mountains north.''

"With all the posters and rewards on that varmint, you'd think someone would have killed him by now.'' Sundon removed his hat and wagged his head.

"With Morton, it's never been that easy. We know that he uses an underground system—special people working for him. They're like spies, gang members that he sends out or uses to scout about and report back to him. He's always worked that way. That's what makes him so hard to capture.''

"What the devil could he want with my town?''

"Nothing good, I can tell you that. But we do suspect he is interested in a stage run somewhere out of Midas. One of Morton's henchmen, a man named Liddicoat—a dangerous chap and a hell of a good rifle shot—was recognized asking about stage schedules.''

"A robbery?''

Landry shook his head. "There just aren't that many gold or payroll shipments through that area anymore. It's more ranching and farming now.''

"True.''

"We're guessing he's interested in somebody traveling through, probably from the Central Pacific rails up north.''

"Somebody important. A kidnapping?''

Landry smiled tightly. "It's all very speculative, of course, but yes, that was our first consideration. We checked the schedules and rosters by telegram and can find no one of real importance. But that doesn't mean much, because we don't know who or what we're looking for."

"Wish you knew more."

"Wish I did, too. All we know is he's headed this way."

"What do you suggest?"

"That you deputize some more men, but don't make it obvious. Morton can smell a trap a mile away. Station your men around where they can see what's happening. Keep in contact with them. And I'll keep in contact with you." Landry rose. "You should go to that funeral. Interesting people often give their last respects to a murder victim."

"It's good they see a lawman there anyway."

"But first I'm going to see if Eve's moved out, you coming?"

"Sure, I always like looking at a pretty lady. Seems to me she's caught your fancy, too."

Relaxed in a tweed coat and derby, Willard Dragmire drove the pacer steadily down the road toward Whiskey Springs, the fringe-topped wagon rolling smoothly, shading him from the morning sun. He would deliver some orders of revolvers and ammunition there and would repair what guns had been left for his special talents. He would be back for a late supper; he enjoyed the outing alone. Dragmire took a swig of expensive brandy and tucked the bottle under his seat. He still seethed inwardly at his boss, Noah Cheveny—the pompous little hypocrite. The first minute Dragmire reported for work, Cheveny had accosted him for fouling up an order and for not expanding his sales more cost effectively in the outlying regions. Cheveny played the God-fearing, good citizen and husband. But Dragmire knew that his boss had not been faithful to Mrs. Cheveny, although he couldn't blame the man. Haughty, frigidly cold, she tormented Cheveny with her constant nagging, and that thought made Dragmire chuckle. What galled him was Cheveny's self-righteousness, his demeanor of superiority. Dragmire suspected that Cheveny had cleverly juggled his books at times to cheat the distributor in the East. But someday someone would find out. And someday his indiscretions would catch up with him. From one of those outlying towns, the words of a free-talking prostitute would work back to Henrietta Cheveny. And Dragmire wanted to be around then.

He took another drag of brandy. The day was pleasant and he had time. He wheeled the horse from the road for a quarter of a mile and stopped under a fractured bluff, a continuation of the rimrock after which his hometown was named. From a tool trunk he removed a belt and holster and a box of cartridges. Deftly he strapped the revolver on, checked the cylinder, and walked a hundred feet into a box ravine. For half an hour he practiced, winging away rocks and sticks that caught his attention. He tried some fast draws, but mostly he worked for accuracy, holding the .44 at arm's length. Every day that he was on the road he spent time perfecting his sense of timing, his aim, his trigger pull, his movements. Some days he drilled with a Winchester rifle, other days with a shotgun. He would toss cans into the air or hunt sage hens in the bottomlands. He had become rather proficient at throwing a knife. When satisfied, Dragmire returned to the horse, which was swishing patiently, placed the gun and belt in the trunk, took another sip of brandy and drove on, whistling a merry tune.

Halfway between Broken Bluffs and Whiskey Springs, Dragmire watched six horsemen approach along a narrow benchland of jumbled boulders that paralleled the road in the flat. Always suspicious of travelers who avoided the main routes, he loosened the rifle in a scabbard next to the passenger seat and secured his belt where a pistol lay angled. They came on, barely giving him notice, but even in the distance he could tell they were a motley, hard lot that seemed disturbingly familiar—especially the leader, short and powerful, with a slouch hat; and the last man, hefty as a bear. He had not seen the faces of the robbers who had accosted his wife, but he could not suppress the violent shivers that surged through him as dark troubling memories filled his being.

Outside of Whiskey Springs a boy of twelve in a straw hat and bibbed coveralls rode out bareback on a trotting mule. Dragmire pulled his horse up. "You coming from Broken Bluffs?" the boy asked.

"Yes."

The boy seemed anxious. "Sheriff Sundon or his deputies there?"

"Last I knew. Why, what's wrong?"

"A gang rode in and robbed Mr. and Mrs. Campbell, then shot up the place and hurt Mrs. Campbell."

"The Campbells?" Dragmire asked angrily.

"Mr. Campbell says it was the Morton gang."

Dragmire nodded, thinking about the suspicious riders he had seen. "Let's take a look." He slapped the reins across his pacer.

A few frustrated citizens milled outside the store. Without a constable or any symbol of authority, they had no alternative than to seek assistance a day's ride away; by then the culprits would be long gone. Dragmire found the couple inside their quarters next to the store, attended by a Mexican woman and a few acquaintances drinking whiskey in sympathy. Mrs. Campbell lay on a bed, more in shock than hurt, although a shard of glass had penetrated one fleshy arm. "It was Morton's crew," the proprietor assured the gunsmith. "I seen him before, and one don't forget."

"They passed me hours ago," Dragmire said soberly. "Best I hightail back. Appeared like they might be heading for Broken Bluffs."

"I pity anybody in their path," said Campbell.

Lilli's parlor offered all the opulence that a Victorian heart could wish for, and Lilli could well afford it. The brightly lit interiors contrasted dramatically with the dismal hovels that most miners or range hands lived in. The house, with its warmth and finely arrayed women, gave men an identity with distant homes, a sense of gentility in harsh surroundings. The chandeliers, the costly mirrors, numerous decanters on carved wood tables, pastoral paintings, a pianist at a grand piano, and the sporting ladies in the finest of Parisian dress, made a lasting impression; especially since Lilli's place featured great flowing curtains, plush tapestry chairs and sofas, polished walnut or mahogany hutches, and long tables filled or set with glittering champagne glasses; the walls festooned with hand-painted plates and scenic tapestries, the thick rugs and wallpaper feathered with matching designs. The tables and the carpeted staircase featured balloon shaped lights filigreed in gold, and silver, and copper.

Lilli met her patrons, usually established customers, in the parlor, where they were presented a choice: whiskey, beer, imported wines, or liqueurs, and cigars, if they so desired. The girls, in short-scalloped dresses that revealed dainty boots and shapely calves, were strolled into the parlor for scrutiny. The fine frills, the low-cut tops framed with beads or cameos, offered succulent flesh. Most of the girls were Caucasian, but Lilli liked blending attractive Chinese, Mexican, and Negroes when available. ''Spiced variety,'' she boasted.

Lilli, a squarely built redhead with braided hair, was all business, tolerating no shenanigans on the part of patrons, although she allowed men to toss gold nuggets between ample cleavages, or to sprinkle gold dust into the high, piled hair, usually providing a tidy bonus when washed later.

Understandably, dancehall girls—such as those in the Glacier Palace—averaged fifty dances a night, a feat of endurance, considering the vigorous stomping and whirling of tipsy partners. Nearly all were anxious to land a job in Lilli's prestigious and eloquent setting. Although some girls worked different shifts, most offered their charms between noon and four in the morning. The madams of most establishments preferred to label their girls "Lady Boarders." And indeed they did receive two meals a day, in late morning and early evening, but the "boarders" split their earnings fifty-fifty with the house. The attractive clothing they were required to wear—usually a casual afternoon outfit and a more flamboyant evening dress—were charged at their own expense to local merchants. And the honorable city fathers who frowned upon these wasted women felt little guilt at raising costs at least twenty percent. But Lilli never lost at the round table transactions. She simply upped the girls' asking price, knowing that many shadowy patrons were the men who righteously condemned.

Marshal Landry entered the parlor before dark. "The party won't roar for hours yet, Marshal," Lilli greeted, "unless you're awfully anxious for company right now."

Landry smiled wryly. "This is all business. I want to talk to your new girl, Eve."

"Now, Marshal, her time is money. You going to pay or you going to charge it to Uncle Sam?"

"Government business, Lilli. Government business."

Lilli grinned widely, her broad nose crinkling with amusement. "She's at the top of the stairs, down two, number seven." She placed a foot at the base of the rise and cupped her mouth. "Lawman coming up."

Landry climbed the curving stairs; he could hear giggles and smell steam from hot baths. Several girls in flimsy petticoats sauntered from room to room, indifferent to his presence. At the top he looked down the white-paneled doors for number seven, approached and knocked.

"Yes."

"It's me, Eve. Landry."

"The door's unlocked."

Landry stepped in and found the girl in a spacious bed, a goose-down comforter clutched tightly around her, leaving her arms and shoulders and upper chest bare. He did not know whether she was partially clothed or not. "You shouldn't leave the door unlocked."

"It's house policy."

"Then I'll talk with Lilli."

Eve turned her head away like a pouting little girl.

"Aren't you supposed to be preparing for evening events?"

"I'm almost ready. Just have to put on my gown. I'm on a late shift. This Virginia Sue thing has tired me, that's all."

"Well, Eve, I want to talk to you, the way your papa should have if he'd lived." Landry worked his mouth, uncomfortable in the role.

She looked back at him condescendingly. "Oh, Uncle Dirk, I've heard it all before."

(3)

Frustrated after an intense bout of arguing, Landry rose from a chair carved with laurel leaves and cupids to nearly knock over a pink-shaded lamp next to it. He paced back and forth. "Damn it, Eve, luckily you're beautiful still, but you're so stupid and naive, it sickens me."

Eve completed her grooming behind a dressing screen, dabbing herself with perfume for a late shift. "Broken Bluffs is not my first time, you know."

"I would suspect so."

"I don't care to discuss the past. What is behind is behind."

"While you short-change your future." Landry glared at her. Had she been a young man, he would have kicked the kid all the way down the stairs and into the street and maybe thrashed him within an inch of his life. But this was a female, a niece that he recalled holding as a toddler: the youngest, the most spoiled, the most impudent and bullheaded of his sister's four children. Eve, he believed, may have been her favorite. He was glad that his sister had not seen the result. She had died of pneumonia before the girl's third birthday. Geoffrey, the father, had tried to raise the children, but two had succumbed to childhood illnesses, and the oldest boy, working a man's job, was killed from a felled timber somewhere in the Sierras. Landry had tried to assist as much as possible, but his job took him to far corners of the West. He guessed what really killed Geoffrey prematurely had been

Eve's running off at age fourteen with a saddle tramp, and the resultant child, which she gave away to an orphanage.

"What I do is my business. I'm of age."

"Honey." Landry softened. "One of your coworkers, your Virginia Sue, was of age. She was buried today—murdered. Doesn't that mean anything?"

"I'm sorry for her. You know I've been very upset."

"But doesn't that tell you anything? And to make it worse, the killer knows that you saw him."

"I can't identify him." She fumbled her words slightly. "Maybe his eyes. I'll never forget his eyes. But nothing more for certain."

"But he doesn't know that." Landry moved closer. "Do you realize how many of your fellow hostesses here will eventually rot their guts from cheap liquor? Do you know how many will someday commit suicide with morphine? Do you know how many will end flat broke? Most won't have a gold pinch to buy some soup or a sack to lay on. Have you ever seen a used-up whore, old and ugly years before her time?" Landry felt a little mean. "You're pretty now, but you won't be for long. And when you're used up, they toss you out. Because there's always someone new and younger coming along."

"I'm not going to work any eighteen hours a day sewing duds in some stuffy shed for some fancy ladies," she shouted. "Nor am I going to scrub floors, or wait tables for barely enough to live on. Here I get good money, real money and sometimes tips. I get square meals, and I can wear beautiful clothes. And I like the way men look at me." She smiled saucily and somewhat arrogantly. "You can't frighten me."

"Sure, but who really gets your take? It's Lilli. Who do you think pays for this fancy place, for the bartenders, for the bouncers, for the piano player, for the fees—ultimately you, sweetie."

Her eyes blazed. "And someday I might manage my own house, or meet a rich man to my liking and leave."

Landry's chiseled features twisted with a smirk. "About running a house, you have no idea, child. A madam's got to be ruthless in business. She's got to be able to boss men, supervise the organization, throw out rowdy drunks, and water down the cat fights among her girls. She's got to be tough and motherly all at the same time. That you?"

"In time, maybe."

"As for Mr. Prince Charming, if you survive and hold your looks long enough, he may chance by. But by then you'll have diseased yourself, so you'll never give him children."

Eve pressed her hands over her ears and shook her head violently. "Damn it, I don't want to hear anymore," she screamed. "Get out. Get out, out, out."

Taken aback, Landry held more words about to erupt. He nodded, put his Stetson on and moved to the door, but turned back to point a finger. "When I leave this town, even if I have to trump something up on you, you're going with me."

"And I'll come right back."

Before Landry could open the door, someone knocked. "Yeah, what?" he demanded, jerking the door open.

Lilli stood before him. "Well, Mr. Marshal, I'm sorry to intrude. You do look a little out of sorts, not that big collected self I always see."

"Never mind. What do you want?"

"Well, it seems, apparently, while you been pleasurin' it up, you missed your chance. The big one just went through right under your nose."

"What the hell you talking about?" Landry growled.

"There's a deputy downstairs looking for you, claims you should come quick, that a Rattlesnake Morton pulled off a robbery and got clean away."

Landry pushed through the early dark with the deputy to the Cheveny Gun Shoppe. Sundon and Willard Dragmire stood in the back apartment where Henrietta Cheveny sat hunched in a rocker, her face pale, checkered with wrinkles of strain. Her lean face, squared by narrow glasses perched on a pointed nose, and her gray hair pulled tight in a pug, made her look older than she probably was. Cheveny lay on a couch, one hand touching his head, his eyes dilated, his face puffy and swelling. Landry assessed the situation. "How bad is he hurt?"

"Bruises, a headache, but no broken bones. He'll have some sore ribs," Sundon answered.

"Robbery? What? Cash, guns?"

"Rare guns. Collector's items."

"He came into the store just before closing," said Mrs. Cheveny. "We thought he was an old Mexican."

"Mexican?" Landry's perplexed eyes darted over those before him. "Your deputy here said it was Morton."

Sundon answered. "Morton only, apparently; none of his gang was around that we know of. That's why my deputies never got suspicious."

The deputy next to Landry spoke up. "I was patrolling the main street, Marshal, and I seen an old Mexican all hunched over ride in. He was draped in a blanket and had one of them broken-up sombreros—you know the kind they all wear. I didn't think nothing of it, except . . ." He chewed his mouth.

"Except what?"

"Except the horse was better flesh than you normally see an old greaser ride. But I thought nothing more of it at the time."

"But how can you be so certain it was Morton?"

"I showed Cheveny here a poster. He said he was sure of it."

From the couch, Noah Cheveny, his voice faint, said, "Not only am I sure, Marshal, but I seen Morton once outside Virginia City when he and his companions lifted a family watch from my vest. You don't forget his face."

"What exactly happened?" Landry looked at the woman.

"You, Mrs. Cheveny, it might be easier for you than for your husband."

"As I said, we were about to close when this Mexican walked in and began looking at rifles in one of the cases. He had his back to us, and when my husband offered to assist him, he turned around with a gun in his hand."

"Then?"

The words came with difficulty. "Then he forced us back here. He said he knew that Noah had a gun collection, and he wanted to collect a few of his own. When my husband refused, he began beating him." She coughed and put a hand with a handkerchief to her mouth. "I was the one that broke, because he threatened our lives. So I told him they were in Noah's office. Besides, I knew it would be only a matter of time until he discovered them himself. He marched us back into the office and forced me to unlock all the cases."

"He had damn good taste," Cheveny said tightly. "He took a gold-plated Colt with ivory grips once owned by Emperor Maximilian. And a flintlock pistol, and an Irish percussion sidearm with a dagger that can be activated, and a .41-caliber Starrs derringer—rare, you know. How much more he took, I haven't been able to check yet. But I seen those go that I mentioned. He filled a sack."

"But that wasn't enough," said Mrs. Cheveny. "He said he knew Noah had some priceless guns with signatures of great people carved on them."

"I think he was considering killing me," Cheveny said wearily, "but I convinced him I did have some but that they were locked up in a vault in the bank."

Sundon said, "Their assistant, Willard Dragmire here, alerted me."

"I come right after," said Dragmire. "Ten minutes earlier I might have come upon 'em and stopped it."

"Or been killed," Landry admonished.

Dragmire stiffened slightly, offended by the suggestion of

incompetency. "I was purposely headed here because of Morton."

Everyone in the room held their attention on the slender gunsmith. "You're here because of Morton?" Landry asked skeptically.

"Yes, I saw him and his gang, six of them, pass me heading this way today. Then in Whiskey Springs I learned that this Morton had robbed the main store there and wounded the proprietor's wife. The man recognized Morton. That's when I decided to hightail back here. Figured this is where Morton was headed. Never dreamed he'd be after my own boss."

"Looks like your hunch and your informant was right," Sundon said to Landry.

The marshal nodded and turned to leave. "I've got to telegraph Sheriff Brent Cole up in Midas. Somewhere outside of town there's a stage that's going to be hit. Wish I could be more exact."

"Will you be leaving us, Dirk?" Sundon inquired.

"I may have to, but I don't want to abandon you just yet, not with these murders on your hands."

"Well, I'll be leaving for Midas soon as my head quits ringing," Cheveny said, grunting to a sitting position, his face more flushed than usual.

"You fool," said Mrs. Cheveny. "You best forget that trip. You're in no condition to travel anywhere."

"If that's the direction my collection is going, that's the way I'm going."

"And what could you do?" she countered with disgust. "That's a lawman's job."

Cheveny held his head in both hands. "Hell, woman, you know we been planning for weeks on my going there."

"What's so important there?" Landry inquired.

"A growing market for guns. I'm expanding. Oh sure, there's tough competition, but that's the challenge. A top distributor from the Colt Company is meeting me there tomorrow.'' He looked at his wife. ''You, my dear, will handle the store magnificently as always, and Willard here can handle the circuit adequately.''

''You are a fool.'' Henrietta looked down her long nose at him. ''No amount of money is worth killing yourself for. And the way you must hurt, it won't be pleasurable.''

''Night's rest and I'll be fine.''

''I need a pot of tea,'' said Mrs. Cheveny, rising.

''I'm not going to let the likes of Morton hurt my future,'' Cheveny mumbled.

''Well, for now,'' said Sundon, ''if you possibly feel like it, we better find out what got stolen.''

As Cheveny and the lawmen moved to the back room, Willard Dragmire climbed the stairs slowly to his room and looked out onto the back alley at the spot where the drunk had lain. He decided he needed a drink in one of the quieter saloons.

Before dawn, at the valley rise known as the Silver Lode Summit, where the road curved steepest in the final pull toward Midas, the Morton gang hid in readiness. They had pushed their mounts hard across the moonlit desert, taking a two-hour rest after midnight. Now they waited anxiously in a jumble of brush-cloaked boulders; Morton and Riles on the upper side, mounted; Fang and Beatty on the down side; Liddicoat hidden above, overlooking them all, his rifle pointed, his horse posted near him. The moon settling low on the horizon cast a red, eerie glow over the sparse valley, a dark swathe between two high walls of mountain range. A cool wind rustled the sage and swayed the juniper. Some coyotes chorused from the dark. Several miles to the south, in the foothills under the escarpment of high mountains, lay Midas, a thriving gold and silver camp, and center for most of the outlying cattle industry.

Riles turned his head. ''I hear something.''

''Yes. Yes, I think I do, too,'' Morton agreed. ''Beatty,

Fang, Liddicoat,'' he called, but not loudly. ''They're coming.''

From down the road a distinct jangle of harnesses and creak of wheels sounded, the multiple clip-clop of trotting horses, slowing with the weight, the animals blowing and snorting, the driver's voice high and urging. They came on steadily. The setting moon faded, but in the flush of pale light, the outlines of horses and stage appeared, the driver and guard alert, with several passengers on top swaying with the movement, their heads bowed in troubled sleep.

Morton raised his pistol and fired once into the air, the sound jolting in the cold morning air. At the signal, the four outlaws spurred their horses out of the shadows and up beside the stage. The messenger tried to defend, but a bullet from Liddicoat splintered his stock, then ripped away through the flesh of his left shoulder and nicked a passenger behind him. Both men cried out as the double-barreled gun tumbled to earth. Startled sounds of fear came from those aboard. Before anyone could respond, Morton and Fang had the stage doors open, with guns thrusting in. The horses pulled and bolted in their traces as the driver jerked to a halt. ''Ain't nothing but mail and sleepy travelers,'' he shouted. ''We don't have nothing worth your while.''

''Shut up,'' Morton snapped. ''We ain't here for money. Just for one person.'' His black eyes scanned the stricken faces, all distinct in the growing light. Two women rode inside; one middle-aged, her hair pulled back tightly in a pug, her thin face and chin set defiantly; the other a teenager, comely, white-skinned, with a pouty mouth and violet eyes. Dressed in a dark green traveling dress with matching hat, she sat wedged between a young soldier and a big-chested man in a buckskin coat, probably a cattle buyer. ''It is you, Miss Kurt, that we want.''

''You don't know who I am,'' she said, recoiling.

Morton grinned triumphantly. ''Oh yes, we do. And you

look just like in the pictures with your proud pappy." Morton reached in. Startled, the girl pulled back.

"Leave her be," said the man in the buckskin; but before he could utter another word, Morton delivered a cracking blow, a gun barrel across the forehead. The man slumped to the side. As Morton grasped the girl's slender wrist, she punched her parasol into his stomach, doubling him.

The young soldier started to rise, his hand fumbling at a gun flap. Morton cocked his revolver and pointed at the youth's belly. "Don't be a hero, soldier boy," he managed in pain.

Riles was then beside Morton, pulling at the girl. She slammed him across the head with the parasol to knock his hat off. He thrust his gun into the holster, tore the parasol away, and lifted her kicking and struggling from the stage, only to wail in pain as she sunk strong teeth into a hand.

"You'll pay—whatever you're doing. My father will follow you to the end of the earth," she screamed, kicking him in the shins until he yowled and danced about, holding her on his hip and under one arm like a sack of flour.

"We know who your old man is," Morton said, mounting his horse and backing away. "And that's why you're going with us. Where's her baggage?" A nervous little man above pointed to a buckled piece of luggage and to a large trunk. "Just toss down the luggage!" Fang caught it as Morton moved to the driver and handed him a sealed letter. "In Midas, this goes to Franz Kurt, you understand?"

"Yes, sir," said the driver.

"Details are all there. And I want you to hear this, driver. And you, too." He looked at the bleeding guard, woozy with shock. "Any and all of you. Her old man has forty-eight hours to deliver if he wants his daughter back well and healthy. Forty-eight hours. All he has to do is follow orders. Now get going. Get the hell out of here," Morton shouted, firing once more into the air.

The driver lashed the team, bolting them and the rocking

stage uphill to the summit a hundred feet ahead, as Riles pulled the girl onto the saddle in front of him.

In Broken Bluffs a strong wind pummeled the buildings in the dark of early morning, streaming sand and dust like wispy smoke through the dry streets and the empty alleys. From the Glacier Palace and from the Wrangler Saloon, music drifted in sad discord. A few horses stood forlornly at the rails, their heads bowed, their tails and manes rippling. A drunken cowboy lurched uncertainly toward the feedlot south of town, to bed down in the hay. At Lilli's, the piano player had waxed into a nostalgic mood of sentimental reveries, the notes clear and sweet. Business continued, although slower. The shaded windows made dim squares of light against the black buildings.

A thin form, bulked in a coat, had slipped up the backstairs of the Glacier Palace and stood huddled against the outside exit. A shawl encircled his face under the floppy hat, revealing strange eyes that darted hypnotically. The full of moon irritated him. Angrily, he would glare up at the soaring orb, for the pale light exposed him, bared his existence, if not his tormented soul, to any curious eyes that might chance by. He had tried the door and found it locked, as expected. Now he stole along a narrow balcony next to the window where the blond girl had emerged, the one who had seen him. He waited, his heart pounding, the tension building, the excitement exhilarating. From the room, shadows played across the window. The girl within had a patron, he was certain. Filthy whore. Creature of scum. His face tightened with indignity; his mouth pinched with a curl of superiority, of sanctimonious pride. He tried to peer through a yellow crack of curtain. He glimpsed here and there movements of a woman half undressed. And then he was certain she was alone, cleaning herself at a nightstand, patting herself anew with perfume, fragrant whiffs that seemed to exude through the woodwork. But he could not see her features, only the form.

He took the knife from his sheath and pried slowly at the window. He sensed her freeze, to listen. He, too, froze and listened. The wind moaned around the eaves while pelting the siding with fine sand. Inside, the woman turned up her lamp and continued her toiletry. The man began a quiet, methodical probing where he knew the latch rested. Then he saw the girl swirl some clothing on, move across the room, and leave. He heard the door close. She had put on a robe or a gown, he decided, and was greeting or entertaining another customer. Quickly, industriously, he set to opening the window. And when he felt it give, he sat down outside and drew his coat tightly around him. Eventually she would be alone again, after the last customer. He would be waiting.

Earlier that night, Willard Dragmire entered the Golden Bird, the most sedate bar in town. The bartender, a rotund fellow, acknowledged him as he purchased part of a bottle and took it to a dark corner. He liked the spot, with its smoky chandeliers, the flowered walls, the huge mirror behind the bar flanked with brightly labeled containers. He admired the mammoth elk, and deer antlers adorning one wall. However, he felt self-conscious over all the nude paintings of plump ladies artfully posed on ottomans that lined a second wall; and on a third, where blendings of history and mythology featured more nudes, *Susanna and the Elders, Satyrs and Nymphs, Aphrodite Emerging from the Bath, Rape of Lucretia, Innocence Betrayed.* Dragmire had seen displays of great art as a youth in the East, and he knew that the paintings here were replicas of immortal masters. He appreciated anything that demanded talent and creativity and revealed exactness and precision, despite the showy display of flesh. He often envisioned himself as a creative artist—his talent with guns, in the shop or in the field, was far more than a craft, he felt.

A few businessmen discussed matters over a beer at a far table, and a pretty waitress stood near the bar, talking to the bartender. In the back room he could hear the slap of cards and the mumble of male voices. The aroma of expensive cigars drifted on the blue smoke. Select clientele—ranchers, doctors, lawyers, merchants, bankers, mining speculators— all habitually gathered here for relaxation. Yes, he liked the setting. That is why he felt uneasy and imposed upon when the two drifters came in. The larger was whiskered with a craggy face and a perpetual scowl. He wore a peaked hat, sweat-stained, tugged low over sullen eyes. The second was wiry, gaunt, with a girlish mouth and a twisted nose that gave him a weaselish appearance. He had hostile eyes that roved about the room. His rounded hat tilted back almost to his neck, with a string tie pulled tight. Both wore greasy coats that had the look of time and distance. They ordered whiskey, paid for and poured several shots which they gulped down and poured again.

Dragmire tried to recall where he had seen them. "That marshal is still grubbin' around," he heard one of them say.

"Don't matter," said the other. Then they lowered their voices so he could not hear. But he could tell by the thick slurring of their words that they had been drinking heavily already. The waitress looked at them with disgust, backed off, and busied herself arranging glasses.

"Don't like our company, lady?" the weasel-faced one said. The girl angled away and did not reply. "Talkin' to you, lady."

The bartender interjected, his face flaming red. "This is a respectable place, gentlemen, I suggest you watch your manners or leave."

"Watch our manners or leave." The larger of the pair tilted back his head and roared with mirth, then tossed another whiskey down. They walked to a free lunch table where the food lay drying and thoroughly picked over. "Ain't got much left for a hungry customer." Both pawed up big slabs of rye bread and layered them with sardines, pickles, and Swiss cheese, then munched into them with gusto.

"There will be fresh food tomorrow morning," the bartender explained condescendingly.

"That don't do us any good now," said the smaller one. "You got some boiled eggs? I got a hankerin' for boiled eggs."

"No."

"They ain't too hospitable here. Are they, Dade?" He looked at his partner and grinned cruelly. The businessmen at the far table rose and left quietly. Dragmire looked down into the dark of his drink.

"You know, Schick, maybe they should just give us some free beer to wash this crap down with." The bigger man chewed mightily, his mouth open.

"Yeah, if they don't got boiled eggs. That ain't rightly accommodatin'."

"Look, I warn you." The bartender pointed a sausage-shaped finger. Stealthily he reached under the counter, possibly for a club or a weapon.

Both men confronted him. The one referred to as Schick raised his gun with the quickness of a professional. His face turned dark and mean. "You threaten us—and you're going to find yourself in bad trouble." He advanced. With his left hand he pushed the bartender back. "Now you mind your business and you just take care of our needs like you're supposed to." The busy clatter of coins and husky voices ceased in the back room. Several older men in suits appeared in the doorway. "Ain't none of your business, either," Schick threatened. The men disappeared.

"You, girlie," said Dade. "Bring a couple of beers." The bartender poured two steins full until they foamed over. The girl wiped them, placed them on a tray, and approached with trepidation. The men grinned, looked her up and down, and took the glasses. When the girl turned around, Dade swatted her soundly across the buttocks. She cried out with anger and scurried away. The two laughed and gulped thirstily, wiping their faces with a backhand. Schick then saw Drag-

mire in the corner watching. The gunsmith's face had hardened with contempt so lividly that Schick both saw and felt
it. The drifter's face went sober.

"Well, lookie back in them shadows. The boy there, he
don't take much to our doings." Schick swaggered over to
the table where Dragmire sat, looking down at his drink
again. The bartender and the girl watched, their faces pained
in anticipation of something frightening. "You, boy, what
you got against me and my friend? We was just funnin'."

Dragmire shook his head. "I don't want trouble."

"Speak up, boy, I can't hear you. What you got against
me and my partner?"

"Nothing," Dragmire managed.

"What?"

"Nothing."

"Say it again."

"Nothing."

"You need to be taught a lesson in respect, son," said
Schick, his girlish mouth pursing. "You're a hothead. You
need to cool off." He reached down, lifted Dragmire's whiskey bottle and poured the remains slowly over the gunsmith's
head. Dragmire closed his eyes, his body quaking as the
liquid splashed and streamed over his face to drip down his
front. But he did not respond in any threatening way. Dade
roared with laughter. "Come on," said Schick, smashing
the bottle against the table, the shards spraying across the
sawdust floor, "this place is dead. Ain't no life here." They
scooped up another bottle, some bread and ham, and
clumped noisily out.

The bartender stood enraged, his face bloated, his thick
fingers white-knuckled, clutching the bar.

The girl rushed to Dragmire with a towel and began patting his wet shirt and vest. "I'm so sorry," she said. "Are
you all right?"

Dragmire did not reply. Shaking with frustration, he rose,
knocking his chair over, and moved out the back door into

the windy night. He had remembered the two. He had seen them once in the gun shop talking to Henrietta Cheveny about some merchandise. He checked his sidearm and stole into the night.

(4)

From the Golden Bird, Dragmire rushed down the back street, attempting to parallel the drifters. He then slipped into a dark alley, nearly stumbling over a drunk cradled between two rain barrels. Cautiously, with his gun drawn, he moved toward the front street and peered around the edge of a building. The two had stopped on the other side of a freight wagon half filled with lumber. By their conversation, he knew they were passing the bottle back and forth. He heard one mention Lilli's place and make a vulgar comment. Dragmire squatted down. He could see their booted legs in the faint light. He considered stepping around the wagon and gunning both, then fleeing down the alley, where he would slip to his room. But he hesitated, knowing that they were dangerous. If he should only wing one, that survivor could return a deadly fire before he managed to reach safety. He decided to wait and watch, for they might move into a better position, where he could take them out quickly and easily.

"You two, I want to talk to you," came a sudden voice. "I'm Hal Sundon, sheriff in this town."

Dragmire dodged back into the shadows and waited.

"We ain't done nothin', Sheriff," said one of the pair.

"Got a complaint from a peeved customer out of the Golden Bird that you two was raisin' a disturbance. Seen you walk out of there pretty cocky."

"Just havin' a little fun, Sheriff."

"Turn around and spread your arms up on that wagon. And drop the bottle," said Sundon, his voice firm.

"Hell, Sheriff, you ain't being hospitable."

"May just take you in for the night, let you sleep it all off."

"You're making a big mistake, Sheriff."

"Recognize them, Hal?" came another voice.

Dragmire got down on his hands and knees to see better. The second lawman was Dirk Landry, backing Sundon on his regular night rounds.

"Not yet."

"A Mr. Dade and a Mr. Schick."

"Well, damned if you're not right."

Landry's voice was deep, resonant: "Whose gun you hired for this time?"

"We was just passin' through," said Dade.

"You two never just pass through."

Sundon took their sidearms and knives and felt for any other weapons.

Schick said, "We are legal; we're law-abiding bounty-men. You can't hold us for nothin' wrong."

"Except for disturbing the peace," said Sundon. "You know where the jail is. Get going."

"Tin star bastards." Dade twisted around, but Landry, who had stepped in, brought his gun barrel down with a squashing sound across the drifter's head, flopping his hat away as he collapsed heavily to lie in a mound, his legs drawn up. Landry reached down, caught Dade by the collar and hoisted him to his feet. The drifter wavered dizzily, then found his balance as they marched toward the sheriff's office.

Dragmire watched with some satisfaction, hoping there might be another time and place.

Men both hated and admired Franz Kurt. In a little more than a decade he had built a small empire of both mining and cattle interests that was rivaled only by the Donnovan brothers, a family that had become resolute in their competition. Twenty years earlier he had immigrated from Prussia with a degree in engineering, an interest in geology, and a consuming ambition. The California mother lode, where the flush of easy pickings had turned into hard-rock mining, proved a natural for him, and he soon rose to foreman with one of the larger firms. In time, some wise judgments as to where the fickle veins flowed brought him a junior partnership. He saved, married a plucky Bavarian girl, and eventually transferred to Nevada as the gold in California faded and the silver boom in the Basin country offered unlimited opportunity. The rest had been history. A good-producing mine, solid investments from the eastern establishment, some shrewd manipulations, and he eventually headed his own enterprise. He had purchased a princely mansion with extensive stables in a lush valley between the staid city of Limbo and the boomtown of Midas. He took pride in having cooks and servants, and thoroughbred horses. Life had been good, except for the death of his wife following complications with the birth of their daughter.

Beautiful and spoiled, Kellie Kurt had been the center of her father's universe. She was an accomplished rider at seven, a classical pianist at twelve, and a polished hostess to the businessmen who frequented their home. For her sixteenth birthday Franz sent her to Germany with a nanny to visit relatives. While there, she toured Paris, Vienna, Brussels, Salzburg, and the Rhineland. Now she was at a finishing school in Baltimore, and that was the problem. Bored and homesick, she missed wearing riding britches and galloping across the open land on her Arabian horse. She had hungered for the excitement, for the people, and for the flavor of the big land. She hated the eastern schooling, the pretense, the petty snobbery—a foreign world that she wanted no part of anymore. She had telegraphed her father that she was coming home, that she would arrive in Midas on the night stage via the Central Pacific sometime after six in the morning,

August 4, and that she had made her mind up and wanted no arguments. Franz Kurt had fired back an angry retort, demanding that she come to her senses and stay, only to learn she had already left. Furious, he nevertheless respected her headstrong spunkiness, which reminded him of himself. What concerned him: she was traveling alone, a vulnerable rich girl.

Kurt sat his horse stolidly, flanked by six of his riders and a foreman. Smallish, he had the distinguished look of a man who gave orders. He had the lean, set features of his east Germanic background, with thick white hair, sideburns, and curving mustache. His dark frock coat, high hat, striped pants, and polished boots set him apart. Grimly, he watched the stage jolt up the main street toward the Wells Fargo station, the driver and messenger looking harried, the passengers hunched. "Something ain't right," Kurt uttered, spurring his horse ahead.

Sheriff Brent Cole and a deputy pushed through the gathering crowd. Handsome, with a bronze face and a pencil-thin mustache, Cole confronted the driver as the passengers stepped wearily out.

"Rattlesnake Morton and his gang," the man responded dispiritedly, and handed the message to Kurt. "He done this to us on Silver Lode Summit."

His face gray, Franz Kurt read the words. "Bastard took my girl," said the mining magnate, and passed Cole the letter. "I feared this. Little fool—she should have used her brains."

Cole read and whistled slowly. "One hundred thousand dollars in forty-eight hours?"

"If that son of a bitch harms one hair on my daughter's head, I'll use every nickel I've got to do him in." Kurt twisted his reins, tightening the bit and forcing his horse to twist and stomp uncomfortably.

Cole continued reading aloud. " 'One man, alone, unarmed. Bring cash in sack or saddlebags to white rock fifty feet uphill, east of road on Silver Lode Summit. Leave it. If money is all there, and there is no tricks, your daughter will be let go where I choose. You have forty-eight hours from time you read this, no longer. Leander Morton.' '' Cole looked up. ''I know that rock. It's an odd tooth of quartz in a wooded clearing.''

''I'm not sitting still,'' said Kurt. ''I'm going after my girl, but I'll need your help, Sheriff.''

''I'll do what I can, but it's mountainous country he's waiting in.''

''If he's expecting me and the money, he'll be there somewhere.'' Kurt turned his horse restlessly to one side and then to the other. ''But first I need to send some telegrams. I'm going to bring in the rest of my men, and no disrespect to you, Cole, but I'm contacting Marshal Landry. I understand he's south of here in Broken Bluffs. Morton is his charge. He's gotta be in on this.''

''I couldn't agree more,'' said Cole. ''But you best raise the money first.''

''I can't just sit around. Give me half a day; at least me and the boys might find out where he's holed up.''

The sheriff pursed his mouth and chose his words. ''Trouble is, he's got the cards on his side—your daughter, forty-eight hours, and rough country.'' Cole looked up steadily at Kurt. ''If he thinks we're double-crossing him, not only is your daughter in danger, but he could draw us right into an ambush. I don't think you have any choice but to play his game until you get your girl back.''

''Damn it, man,'' Kurt blustered. ''You suggesting I just cave in, just give him what he wants without a try? He don't dare hurt my girl.''

Cole did not buckle under Kurt's withering look. ''You may not have that much choice. You may be powerful in this territory, Franz, but Morton, he don't fear the Devil himself.''

Kurt considered the words and acquiesced some. ''If I

knew where they're holding her, we might get a crack at them after Kellie's released.''

"You have a point," said Cole. "But it's a dangerous gamble in my estimation.''

Kurt squared his jaw. "I didn't get where I am by crawling, not to the likes of Morton.''

Midas stretched from the base of a high bluff out onto an alluvial plain, the foot of a wooded canyon in the rugged Toquima Range. Below stretched a steep slope that flattened in a great blue valley of sage which ended in the abrupt rise of the Toiyabe Mountains to the west. Just south of the Silver Lode Summit the town offered all the amenities of a prosperous mining and cattle center: stores, hotels, churches, laundries, bakeries, assay offices, cold storage lockers, a lumber company, a livery stable, cattle pens, a theater, a school, a brewery, a fire department, numerous fraternal halls, a half-dozen stamp mills on the back hills, and the usual sporting district: fandango houses, gambling palaces and saloons, the latter disproportionately evident. With an ample supply of wood, water, rock, and clay, the townspeople had constructed many substantial stone and fireproof brick buildings as well as numerous frame structures. Nine thousand people found their livelihoods in the high tide of an exciting prosperity, as mule freighters toiled in and out each day, churning dust as they hauled away high-sided wagons of ore or brought in supplies and basic goods and often bigcity cuisines: iced oysters, champagne, and strawberries that those in the flush could afford.

Cole, Kurt, and his foreman, Bradly, found their way through a busy crowd to the telegraph office where an impatient Kurt sent telegrams: first to his business manager, and then to the sheriff in Limbo to notify his men.

"Doubt if all your men are going to help much," said Cole. "Doubt if you ever get a chance to face off with Morton.''

"Eventually, someplace, somewhere, I'll get a chance,

and when I do, I'll want the forces to wipe them out.'' Kurt dug into his vest pocket for coins and laid them on the counter.

"This is important, Joe," said Cole to the telegraph operator. "We want to get through to a Marshal Landry." From under a green-shaded cap the man regarded Kurt with curiosity. He scribbled the messages, nodded curtly, sat down before the circuit and flipped on the current.

Kurt watched the operator, not understanding Morse code but taking satisfaction that the words were being transmitted. He said to his foreman, a husky man with sagging jowls and a walrus mustache, "Bradly, I'm leaving you here. I want to at least look over the situation. Maybe I can learn where they've taken her."

"I understand, but I would rather be with you, sir."

"No, you're the only one I can rely on. I want you to wait for Landry and for the rest of the boys. If we haven't returned before they arrive, you know we'll be in the Silver Lode area. Landry's a good tracker. He can find us and probably find that bastard with my daughter."

"Forty-eight hours ain't very long," Cole advised. "It's your daughter and your money, but maybe for precaution's sake you should arrange for the money before doin' anything. I think you're going to have to hand over the ransom and go after Morton afterward."

Kurt scowled. "I plan to; it's just that I hate to dance to Morton's tune. It's going to take time and some amount of juggling to get that sum together. My business manager, he'll have it all by today sometime. He's going to have to borrow against different accounts and securities. But in the meantime I want to take my boys and scout around. And I'd be much obliged if you and some of your deputies will go with me." Kurt added soberly, "I'll arrange the money first. But you must understand, when my boys arrive, I've got to go out there. The site's less than an hour's ride. You understand?"

"I think it's dangerous and wrong," said Cole. "If I was

you, I'd wait for Landry. If he don't come, then take the money to Morton. Get her free first. Goin' up there in force— you could ride into a trap, especially if you anger Morton. But if you insist, when your men get here, I'll deputize them.''

"You won't come with me, then?"

"I'll ride up there on one condition."

"What?"

"We'll look things over. If I don't like it, we're coming back. I'll not jeopardize my men, and you shouldn't yours. Agreed?"

"Agreed."

"I'll round up some of the boys," said Cole, hitching his gun belt.

"How much reward now for Morton?"

"Ten thousand."

Kurt called after the sheriff. "I'm going to double that."

On a plateau, forested with pinyon and juniper, four riders approached a squat wood cabin partially hidden by willows in the shadow of a bluff. From an adjoining cedar corral a saddled buckskin raised its head and nickered. Rattlesnake Morton led, followed by Riles holding the Kurt girl in front of him, with Jenson and Beatty behind. As they cantered to a stop, a baldish man, stooped and moving stiffly, emerged from the cabin. "Said you'd be here today, and you are—just on time." The old man spat a ropy length of tobacco, his face widening in a toothless grin. He held a roll of blankets under one arm. "Seen you comin'. I'm ready for whatever."

"That cabin in the Monitors," said Morton. "You know, the one east of here. . . ."

"Sure do."

"Just like with this one, I want you to keep it supplied, and keep anybody nosin' around the hell out."

"And if somebody's already there?"

"Take care of 'em, like you done before."

"That for the next haul?" the old man asked cheerfully.

"Depends on how good we hit it with this little girl's old man."

"You're not going to get anything out of my father," Kellie Kurt shouted.

"Remains to be seen."

"You going back now with Liddicoat and Fang?" Jenson asked.

"Yeah." Morton slid from the saddle. "They and me are going to wait. Eventually Kurt or someone will come with the money. He don't have no other choice. Oh, he may snoop around first."

"That Kurt feller, he's got a lot of pull. He might not cooperate so easy."

Morton looked slyly at Jenson. "That's why you're going to ride back to Midas. Get in there tonight sometime undercover, like you've done so many times."

Jenson smiled proudly, his sharp face twisting. "Like a mouse; like always, I'll be just like a mouse."

"You know who to contact. He'll know what's happening. If something goes wrong, if you learn of problems, get the hell back here."

"Like what?"

"Like Franz Kurt dropping dead before he can pay, or of an army comin' after us, or of that big marshal, Dirk Landry, on the prowl." The men laughed.

"That never stopped you before." Jenson grinned.

"And it ain't gonna now." Morton chuckled from the gut. "But you keep on your toes; keep your eyes open, you hear?" Morton grew serious. "I never dealt with Franz Kurt before. I don't know exactly what to expect. And you're right, he's a big man in the state. Rich men are proud. Even though I got his little girl, he might try something foolish."

Riles swung from the saddle. Holding the reins in one hand, he tipped his Stetson in an exaggerated sweep. "Welcome, my princess, to your palace." When he attempted to lift her down, she kicked him in the chest, knocking him back. Beatty and Morton laughed. Cursing, Riles rushed back to drag her off. He stood her straight and shook her. "Little bitch." She slapped him resoundingly. He yanked her to him, held her and kissed her neck. She bit his ear. He cried out, stood back and slapped her. She cried out angrily, like an abused little animal, and swung her knee for his groin, but he caught her in time, his arms enveloping her as she struggled.

"Let go of me, you stinking hog," she grunted. Riles loosened her and flung her toward the cabin. She almost lost her footing, but he was behind her, grasping her and flinging her through the open door. He pushed her past the first room into a second, a storage area with a bunk and low bureau. She spun around, her back to the wall, her breasts rising and falling with emotion.

Morton came in, lit a coal oil lantern and walked into the room with Kellie. Beatty and Jenson entered the cabin and stood back, uncertain. Morton laid the lantern on the bureau and pawed through her luggage for weapons before setting it down. "There's no way out, just that little window overhead for air. But you have all the comforts of home: water, a washbasin, a bed, a chamber pot in the drawer. We'll have some grub for you shortly. Ain't what you was brung up with, but it's gonna have to do."

"Go to hell," Kellie spat. As Riles left and Morton bolted the door shut, Kellie crashed something against the wooden planking.

"This ain't going to be so easy," said Riles, wiping his brow with a neckerchief.

"Ain't your problem," said Morton. "You ain't getting near that girl. Too much could happen."

"I can handle her," Riles protested.

"You're going to keep away. Like I told you earlier, you hold watch outside there until we get back." Morton motioned toward Beatty, who lumbered forward. "Take over;

guard the girl good, and attend to her needs.'' Beatty nodded slowly and ran a purple tongue over yellow teeth. Outside, the old man, still shaking his head, pulled the buckskin from the corral and climbed stiffly aloft. Jenson and Morton joined him. ''From here, you best take the mountain cutoff,'' Morton told Jenson. ''You can make it to town in a couple of hours. Keep on top of that couple we hired. We may need them if things get rough. They'll be contacting you tomorrow afternoon as planned.'' He turned to the old man. ''I'll be seeing you; figure on us joining you in a couple of days or so.'' As the three rode their ways, Riles watched sullenly. When they had disappeared into the trees, he looked back at Beatty and at the locked door; a smile of anticipation curled his lips.

''Mime dead? In my old room?'' Eve cried in horror. Tired and a little bleary-eyed, she stood before Landry in the parlor, fetched from her room by Lilli, who was opening the heavy curtains to let the early morning light stream in.

Landry nodded solemnly. ''I'm getting you out of here for the time being. I'm taking you north, probably to Midas. I know a woman there with a lodging house that can keep you until all this is solved.''

''In other words, Mime's killer thought she was me.'' Eve stood tall, her jaw thrust in feeble courage.

''Ordinarily I'd give you a bad time,'' said Lilli, ''about hankering for my girl here. But we heard the rumor earlier this morning. Things travel fast in a town like this.''

''They must. Mime was found strangled only a few hours ago.''

''You best get this girl where she's safe,'' said Lilli. ''I don't want that kind of trouble around here.''

''How soon can you be packed?'' Landry asked.

''In no time. Just have a few changes and my personal things. But how can you leave just for me? Weren't you assigned here?''

"Well, it's more than that. I received a telegram this morning, some big things are breaking north of here. You be ready. I'll be back shortly." Landry acknowledged Lilli and walked out. When he reached the law office, he found Sheriff Sundon releasing the two bounty hunters, Dade and Schick. Sobered, the two men strapped on their empty guns and looked heatedly at the officers but did not speak.

"Just don't forget that you ain't welcome in this town," Sundon told them. Sullenly the lawmen watched the two plod toward the livery stable. "So Morton kidnapped Franz Kurt's daughter. Kurt's a damn important name here in the Basin country."

"Big enough that all hell could break loose."

"You pulling out now?"

"Soon as I get my horse and one for the girl."

"Best you get Eve somewhere safe. Don't seem to be a hell of a lot we can do to protect these women." Sundon rubbed his eyes. "Some crazy mind out there. But where do you start? As long as women ply their trade and someone hates them for it, this thing is going to happen."

"I'm sorry to cut out on you," said Landry, "but Morton is too big, too dangerous to ignore. I been on his trail for too long. And not this close for some while."

Sundon returned to his desk and shuffled some papers. "Well, there's not a lot you can do here that me and the boys can't do. With no solid leads and no suspects except what that Eve girl saw, which wasn't anything really, we don't have much to go on."

"Well, I'm not off this case yet. Keep me posted by telegram," said Landry. "I'll be back."

At the Wells Fargo stop in Broken Bluffs, Willard Dragmire assisted Noah Cheveny onto the stage. Stiff, a cheek bruised, he moved with difficulty. "You are a fool, my husband," said his wife, Henrietta. She had been harping at him steadily since they had left the store in Dragmire's rented wagon.

"You know I got an appointment in Midas. You know that I've worked too hard to cancel this one. Biggest connection I've ever made," said Cheveny, wrapping a scarf around his neck in protection against the morning chill. "Possibility of big sales there. It's a booming town, not like here. You know that, Henrietta. We just might start a store there. Maybe even move there if things work out."

"You talk dreams, my battered husband."

Cheveny dismissed her haughty manner. "Besides, I'm going to talk to the sheriff up there about my gun collection. Brent Cole is his name. He's a good man."

"That Morton man will have sold it somewhere by now," the woman scoffed.

Ignoring her, Cheveny eyed Dragmire. "I hope to hell you can handle things while I'm gone."

Dragmire stiffened. "I know my routes, sir. I've never failed you, have I?"

"Hell, boy, as a gunsmith you're not bad, as long as I'm looking over your shoulder, but as a salesman you got a long ways to go. It takes gumption, drive. Like me going to Midas beaten and sore, but that don't stand in my way."

"Yes, sir."

"He'll do fine. You got everything you need?" Henrietta asked.

Cheveny patted his satchel. "Got all I really need right here."

As the stage pulled out, Dragmire saw the self-proclaimed bounty hunters trotting their horses out of town, their stone-hard faces pointed straight ahead. Dragmire felt an itchy discontent come over him. The no-good bastards were riding northwest, the direction he would be going. The thought appealed to him. He made note that the man named Schick rode a brown with white stockings, and Dade rode an Appaloosa. Henriette Cheveny watched them with interest, too.

Dragmire took Mrs. Cheveny home and loaded his spring wagon with boxes of ammunition, Winchester rifles, Colt revolvers, a few shotguns, and a couple of derringers. He went to his room and packed extra clothes for the week's circuit. He studied the faded picture of his wife on the table. He recalled the stage robbery, the man with the flat face and arrogant way, his wife swooning, his reacting and being clubbed senseless; then later that dark night, finding her, dead, strangled, laid carefully across the bed. The sight was never clear in his mind, always hazy and squirming, fading in and out with distorted shapes and images that swelled and shrunk, until he pushed it all away. Dragmire felt nauseated. He laid her picture facedown. He had to. A pounding headache filled him to bursting. He found his hands shaking. He had been thinking about her more often, it seemed, the effect leaving him weak and expended afterward. Dizzily, he found his way downstairs, where Henrietta Cheveny was studying him. "Are you all right?"

"Yes."

"What happened?"

"Nothing." He took his orders from the countertop. "I will be back in a week," he told her. "Will you be all right?"

"Yes. I can handle things. And I'm sure my husband is in no condition to forget business."

Dragmire was not certain what she meant. "Keep your doors locked."

"I will." She sighed. "But surely the likes of that Morton are long gone."

"There are others like him."

"It's too bad that people like that can drift in and out, hurting and killing," she lamented. "Dirk Landry's in town. He's good, but he's too few. We need more lawmen."

"Oh, there are citizens—people around to help," Dragmire said, his features transformed, confident.

"There are plenty armed, for certain. But how helpful, I don't know."

"Oh, there are some, only a few maybe, but some who are willing to act." Dragmire lifted the last of his luggage and walked toward the waiting horse and wagon. Down the street he saw the marshal and the girl named Eve turn a corner to head into the desert.

(5)

Marshal Landry pulled a halt in the shadow of a rocky spur where a spring pooled bluish green and the grass grew lush near a cluster of thick willows. Ahead, the flat of sage and shad scale stretched to a bluish rise of mountains, the southern end of two ranges, with the valley between like a great yawning mouth. He and the girl dismounted to let the horses take their fill and graze for a time. Landry studied Eve. He could not believe the scrawny little girl in pigtails that he had especially remembered was now a strongly built woman, full and rounded.

She sensed his eyes upon her. "You must have been a devoted brother. I understand Mother always spoke of you with much respect."

Her sensitivity touched Landry. A man who seldom delved into emotions, he turned away and adjusted the cinch on his big chestnut. "You're my family. What do you expect? If you were mine, she would have done the same for me. Besides, she was always my favorite."

Eve looked at him curiously. "I can't remember her much, except the terrible coughing and suffering before she died. Oh, I remember a dress she sewed me with frills." The woman smiled, her eyes distant. "And a rag doll she made me." She looked away and shuddered. "I don't want to talk about it; it's all past." She hoisted her shoulders. "Now, about where you're taking me."

"I told you, to a boardinghouse. You'll like Mae. She

takes good care of her customers.''

"I don't have much money on me.''

"This will be courtesy of the U.S. government.'' Landry filled his canteen where the water emerged clear and cold. He handed her the container and she drank with pleasure. "Midas is one of the few booming towns remaining in the Basin, an interesting place.''

"I've heard of it. Is it safer there?''

"Safer for you, yes. That's why I'm taking you, but also I have business there. A man—an influential man's daughter has been kidnapped.''

"A poor little rich girl?''

"Yes.''

"And you are going to rescue her?''

Landry smiled. "I'll do my best.''

"She is the type I would ordinarily envy and despise, but I feel sorry for her. I guess even the powerful and the rich can be hurt.''

"Of course they can. I've known her and her father for years. In most situations, Kellie could take care of herself. She's feisty and spoiled rotten. Ordinarily I'd say she might be a match for whoever took her. But Leander Morton is not one to fool with.''

Eve rubbed the neck of her horse as it ripped up mouthfuls of grass. "Leander Morton. I've heard that name.''

"No doubt you have. Rattlesnake Morton is what most call him. He's raised hell in this land for years, and so far no one has been able to stop him.''

"Not even you?''

"Not even me. Oh, I put him behind bars once, until he escaped. And I once shot him out of a hoist into an abandoned mine, but he escaped that, too. I thought I had him with all that timber and soil falling in on him.''

"He must live a charmed life.''

"He's smart and he's been lucky. But sometime his luck is going to run out. And I intend to be there when it does.''

Eve started to respond, paused, and asked, "Where do I go when all this blows over? If you find the killer."

"Probably to Limbo. It and Virginia City are the old queens of the territory. Glorious pasts. Sedate and quiet now, but thriving, a place where one could get lost and start over."

"You won't take me back to Broken Bluffs?"

Disappointed, Landry looked at the girl. "No. Never. You are pretty. You can be somebody, Eve. Marry somebody decent. There's no reason whatsoever to choose Lilli's way."

Eve's soft voice took on an edge of hardness and her face grew taut with resistance. "I came with you because I am frightened. But afterward, I owe you nothing, Uncle. You are not my guardian. I am my own person, and I will choose to do what I want to do."

"Right now you're being a jackass," said Landry. "Mount up, we're moving on." He quickly examined the cinches on her saddle and hoisted her up with a vigor that made her grab the pommel to keep from going on over.

For several hours Franz Kurt, Sheriff Cole, and their men pushed into the timberland east of Silver Lode Summit, but without success. They found hoof marks and fresh droppings, but the trail became less defined and soon indistinct as they went higher and the soft andesite gave way to hard slate and granite. The squeaking of leather, the clop of iron on rock, and the blowing of horses drifted through the wooded aisles, driving deer to thunder away and jays to shriek in protest. "Anybody would hear us coming two miles away," Cole called to Kurt. They all swung their horses into a loose circle to consider the situation. "I have a suspicion that some of Morton's men may be decoying us," said Cole, his face pinching derisively.

"How is that?" Kurt growled.

"Have you noticed, we've been swinging in a loop? They've drawn us up toward open country. Now we're turning back down toward where we started."

"Hadn't noticed. But I see what you mean."

"They're toying with us," Cole snorted, "leading us on until we come to our senses and pay the ransom. They could have blown us out of the saddle anytime."

"Hell, we need a man who can track," Kurt blustered. "None of my men are good that way."

"I ain't too good a tracker, either," said Cole. "If Landry was here, he'd see things we don't."

"But he ain't."

"I have a feeling part of them pulled us away from the ones who took your daughter, and now they've left us," said Cole. "There's a good number of old miner cabins in these hills. My guess is that some of the gang has holed up with your girl in one of 'em. But which one and where is impossible to guess."

Frustrated, Kurt removed his high hat and wiped his face. "Time is so damn short. It'll take Landry a good half day to get here, assuming he got my telegram." Out of defiance, Kurt had left a man named Haney at the Silver Lode Summit below Morton's rendezvous spot to await Bradly and the marshal.

"Like I tried to tell you before," Cole said firmly, "Morton's in control. We're wasting our time here. Until you get your girl back safe, I suggest you do as he says."

"Looks like I don't have much choice," said Kurt. "At least for now, you were right. But that bastard will pay. I'm not used to being pushed around." Kurt kneed his horse down the slope. "Let's pick up Haney and get back to town."

Two hundred yards above the posse, through a leafy glade of alders, Liddicoat and Fang watched the riders wander, confused. The two stretched out behind a jumble of angular boulders. Liddicoat, his face waxen, emotionless, played with his rifle, aiming at the nearly dozen men. With quiet pleasure he made trajectory judgment on Sheriff Cole, then

Franz Kurt, and back to Cole again. Even at the distance and steep angle, he figured he could kill either with ease.

Fang grinned with satisfaction, his snaggled teeth gleaming in the late morning light. "It worked. Morton's too smart for 'em," he gloated. Although ordered to oversee the delivery sight, the two gunmen had been warned that Kurt might try to follow with his hired guns, an emotional response of a proud man. And if he did, they were to lead him and his men astray. Upon seeing the posse, Fang and Liddicoat had dutifully obeyed by veering to the right and climbing through the pines, while leaving a decided trail at first. Previously, Morton and the others, with the girl, had doubled back and had slipped their way across the plateau to the cabin.

"Best we sneak down to the road again and keep under cover," Liddicoat said tersely, sighting his rifle continuously. "Morton should be joining us soon."

After deftly avoiding the posse upon return, Rattlesnake Morton had left his horse in a wooded recess above the Silver Lode Summit to approach an armed intruder. Franz Kurt was not cooperating and would have to learn that he meant business. Morton was not surprised or too irritated; he had rather expected the bullheaded Kurt to come plowing after his daughter in blind rage. It was the tycoon's nature, and after all, he had over forty hours yet. Not far from the stone tooth where the money was to be delivered, Kurt had left a guard, probably as a liaison for the law or for someone following, a rebellious gesture that amused Morton. A soft wind rustled the brush, and the warming air brought pungent smells of pinyon and sage. Bees hummed among the summer blossoms. The guard leaned back, his head nodding then jerking up as he squirmed in discomfort, his rifle cradled askew across his lap. Sullenly, Morton gauged the distance and studied a possible approach. A glow of anticipation filled his dark eyes. He checked a vest pocket for a pencil and piece of paper, took his bowie knife from its sheath, crouched forward and stole forth.

The man named Haney yawned. He had not seen anyone or heard anyone since his boss and the others had ridden off. Bored and hungry, he wished they might return so he could get back to Midas. He had a strong hankering for a drink. With the high elevation and the proximity to packs of lingering snow even in the heart of summer, all the saloons in town featured ice-cold beer. The thought made him lick his dry lips. He sat up a little straighter, for his back ached and the shade had shifted. He laid the rifle at his side and yawned again. He pulled a chew of tobacco from a pocket.

As Haney opened his mouth, his features froze, stricken. A catlike form sprang from behind, clutched the man under the jaw with one hand and sank the broad blade into the heart with a downward sweep of the other arm. Haney cried out slowly, like a bellows losing air. His upper trunk toppled to the side, his green eyes wide and sightless, his mouth still open as blood pooled beneath him. Morton jerked the knife free and wiped it clean on the man's backside. He then scanned the valley below, the hill he had just descended, the road. Certain that no one had observed him, he removed the paper and penciled a message: "You did not follow my orders. Now bring the money. One rider, here. Try something again and your girl will end like your man here. You have just over one day." Morton then dragged the body down to the granite tooth and propped it into a sitting position. He found a small hunting knife on the corpse, removed it, placed his message over the right side of the chest and stabbed the paper in place.

Dejected, the riders—led by Cole, with Kurt a half length behind—filed down the hillside. "Got to get back," said Kurt. "All my boys are to meet me at the Nugget Hotel. Landry might be there or on the way here with Bradly."

"The horses are tired," said Cole. "We can push them

just so hard.'' They eased their animals toward the stage road. The horses clicked and stumbled and caught themselves in a choppy rhythm, their eyes wallowing. ''Be glad to get them on the level down there.''

One of the deputies cried out, ''Look. Look at that rocky point. Kurt's man, the one we left here. He don't look right.'' All the men saw Haney then, slumped back. His body had slid some, giving him an awkward look. The possemen quickened their pace.

Both Cole and Kurt, his face colorless, dismounted. ''Son of a bitch,'' Kurt uttered. Cole removed the knife, studied the paper, and handed it to Kurt. All eyes focused on him as he read the message, his face anxious and twisted. He cursed again in frustration. ''Morton's around here, close by. He's been watching us. Probably watching us right now.'' The magnate's eyes darted over the setting.

''What did you expect?'' Cole said coolly. ''You've got to play his game for now. You've got to come up with the money, and fast.''

Kurt looked at the quartz rock. The arrow-shaped rise was in the open, easily surveilled and totally vulnerable to a bullet. Morton had chosen his site well. ''I know,'' he said with deep resignation. ''Let's get the hell back.''

Kellie Kurt searched the room. Sparse, it apparently had been prepared as a prison for her. The storage shelves were empty except for a few blankets and some staples, sacks of flours, beans, rice, coffee, and a can of kerosene. But any tools, pieces of equipment, or miscellaneous boards had been carefully cleared. She noticed that the door bolt had been recently removed from inside and installed outside temporarily. The stark walls had no pictures or decorations. The only furniture was a solid bunk built into the wall, a high-backed chair, and a squat nightstand with a wide door. She looked inside. It contained a heavy chamber pot. She pulled the chair over next to the high window and stepped up to test the narrow opening. The daylight brought the sharp scent of pines, but the room was stuffy, the coal oil lantern filling the place with a dull glow and dirty fumes. She checked the sill and the vent slabs. Everything in solid place. In her baggage she had nothing substantial to use as a wedge—a mirror, but the bone handle would surely snap at the first yank. Even if she could break the space wider and hoist herself, she doubted she could squeeze her small frame through. But by dark she would try.

Kellie heard breathing, rattling gulps like that of a large animal. She looked at the rough-hewn door where it met the jamb. The flicker of lamplight reflected a glimmer—an eye. Someone was trying to watch her. Indignant, she walked to her luggage. Her hands trembling, she produced a small sewing scissors, then edged along the wall, her back to it.

Outside the cabin, Riles, growing restless, looked in to see Beatty, his bloated face pressed against the door, his sweat-crumpled hat tipped far back. Saliva drooled around his bearded jaw. He was trying to peek at Kellie. "Keep your damned eyes to yourself," the girl shouted, punching the scissors partially through the crack.

Beatty snapped his head back, caught his face in a clumsy grasp, and hulked backward. "Jesus Christ, she tried to stab me," he roared.

"What the hell you doing?" Riles hissed, replacing his rifle on his horse.

"Nothin'!"

"Serves you right, you dumb bastard." Riles laughed. "Now get the hell back outside. I'm taking over here."

Untouched, but shaken, Beatty looked at Riles, his ponderous features registering displeasure. "That ain't the orders. Morton said for me to take care of her needs. That's what he said."

"Well, he ain't here. And when he ain't here, I'm in charge. Always have been."

"I was just seein' what she was doin'." Beatty blubbered. "She was on a chair, tryin' to break out."

"She can't break out, you know that. Now get out front."

Beatty hesitated, then weakened. "Morton, he won't be happy."

"He ain't comin' back for a time. It's just you and me and the girl."

Beatty picked up his rifle and walked outside.

Riles pressed against the door, his words intimate. "What's going on in there, honey?"

"Go to hell."

"We could be here some time, honey, especially if your old man gets stubborn. So you best cooperate. Be nice and good."

"I'm not your honey, you pompous ass."

Riles smiled with great pleasure. "Well, well, well. We got a little mountain lion on our hands."

"You push me and you'll see a mountain lion."

Riles leaned against the door on one hand, the other cocked on his hip. "Best you pleasure us, ma'am. Make it easy for us and for yourself. Because you ain't goin' nowhere. And you ain't goin' to do nothin' that interferes with our gettin' your daddy's little gift."

"He'll see you hanged."

"Honey, right now he don't have no choice. He's got the money and we got you. One hundred thousand in exchange for your pretty little self. Now that seems mighty fair and mighty wise."

The door shuddered with the impact of a thrown or swung object, toppling Riles back. The girl apparently had heaved a chair against the door. Riles stepped to a wall and removed a short coil of rope from a nail. "Guess we're going to have to bulldog and brand the little heifer," he said with delight, tucking the hemp in his belt. He slid the wooden bolt and eased the door open. Kellie threw her body against the door, knocking Riles back, but he laid his superior weight against it and forced his way in. She hit him with a right, her doubled fist catching him solidly on the nose.

"You damn little bitch." Riles threw up his arms to ward off a pummeling blow as she swung her baggage, catching him off stride. He nearly fell, grappled with her, and managed to grasp her upper arms. He heaved her hard, crashing her across the bed. He was on top of her, pinning her; she writhed under him, entangling them in the blankets. "God, you are a she-lion," he whooped ecstatically. He pressed his scratchy face to her neck and sucked at her flesh, but she twisted aside and bit his cheek with all her might. He howled, rolled off, and hit her with an open hand, but with such resounding force that she cried out, her head hitting the wall. Momentarily stunned, she lay groaning as he bound her hands together, his teeth gritting. Struggling to keep him from immobilizing her, she shook the fuzziness from her head and tried to knee him, then gouge his eyes; but when his strength held her, she spat in his face.

Beatty appeared at the door, the rifle still in one hand. He giggled, his small eyes red, alive with pleasure. Riles roped her hands to a cross board at the foot of the bunk. Then he stood back and looked down at her triumphantly. Kellie glared at him, her features blanching with defiance, with fear. He spoke like a superior master. "You been a bad girl, honey." Suddenly Riles was aware of Beatty. "Get the hell back out where you belong," he ordered, while smiling menacingly at Kellie. "I'm completely in charge here."

Beatty backed up hesitantly. "That's not Morton's orders. He'll skin both of us alive."

"That's between me and Morton." Riles did not look at the big man but kept caressing eyes on the girl, absorbing her. Softly he said to her, "Me and you might become good funnin' friends." His eyes concentrated on her perky bosom. "I ain't ever had close company with a rich lady before."

"Touch me, and if your boss doesn't kill you, my father and his men will," Kellie cried with icy scorn.

Riles closed the door and stepped beside her. She cringed helplessly as his unerring fingers unbuttoned the dress at her neck. He caught a foot and held tightly despite her vicious kicks. As his eyes roved along the white taper of her leg to the frilly pantaloons, Kellie's proud rage turned to desolation.

Willard Dragmire had enjoyed a pleasant day in the spring wagon with the fringed top, his horse trotting steadily. He had visited three outposts northwest of Broken Bluffs before the sun had arced to its hottest, and he had made several sizable orders, enough to open Noah Cheveny's eyes. This time the old bastard would have to sit up and recognize him as a man coming into his own.

Feeling content and happy with himself, Dragmire had taken an early lodging in Bullion, a prosperous little camp in the rolling hills southwest of Midas. To shake the desert dust, he had gotten a haircut and a bath, then chose the best restaurant in town, one with chandeliers and tablecloths. He had ordered some imported wine, a porterhouse steak with potatoes and gravy, and fresh fruit. He had finished with several cups of hot coffee. Afterward he had bought a local newspaper, then strolled casually along the boardwalk to watch the movement of people and animals and to enjoy the gradual cool of late afternoon with the sun slanting golden against barren hills.

On a corner on the western side of the main street, a woman watched him approach. She stood tall, in a long hourglass dress with a little feathery hat on her upswept hair. He stopped abruptly, for her general image reminded him of his murdered wife. A dark-heavy pain surged through him. He saw her smile, eye him, and lick her lips. Then he knew: a prostitute. A whore soliciting him—a whore who looked like his wife. A whore in the image of his fetching wife! Flushing, he turned away and walked quickly back to his hotel. He twisted around once to curl his mouth at her. She was watching him still. Brooding thoughts, memories, images, haunting, hurting, gnawing, searing, all rushed upward through him—he reeled down the street toward his hotel. People stopped, looked at him, dismissed him as drunk or crazed. But it hurt so, a beautiful woman, strikingly like his wife. Why did life have a way of always reminding him of his loss? And he did not understand, except whoever, wherever that killer was, the one who had destroyed his love, the one who was now out there—all those who killed and maimed and deprived had to pay. Willard Dragmire smiled inwardly, secretly, and he knew.

In the room, Dragmire removed his jacket and boots and stretched out on the iron bed. Jerkily, he took several long gulps of brandy, letting the liquid sink into his being until he felt a buzzy relief. Again he drank deeply, and then once again, before shoving the bottle and glass onto a nightstand. He lay back to absorb the flowing sweep of relaxation. He rested for a time and then tried to read his paper, tried to steady the pages as the words swam and swashed and rolled in slow waves.

Next door a man and a woman continued arguing, both attempting to keep their voices under control. He had heard them earlier when he had rented the room. He rolled on his side and tried to ignore them, but their insistence and sharp words grew progressively louder. The man's voice seemed familiar, somehow.

"And for one more thing, you're not worth the price," he heard the man say.

"You and that cheap partner of yours," she shouted. "He was bragging about all the big money you're coming into."

"Ah, shut up. We'll pay you then."

Curious, Dragmire left the bed to press against the wall and listen.

"You owe me, now," she demanded. "You've had your way—for hours."

"Go to hell." Dragmire heard the man strike her. She

wailed in pain and frustration as he slammed out, clomping by. Quietly Dragmire eased the door open a half inch and watched the man move down a stairway. He recognized the girlish mouth and weasel face of Schick, one of the bounty hunters who had humiliated him the night before in Broken Bluffs. Closing the door, he moved to his street-side window and watched the drifter exit and stalk across the thoroughfare into a saloon called the Aurora. Dragmire stood for a time, staring at the building and at the customers moving in and out. Am ember of anger took flame within him, fanned by the brandy into an inferno of hate. Bullies, trash, lower than creatures that crawled, Dade and Schick had no right to exist, he thought. They were scum, dung that should be buried. He put on his jacket, placed a Colt revolver in his belt, checked the bowie knife in the sheath at the back of his neck and the derringer concealed inside the breast pocket, and left for the Aurora.

(6)

Landry's first priority when he reached Midas was to settle Eve in the boardinghouse, a homey two-story building on the south edge of town. Mae, a buxom, round-faced woman with hair braided over the top of her head, extended a friendly hand to the girl. Eve accepted her shake graciously but nervously. "The young lady will be with you for a few days," Landry said.

"We got good grub, courteous customers, and the best goose-down comforters in town. And I'm going to give you a second-story room with a view of the mountains," Mae said, beaming. " 'Course, you ain't the first customer the marshal's brung here."

"I'm much obliged," said Eve, her eyes roaming around the big room with its long dining table, ticking grandfather clock, and a wall adorned with painted plates and deer antlers. A middle-aged man, reading a newspaper in a plush chair, looked up with an admiring stare to catch her eye.

"Bad news for Franz Kurt about his daughter," said Mae.

"News travels fast."

"I figured that's why you're here."

"Partially."

"Well, we're all sick of that Morton man making fools of us—just robbing the territory blind; but at the same time, I don't think there's too much sympathy for that Mr. Kurt."

After Landry saw Eve safe in her room, and after he had instructed her in the use of a derringer and to stay put and out of sight, he rode to the livery stable to board her horse. Mae was right—several of the workers, upon seeing the marshal's badge, inquired about the kidnapping. Landry acknowledged the fact and found his way to the Nugget Hotel, an imposing brick structure designed by a San Francisco architect. The front hitching rail was congested shoulder to shoulder with horses, carrying the K Kurt brand. Along the boardwalk and inside the hotel saloon the Kurt hands drank or played cards, some sulking impatiently. Landry estimated that the tycoon had close to a dozen and a half cowhands, all acting gunmen, an impressive little army that would be of no avail against the likes of Rattlesnake Morton. Bradly, the foreman, red-faced from drink, smiled broadly and rose to greet the marshal. "Got your telegram that you was coming."

"Where do things stand?"

"Mr. Kurt, Sheriff Cole, some deputies, and our boys here went out looking—but nothing came of it."

"A dangerous waste of precious time," Landry said without sympathy. "Cole should have known better."

"I think he did, but you know Mr. Kurt. And we lost one of our hands, Joe Haney—knifed by Morton, who left a message of warning pinned on him."

Landry nodded soberly. "Has Kurt raised the money?"

"He's been runnin' between the National Bank and the telegraph office the last couple of hours. His business manage rode in with the boys. It's all too big for me, but I guess they're making arrangements, collateral and all that."

"Where's your boss now?"

"Just saw him and Cole walking over to the telegraph office," Bradly said. "Tell me, Marshal, just how we going to get that girl back all safe?"

"By doing exactly what's being done right now. And Bradly . . ." Landry's gray eyes narrowed. "Don't drink anymore. I just may need you."

Admonished but pleased, Bradly snapped a salute.

* * *

Although the overhead sun warmed the day, a cooling breeze came down from the mountains, mingling a pungency of sage with the acrid odor of animal dung, churned dust, and green timber. Midas, at nearly seven thousand feet, clung to the western slant of a short mountain range, the north side abrupt against a steep bluff where the newly rich were building mansions; on the south side, the pitch of land lay open through an extensive swale of sage and willows that led upward to a canyon, a deep slice that continued on toward the peaks.

Landry dodged his way through a flow of buggies, big ore and wood wagons with their creaking teams, the shouting of bull whackers and mule skinners; he found his way to the telegraph office, where he saw Franz Kurt and Brent Cole inside. Both men shook his hand vigorously. "Damn glad you're here," Kurt huffed. His eyes had a harried, woeful shine.

"How the hell did Morton know about Kellie on the stage?" Landry asked.

"Don't know. She must have told somebody."

"She did telegraph you she was coming?"

"Yes. She was coming by train, with the last lap by stage to Midas. Said she'd be in early this morning. I fired one back, hoping to bring her to her senses, but she'd already left."

The telegraph operator peered up from under his green shades and studied Landry. "We can mount a major posse, or several if need be," Cole said, "but I don't think it will do much good."

"It won't do a damn bit of good. I need to send some telegrams," said Landry. "Then we can talk about it in your office."

"Don't mind me, Marshal," the telegrapher said. "I just hope at last someone can get that Morton feller."

Landry scribbled out two messages, one to Sheriff Sundon asking to be informed on further developments in the mur-

ders, and a second to the federal office in Limbo, saying he
was on the Morton case and that he assumed they were aware
of the Kurt kidnapping. The three men proceeded then to the
jailhouse, and in the privacy of Cole's office they set to planning. Cole poured them each a shot of whiskey and said,
"Morton's demands are so big, we've had problems coming
up with enough paper cash in this town. We're going to have
to include some gold dust."

"You have the ransom?"

Kurt wagged his head gravely. "Hopefully, I'll have one
hundred thousand within the hour. My liquid assets don't
flow that easy. Got too much tied up that I have to borrow
against." He helped himself to another whiskey.

"How do you plan to handle this, Dirk?" Cole asked.

"With the girl's life at stake, damn carefully. We're going
to follow Morton's orders. One man will take the money to
the arranged spot. But I'll follow, out of sight and close
behind."

"Just you?" Kurt said.

"Just me. Any more and we will kill the chances of getting
Kellie back."

"What can you do?" Kurt pursued, obviously frustrated.

"Not a hell of a lot," Landry confessed. "I can be there
in case something goes terribly wrong. I can see where they're
headed once they release your girl; then hopefully I can track
them."

Kurt rubbed his mouth in resignation. "Nothing I can do
now but play it out."

"Of your men, who would you trust most? Bradly?"

"Yes, but he's not going."

"Then who is?"

With steely reserve, Kurt replied, "I am." Landry started
to protest, but Kurt cut him off. "She's my daughter, and it's
my money, Marshal. It's between me and Morton. And I'm
not going to jeopardize another man's life for my problems."

The two men looked at each other and sealed an agreement. "All right," Landry said, squaring his shoulders. "Get your gear and horse and we'll ride. I'll meet you here within the hour, assuming you have the money."

"Can me and my boys help in any way?" Cole asked.

"I was getting to you next," said Landry. "It's roughly a thirty- to forty-minute ride to Silver Lode Summit. Give us two hours. If Kurt's not back with his daughter by then, well, you better come looking."

"I'll deputize the rest of Kurt's men," Cole assured.

Landry walked outside to where the chestnut stood big and solid, nickering to him in anticipation of heading out. The ride from Broken Bluffs had been a pleasant warm-up for an animal used to covering the great distances demanded in a marshal's work. The trip to Silver Lode Summit would be another pleasant jaunt for the animal; however, Landry anticipated possible rough going ahead if he trailed the gang as expected. Landry walked the chestnut down to the boardinghouse. Mae was receiving a delivery of ice from a driver who made daily rounds. "You look like you're setting out on some serious business," she greeted.

"I am. The girl, Eve, is she all settled and comfortable?"

"Oh, she's out looking the town over already," Mae said matter-of-factly.

"Looking it over—she's wandering the streets?"

"Said she'd heard about our town and always wanted to see it. I told her I didn't think you wanted her flittin' about. But she didn't listen."

"Hell," Landry spouted. Women were difficult enough to deal with as it was, but a female relative was impossible, he decided. "She probably didn't expect me to come back. Well, you tell her for me that I'm mighty perturbed, and that for her own good she best follow orders."

Eve had walked out of the lodge shortly after Landry left her; not that she didn't respect her uncle's wishes, she just couldn't see the harm. After all, they were a half day's ride from Broken Bluffs and no one knew her here, although Mae's scowling admonishment bothered her some, mostly reminding her of the mother that she had lost and needed for so long. But she had heard so much about Midas, a town built on fabulous riches, which employed the most enterprising men and women now in the state. How could one just hide interminably in a stuffy room when a new, exciting world lay in the offering? She would not stray for long, just enough to get a feel of the place.

Despite the high, warm sun, a cool breeze blew steadily from the mountains—a delightful contrast. Usually, by high noon, Broken Bluffs lay baking, unprotected from the desert rays. She breathed deeply of the good air and strolled farther. The busy pounding of the stamp mills, the movement along the main street, and that peculiar hum of a thriving city filled her with a vague joy that she had not felt for many months— a new city of sawmills, quartz mills, frame shanties, and brick buildings. She walked another block past some small houses with picket fences to where men were loading flat wagons with lumber. She saw them stop work and all look at her, not with lecherous longing, but with that honest appraisal of men who admire femininity at its best. She glanced coyly away, pleased, smiling to herself. Then she remembered why Landry had brought her. Was it so wrong to enjoy a brief outing? Perhaps she should have worn a bonnet, she thought, something that shielded her features. Reluctantly she returned to the lodging house.

Bored, she ironed a dress by a hot stove, sewed some clothes, and washed her hair with a Castile soap and rinsed it with water and vinegar for softness and sheen; then she rubbed it briskly with a towel and dried it in the sun on a second-story balcony; she took care to cover her face and arms, so that her delicate skin would not burn and peel. By midafternoon she felt restless again. She wandered downstairs into the parlor; a few portly men, reading newspapers, regarded her with appreciative glances. She took a yellow apple from a fruit bowl on the dining room table and bit into it; too sour for her taste, she dumped it into a fat ashtray. She meandered around to watch the maids pack out linen from a closet and the cook in the kitchen dicing potatoes. Mae brought in an arrangement of pink and yellow roses that she had cultivated, and placed them in a decanter on the main table. "This will add a little cheer for supper tonight," she said, arranging the buds.

Without comment, Eve rushed up the staircase to her room. She picked up the cream-colored dress she had just ironed and held it before her to scrutinize the effect in a bureau mirror. Satisfied, she chose a jade necklace and matching earrings, and a dark hair comb highlighted with delicate diamonds, given to her by a wealthy patron. Then she brushed out her hair with vigorous strokes until it shimmered with freshness and life; carefully, she began to pile it, pinning and shaping, leaving a band of flowery curls across one side of her forehead. She struggled into the evening dress, her favorite with its soft green ruffles and tan train, adjusting the bustle where the material bunched and gathered. Then she lowered the scooped neck around her shoulders. Admiring the effect, she tripped about with dainty steps, noting the curves of her body and the appealing lines of her face.

She practiced breathing, for the buckled waist pulled tightly, a discomfort that a girl had to live with. But Eve didn't mind. The corsets, garters, and heavy stockings were all part of being feminine, which she loved. She adored the beads, ribbons, feathers, lace, and buttons that adorned the latest styles. And with the extra money that men so freely gave, she had bought the best in Broken Bluffs, lovely outfits that she had been forced to leave behind, although Lilli had paid her for them, but not enough. She wanted to build a wardrobe again. The stores in Midas surely would offer more variety. She wanted to shop, if she could get a little money. Judiciously, she pinned a petite beige hat with green ribbons onto her hair, giving it a coquettish tilt. Not wanting to use rouge, she pinched her cheeks for a flush.

When completed, she picked up her white parasol, angled it open across a shoulder, and swirled back and forth before the mirror to make the skirt swish and flare. The green of her outfit accentuated her eyes. Into the pocket of her dress she tucked some change, a handkerchief, a box of breath perfume, a small brush, and the derringer Landry had given her. She walked primly down the stairs, aware of eyes riveted upon her. As she stepped through the front door, she heard Mae, the voice accusing. "The marshal told me to take care of you. How can I take care of you when you're gallivantin' around?"

"I'm free and of age. You have nothing to worry about." Eve glanced slant-eyed over her shoulder.

"Well, I don't own you, and I can't lock you in, I guess, but I don't like it," Mae sputtered. "Marshal Landry sure ain't going to be happy if you get into trouble."

"I can take care of myself. I always have," Eve said confidently, and swayed out, the hem of her skirt looping daintily about her ankles. She opened the parasol and strolled up the street. The late afternoon sun tinted the brick and raw-wood buildings a mellow gold; substantial new buildings with gaudy signs lined the main thoroughfare, all sporting wide balconies with balustrades that provided walks beneath, a continuous, if irregular arcade. The air blended the scent of sage, pine, wood smoke, and of lathered horses and dust. From the stamp mills on the slope came the life sound of mining, the clatter of the stamps, the thunder of hoists, whirs of machines, shrieks now and then of stream whistles.

The frenzied activity of the morning had tempered some as men lounged along the walks, relaxing before heading back to their respective jobs. Others had come out of the saloons or gambling halls for a breath of fresh air. Eve kept her eyes straight ahead. She could hear the jostle of harness

bells on a team passing behind her as she crossed a street,
taking precautions where she stepped. Droves of flies swirled
and hummed about. Ahead, three Chinese in pigtails, all
balancing baskets from yokes on their shoulders, stopped to
let her pass. Squatting Paiutes draped in blankets watched
her stoically. A Mexican vaquero on a high prancing horse,
his silver-mounted saddle jangling, tipped his sombrero to
her. On she pressed, sensing the gawking men everywhere.

"Gawd, where'd she come from?" someone called out.

"From heaven," another answered. A few men made
smacking sounds and grunts of satisfaction as if eating an
irresistible dessert. Eve held in her stomach and evened her
breathing as she turned into the foyer of the Nugget Hotel,
an impressive building that seemed to draw her with its mar-
ble front, plate-glass windows, glittering signs, and obese
porters in purple. A number of businessmen in suits stopped
their conversation to eye her. The clerk behind a check
counter looked at her suspiciously—a small man, wall-eyed
behind thick specks, he began edging out as if to confront
her, but thought better of it as some important-looking dig-
nitaries acknowledged her with pleasantries. Twirling her
parasol, Eve sat daintily on the edge of a sky blue chaise
longue. Still without looking at anyone, she closed the small
umbrella with care and luxuriated in the opulent setting. More
men descended a white, curved staircase with fancy scrolled
banisters. They, too, noticed her, and she looked properly
away. Hefty urns of potted ferns and banana plants made the
setting junglelike. The floor, parqueted in black-and-white
tile, had a glossy shine, unlike anything she had ever seen.
Trying to hold her composure, she felt like a little girl adrift
in a fairyland.

"You look lost, lady; can I be of help?" Eve saw first the
polished shoes, then the gray suit with a gold-flowered vest,
and then the squarish face, rosy-cheeked with a penciled
mustache and dark smoldering eyes, the hair black and
straight. She judged him thirtyish, a gambler or a speculator

by profession, but not the ordinary kind that she had experienced. She felt him both attractive and threatening somehow.

"Thank you, no." She peered around as if expecting someone.

"You are waiting for a friend?"

"Yes."

"He must be very lucky."

"Thank you."

"Once again someone has gotten you first," he said playfully.

"What are you talking about?" She gazed at him defensively. "I don't know you." And yet she did somehow. For some reason, intuitively, she felt ill at ease about him. For an instant she wished she had obeyed Uncle Landry. Perhaps she was overly jittery, with all the murders, she thought.

"Just that I want to buy you a drink. I'm in town for important business. If all goes well, I'll get a good bonus. So I'm celebrating in advance."

"I, sir, am not in the habit of picking up with strangers," she said defensively.

He sat down beside her and smiled roguishly. "Would you meet me afterward? I'll buy you dinner, champagne, roast duck, whatever. The Nugget here has it all."

The structured routine of the houses she had worked in gave protection. But on her own now, Eve felt frighteningly vulnerable. "It's too early."

"My name is Nathanael. Nathanael Weldon. And you?"

"You are a presumptuous man. I told you I am expecting someone."

"I said afterward."

"What are you trying to say?"

"The one time I saw you, I couldn't take my eyes off you. But you were taken."

Eve felt uncomfortable again. "I must be going." She started to rise.

"No." He touched her arm and said earnestly, "I would like to buy you a drink at least."

"I've known a lot of men, but none that came on like you. You didn't hear me, my friend will be coming shortly," Eve said unconvincingly.

"You know, I don't think your friend is coming." He rolled his mouth and arched an eyebrow confidently. "And if he is, I'll take you afterward."

Eve couldn't shake the strange feeling that there was something familiar about the man, but she couldn't place him. "I must get back." She had pride. She might sell her body, but not to just anyone.

The pleasantry left his face. "Who you kidding? You know and I know," he said, his eyebrows again arching, haughtily now. "Let's get down to business." She started to pull away. "I've never forgotten you. Not since that night I saw you at Lilli's. I wanted you, but you were taken. And I want you tonight. It's that simple. I have the time and the money, and you have the rest."

My God, Eve thought, there was no escape. Maybe her uncle knew more than she gave him credit for. The man's words, although spoken with conviction, had an edge of malice. Taken aback, she fumbled for words. But he pressed on. "Let me buy you a drink for now, just a drink in the dining room. No commitments." He winked at her in a disarming manner. "I want to celebrate, and we can talk. Just talk." He stood up and gracefully took her hand. "I promise you, nothing more for now. I'll abide by your wish. Please?"

"Maybe one," Eve sighed, somehow knowing that she would regret it; but the challenge was new, different.

Cramped and somewhat weary, Noah Cheveny arrived in Midas by stage after a brief business sweep to a neighboring

camp, and took a room in the Nugget Hotel. Wet compresses
throughout the night had relieved the swelling, although he
ached around the lower ribs where he had been pounded. His
pink face had darkened in patches as tender bruises formed,
but he had managed to look quite respectable and to cover a
lump on his head with a light derby that did not bind his
skull. He asked for and got an upstairs room on the fourth
floor—the top at the rear of the hall, which afforded him quiet
and privacy. With effort he carried his one suitcase with both
hands, and the business case under one arm, locked the door
behind him and took refuge on the edge of the bed. From his
window he could see the upper streets that reached toward
some stately homes under construction on the skirt of the
mountain. Signs of profit and good times in the town, he told
himself.

He dug into his trousers and produced a wad of money
that he had been saving secretly from Henrietta. He flipped
through the crisp bills, several worth a hundred dollars. And
he had more stashed in the satchel. He would have a few
good days in Midas, free for a time from the constant weight
of his business; although he had come to talk about expansion
with a Mathew Long, an eastern representative of the Colt
corporation, there would be ample time for the recreation he
sought. Private fun and the chance of a profitable venture
pleased Cheveny, and he gloated with the thought. Midas
was a thriving city that could stand more competition among
the gun and ammunition dealers; he was confident of that.
Wealth, growth, and investments in resources and land meant
needed protection, which added up to arms.

Most certainly he welcomed a break from the townspeople
of Broken Bluffs, who he knew laughed at him behind his
back, who thought him homely and odd if not eccentric. He
welcomed relief from his hounding wife, and from the eter-
nal presence of that insipid Willard Dragmire, so prim and
proper. And above all he looked forward to the young girls,
heavenly temptresses with soft white flesh, whom he had

fantasized about for long months; girls waiting and receptive, sweet-scented with perfume, all ready and willing to
bare more body in one encounter than he had seen of his wife
in all their insufferable marriage. If one had the money, one
could buy dreams and fantasies. One could purchase full lips
and firm bodies with deep cleavages. Many men on the fron-
tier liked their women to look like a draft horse from behind,
but not Cheveny. He wanted more class. He liked clean milky
skin, especially dimpled shoulders and long legs. And the
girls had to be young. Youth touched upon immortality,
sounded of violins and of misty waterfalls, and of forbidden
worlds that Henrietta and the others could not fathom and
would never in their wildest imaginations realize harbored
within Noah Cheveny: unsatisfied hungers of infinite desire.
Here in Midas, unknown, he could fulfill, if only partially, if only for a few stolen minutes, those private yearnings,
those black secrets that deviled always within him. And he
had the money.

One of the more progressive and modern hotels in the
region, the Nugget had colored tile bathtubs on each of its
four floors, with Chinese assistants who brought hot water
as desired, scented soap, and huge Turkish towels. Cheveny
soon took advantage to soak and soothe away his pain. He
closed his eyes and felt the rhythmic slosh of water against
him penetrating every pore of his body. The fact that he was
away from prying eyes and censuring looks relaxed him. But
the bruises and the aches that might restrict or limit any
performance, that might repulse some young maiden, riled
him. He had so anticipated this particular adventure. But he
would manage, he vowed. He would deny himself nothing.
He lit a long Havana cigar, puffed on it and savored its good-
ness, an indulgence that he enjoyed only when away on business trips.

Under the guidance of a black coated maître d', Cheveny
took a circular table in the corner of the dining room, where
he could not see himself in the big mirrors at one end, but

where he could watch those who entered. He liked the array of maroon-clothed tables with dark-wooded maroon seats and backs, and the thick maroon curtains that closed out the crudities in the street and darkened the place like night, although the time was a little past midafternoon. Plumpish waitresses in black dresses and white aprons and caps catered to him, first lighting a candle to glow warmly over the silver setting, although a half-dozen crystal chandeliers, each aglow with numberless coal oil lights, flickered throughout the room in a starlit dance of movement and shadow.

Cheveny ordered a small bottle of imported Chablis, two roast quail with seasoned stuffing, chilled oysters with spiced tomatoes, and broiled white potatoes and cabbage garnished in a Swiss cheese and mushroom sauce. He ate slowly, deliberately. And when he had finished, he lit another cigar and drew deeply, then ordered a bottle of whiskey and a small glass. The room had filled slowly with businessmen, eastern mining speculators and engineers, some ranchers, possibly a gambler or two or traveling salesmen, and the expected investors with their white shirts, broadcloth coats, bright vests, and chain watches, who had ventured in from the nearest railway for an overview of operations and a leisurely dinner.

It pleased Cheveny that there were no riffraff, no rowdy cowhands, no grubby miners, no drifting opportunists. A few men had women companions. The more staid and proper, with tight lips and high-necked bodices, topped by concocted hats, were wives, he concluded. There were a few others, livelier, responsive, with hair that cascaded in waves or was piled tumultuously and richly on top to curl teasingly here and there. Lady friends. Some might be the daughters of a few powerful men who commanded respect and position in the territory, but he doubted it. These particular women knew how to please men, how to pamper their egos, and how to charm them. They were high-paid ladies of the town, he decided. A liquidy feeling made him go weak and flowing inside. A part of him ached for their company. Yet a part of him feared them, despised those who had belittled his manhood.

In his mind's eye he saw himself, elfish, his head eggshaped and bald, his thin pipelike neck, the myopic eyes rimmed by wire-thin glasses. Cheveny poured a double drink. He remembered, once, the whore in a town called Bullion, tipsy after he had plied her with wine—how she had laughed at his nakedness, had laughed really at his being. Cheveny downed another and thought about his wife, so self-righteous, so above it all, so controlled, so demanding, so demeaning. He drank deeply. There was a whorehouse in town called the Monmarte, he had learned, that featured the most attractive ladies in the territory—or at least that was the word. Why not now? He had money, plenty of money. Enough money that no little tramp would dare scorn him.

He rose to leave, when he saw her with a man in his early thirties. Her escort seated her nearby; he kept talking with light abandon. The man had black full hair and a penciled mustache and wore a gold flowered vest on gray. Cheveny knew the type, handsome, fancy-talking, and quick-handed. But the girl—ah, the girl, she was the most beautiful young lady that he had seen in many years, blond, green-eyed, with porcelain skin, her face lean and strong, the nose chiseled thin, her forehead broad. What he noticed were her white neck and shoulders, the cream-colored dress that draped just slightly off the smooth roundness. She wore a jade necklace on her bosom that matched her earrings, and a charming little hat. She acted somewhat distant and suspicious of the man, her small red lips pursed. God, he thought, a rose in the desert. But an evening dress in the afternoon? Could she be the kind? Cheveny experienced conflicting emotions. Such a queenly young woman selling herself to men? The pity. But he fantasized about touching her, watching her disrobe, of possessing her, and went weak. Cheveny sat back down to savor another drink and to observe. The man ordered her a brandy and himself a whiskey. They talked, and by her practiced attentiveness, he assumed she was listening politely. But for some reason the girl was reacting negatively. The man's back was slightly toward Cheveny, while she faced him.

Cheveny tried to listen without staring. The man changed his tone and became serious. He was propositioning her in a condescending way, asking her price, and she was not being cooperative. I'll be damned, a beautiful whore, Cheveny thought, deducing that the man knew her from before, and that she did not like him. "I choose my own patrons," she told him. "And I don't choose you." The man grew surly then, saying some unflattering things. Cheveny removed the wad of bills, more out of a childish impulse than calculatingly, and held it concealed under the flap of his coat but in clear view of her.

Cheveny hung on their every word, stealing a look now and then while sipping his liquor. "Keep your voice down; people are listening," said the girl. She looked around. Then she noticed him and her eyes widened in startlement, then curiosity. Immediately she looked back at her partner. The man was talking louder than necessary now, something about coming into some money. When he turned to order another drink from a waitress, the girl looked again with guarded casualness. He saw her stiffen, her face twist slightly. Was it revulsion? Resolutely, he looked steadily at her, determined not to identify with any resistance, and tipped the roll out in full display, rotating it slightly. Her eyes centered on it and did not waver until her host returned his attention. Dangerous as it was toying with another man's woman, Cheveny could not help himself. The man's voice went low and insistent again, but the girl cut him off. "I wish to leave," she announced.

"Who in the hell do you think you are?" he snarled under his breath. "You think you can dismiss me? Tease around with me? You damned little tramp." Biting her lip, the girl rose and, with her shoulders back and her chin high, left the room. His eyes blazing, the man glared at the customers around him who pretended not to notice. He stood up and finished his drink, lifting it in toast after her. "Her highness the bitch," he said for all to hear, and then stalked out.

Kellie Kurt sat on the edge of the bed in the cabin, tears flecking her eyes and slowly striping her soft face. She had gathered the torn dress and undergarments around her, to sit for a long time hugging one folded knee as she rocked back and forth, trying to piece elements of the nightmare. Her body ached with throbbing intensity and she felt faint still. At first she had kicked and then screamed, but the man named Riles had become more excited by resistance. Nothing had been of avail except to grit her teeth and endure the inevitable. Seeing her submissive and defeated, Riles had released her and left, promising to be back later. At first she had nearly passed out; then she had started to vomit, but got control of herself suddenly as a welling anger replaced the fear and the repulsion; gradually a seething desire for revenge lessened the humiliation. But the loathsome dark of degradation would hold in her permanently, she knew.

Her father would ransom her release in time. Then somehow, someway, he and the authorities would track the gang down. Riles would pay with his life. She relished the thought. Bestial animals like him were not tolerated, not in the big country. But since childhood she had heard of Leander Rattlesnake Morton, never dreaming she would someday be his victim, his pawn. Such individuals were only names mentioned by her elders more emblazoned in newspaper headlines, nothing that ever entered the protected life of a girl growing up on the Kurt estate. Heavyhearted, she recalled that Morton had been an enigma, a phantom character who had eluded all attempts to bring him to justice, although she remembered that he had once been in prison, until leading a sensational outbreak. Morton would not be easily discouraged or easily defeated. While the law and her father did whatever they could, she had to do something here, now, in the cabin. The realization anguished her, weighed on her.

Kellie envisioned the busy excitement, the bustle, the concern about her. The thoughts gave her momentary relief. She smiled slightly, thinking how her father, angered by her impulsive return, would excuse her, would ultimately forgive her after some severe rebukes. She thought of his hired men, most just ordinary cowpokes, with some respectable gunmen among them, all armed and in the saddle. There would be others out of her father's mines and lumber camps, who would be ready if needed. She had not heard the asking price but suspected it would be sizable. And her father would seek the best of assistance, a number of sheriffs, and without question one man, Dirk Landry. Her father respected and admired Landry, although it angered him that the marshal had never taken sides in the rivalry between him and the Donnovan brothers, the other biggest developers in the western basin. But Kellie knew that quietly her father respected Landry for his independence. She trembled. Somewhere in the big spaces out there the marshal would learn of her plight. Dirk Landry, what an important part he had become in her life, although he did not realize it.

She had always harbored a secret, girlhood crush on the big man. She remembered him as a gracious gentleman at their dinner table. She especially remembered him bringing one of her father's hired hands home, a mere boy who had broken an arm when his spooked pony had bucked him off in town. Holding him tenderly in his arms, Landry had lifted the boy down from his proud mount and carried him into the bunkhouse. More etched were the times she had seen Landry patrolling the main streets of Limbo and of Midas, and once in Bullion, backing the local sheriff or constable at twilight when troubles brewed. His presence had been assuring, comforting. His careful deliberation, the catlike movement, the gray eyes that assessed; the effect of his presence had remained long after.

Mostly Kellie remembered that frightening day in her early teens when, visiting Limbo with her father, they had watched Landry march across a street into a saloon. Protectively, her father had rushed her away in their carriage. But she had seen the marshal's face. She learned later that Landry had killed a man, a wanted desperado who had come into town, tanked up on whiskey, with the intent of gunning some lawman down. Kellie could never forget Landry as he bore across the street in determined strides, his features a hardened mask of raw fury—a perfectly controlled death machine. The pale-set mouth, the hard-cold eyes that had laced chills through her being, all remained indelible. She wondered if Riles would eventually face that same human force.

Kellie heard movement beyond the door and some heavy breathing. Beatty was attempting to peer in. When he left finally, she rose shakily, took her luggage, and moved to a corner near the door where prying eyes could not see. She changed into a loose-fitting cotton dress that gave her greater freedom. She wished she had a riding outfit. Then she washed and cleaned herself the best she could from a pitcher and basin they had provided. Her hands trembled with thought again of the ordeal and of Riles. She closed her eyes and swallowed, thinking she might be sick. Clenching her teeth, she fought off any feelings that might defeat her intent. When finished, she studied the room; the lantern burned steadily, its light flickering rosily around the walls. Her eyes centered hypnotically on the wavery flame. A chance, she thought. A chance that could result in her own death, a horrible death if they did not rescue her.

She sat back on the bed and contemplated. If it were only

a matter of waiting. But how long would an exchange take? Meanwhile she was alone, at the mercy of two animals who had no control and no compassion except to satisfy their own debased hungers. Nervously she licked her lips and considered the possibility. Slowly, with resolve, she went to the bureau and removed the chamber pot, a heavy, solid container, and placed it next to the door. Deliberately she piled her torn clothes and the blankets on the bed, except for one that she tossed on the floor in the middle of the room; the blankets had lain on a mattress of dried pine needles. From a storage shelf she lifted down the tin of kerosene and saturated the bed. Woodenly then she stood before the lantern on the table, staring at it for a long time. She reached out, took hold of the base, hesitated, caressed it, squared her jaw and flung it into the corner, the crashing shatter spraying flames and oily glass over the bed. Tongues of orange burst into heated life.

Kellie clutched her cheeks in both hands, closed her eyes, and emitted a piercing, shuddering scream. And then again, and once again. Riles came running, his footsteps pounding. He unbolted the door and swung it open. Seeing the blaze, he flung her aside and grabbed the blanket lying in front to commence whipping and beating the fire in a desperate attempt to smother the leaping flames. Kellie stooped down, lifted the chamber pot and swung with all her might across the back of the man's skull. Riles's hat flew away as he cried out and slumped to his knees, going limp momentarily, face forward. Kellie jerked his revolver free from his holster and swung around as Beatty neared the door opening, one hand clutching his rifle, the other a monstrous paw reaching almost to her. Desperately, holding the gun low in both hands, she pulled the trigger twice. The resounding explosions shook the room, belching smoke over her, forcing her to squeeze her eyes closed. Beatty stopped, caught his gut with the free hand as if to keep the contents from tumbling out. His small eyes and ponderous features registered total shock, a wry twisting of disbelief as the impact sent him back, his footsteps faster. As he passed through the front door, he dropped the rifle, drifted around and pitched headlong onto the ground to roll over faceup, both hands cupping his lower belly.

Hearing Riles stir, Kelly turned back, saw the flames and smoke engulfing the room as the outlaw pushed himself to his feet, swaying, his face constricting with fear and hate. Again she pointed the gun with both hands and fired twice more, not certain she had hit him, as the gun bucked high. But Riles spun backward and went down. Kellie ran, picked up Beatty's rifle, and carried it out to where the two horses tossed and pulled, their reins trailing. Kellie shoved the rifle into the scabbard on Beatty's big bay, curled the reins over the horn and swatted the animal's rump with all her might. The horse rocked off in a steady gallop down the road toward Morton and his men. Riles came to the doorway, hatless, holding a grazed arm, the bullet-torn shirt splotched red. Kellie fired again, forcing him back. Fire was coiling above the back roof. Apprehensively, she approached and pulled Beatty's gun free; the man was alive still, his eyes open but unseeing. He breathed heavily, a gurgling in his throat. Kellie heaved Riles's near-empty gun into some willows, took the outlaw's sleek sorrel and swung into the saddle, her skirt hoisting above her thighs; she turned the animal toward the woods above and kicked it into a run. Riles burst from the building down to his sprawled partner to search for the revolver. Unarmed, frustrated, he ran after Kellie in a futile effort.

Below on the stage road Kurt saw the smoke. And Landry, weaving his way through the juniper several hundred yards behind and some fifty feet above, dropped his horse to the road and raced after the man. "What the hell is it?" Kurt shouted upon hearing Landry approach.

"My guess is it's a cabin burning on the flat above us there." Landry pulled the big chestnut up short. He had a rifle in a scabbard and a ten-gauge shotgun strapped on the opposite side.

"Might be somebody's campfire out of control."

"Might be. But so far it's not spreading, and it's getting mighty big."

"How far away?"

"Less than a quarter of a mile, probably."

"What do you figure?"

"It's just a hunch. But I feel something in my bones."

Kurt looked earnestly at the marshal. "Kellie. You're saying it could be where Kellie is. That something's gone wrong for them."

"It's a wild chance, but a chance."

"I think it best we abandon our plans for now," said Landry, studying the dark puffs rising higher. "I think we gotta look into this. Morton will see the fire, too." Kurt nodded as Landry led the way, climbing toward the terrace of trees.

In the woods overlooking the rendezvous site, Rattlesnake Morton saw the climbing smoke and a glow at the base. He stood up, his eyes narrowing. "God damn," he said through clamped teeth. He signaled Fang and Liddicoat, who had both raised their heads like two turkeys on the alert. With a swing of his arm Morton gestured them to him. He went for his horse and, when in the saddle, looked at the billowing smoke in disbelief before shaking his head and plunging the animal away. From its position nearly a mile away in the southeast corner of the plateau, he knew the fire had to be coming from the cabin. That stupid Beatty and that hot-blooded Riles had fouled up—the bungling fools. He should have sent Riles into town instead of Jenson, he thought, spurring his way up the divide; Jenson never let emotions get in the way of business. Odds were that Riles had tried something with the girl, something that someway backfired.

* * *

Riles raced about in confusion. Kellie had vanished on his sorrel. Still holding his bleeding arm, he leapt over a log and ran puffing down the slope, back to the flat in search of Beatty's horse, but it was nowhere to be seen. The fire burst into a roaring inferno, consuming the cabin and sprinkling cinders, a myriad of sparklers that danced and darted, some drifting toward the surrounding pines. The heat blast ruddied his face and he retreated. He considered briefly trying to pull Beatty clear of any burning debris, but thought better of it as the hot pitch in the pine boards exploded, collapsing the roof. Then he saw a winking movement of patterns that he thought might be some horses and riders. He dived headlong over a moldering stump, to lie still. He waited. Then he glimpsed two horsemen moving along the base of the bluff, approaching the cabin from behind. Damn, he grunted, if only he had a gun. Sweat filled his eyes; blinking, he wiped them with fingers slippery from blood and tried to see. Had someone dismounted? Whoever it was had disappeared in the thick of juniper.

Landry and Kurt held back and watched the spectacular burn; they comforted their mounts, embracing the heads while rubbing noses and necks as the nervous creatures tossed and sidestepped. "My God," Kurt said, aghast. "My God, is my Kellie in there?" He started to edge forward, but Landry detained him.

"Nothing you can do now. We ride out there, we could be walking into a death trap."

"My God," Kurt said, his harrowed eyes looking heavenward at the spiraling smoke. "Where's Kellie?"

"There was some kind of shoot-out here." Landry's words sounded less callous than reasoned.

"Who's that sprawled out there?"

"He's big. One of Morton's men was big like that. A grizzly of a man named Beatty." They stood transfixed, wondering if the enormous blaze would spread, since drifting cinders were plying the bordering willows and some were approaching the conifers farther up. As Kurt stood wide-eyed, Landry looked about for signs of the others. He grasped Kurt. "Look. Look up there." He pointed. "Kellie!" The girl had emerged from a grove of pinyon to cross the spine of a higher ridge. She rode hunched over a sorrel, kicking her heels into its sides.

"Thank God," Kurt choked. "Oh, thank God." He mouthed words as if calling to her. "We got to go after her. We've got to get her before Morton does." His whole being fused both blessed relief and anguished fear.

"I'll go after her." As Kellie vanished over the ridge, Landry said, gloating, "Somehow, someway, she got free. She managed to escape them."

"Amazing girl, my Kellie."

"I want you to go back," said Landry, removing a paper and pencil to scribble a hurried message. "I want you to give Cole this note to send your boys and whatever deputies he can spare for a posse back here. Armed men could make a big difference now; if they can't catch Morton, they just might force him to hightail it empty-handed."

"You know best, Landry. Just get my daughter home safe." Kurt tucked the folded paper in his vest pocket and started leading his horse away.

"I figure Morton and most of his men were waiting near that white rock for us. Of course, they've seen the fire, and I'm sure they'll be here any minute. I'd just as soon not let them know we're here."

"Take the money," Kurt said, removing the saddlebags. "I trust you, Landry. Bury it someplace if need be."

Landry accepted the bags. "It might still be used to barter for Kellie if I fail." Landry secured the bags as they continued moving out on foot, keeping under cover. "If I do fail, I doubt if Morton will harm your daughter, as long as he gets the money. He may be mean, but he's not stupid. But I'll try my damnedest to get your girl and all your money back safe."

"I know you will, Marshal."

Landry spoke with confiding assurance: "We'll beat Morton this time. Now listen carefully: is there some bank official in Midas who you can trust to keep his mouth shut?"

"Yes."

"I want people to think you brought that money back and deposited it for the time being. Except for Cole, it's no one's business what's happened here. Members of the posse—even your men can't be trusted—everybody's suspect for now."

Kurt was walking beside Landry, both moving at a fast pace. "I'll do as you ask, but I don't understand. Is there a special reason?"

"Just a hunch I have. And be sure Cole gets that note. It's important. You and him will have to keep a lid on the town. If I can get Kellie out, you and Cole may just be able to save us."

Kurt nodded. "I don't understand, but I guess I will. I'd rather be with you, going for Kellie now that we're so close."

"We've got no choice. You've got to get that message back. Now go, before Morton gets here."

Kurt tipped his hat in resignation. "Landry, thanks and good luck. And bring my girl back." He pulled his horse away in the direction they had come. Mounting, he felt his way cautiously at first, then urged the horse into a steady pace across the terrace.

Landry mounted his chestnut and let it pick its way through a rift of granite boulders along a spur of trees, the route Kellie had taken. He would attempt to overtake her while acting as a buffer between her and Morton, who would surely be on her trail soon.

From behind the stump Riles waited. He had glimpsed Beatty's horse grazing some hundred yards down the trail, but he dared not go after it for fear of detection. The two riders had not revealed themselves; they could be miners or hunters or they could be the law nosing about. He stared at the coiling flames. Some of the dry sage nearby had burst into crackling life, but the fire didn't seem to be spreading. In fact, it was not burning as vigorously. Morton would be killing mad when he arrived. Unarmed, Riles felt naked and unnerved. A damned girl doing him and Beatty in. If he could get the bay, there might be a gun in the saddlebags. With the horse, he might be able to overtake her.

He started to slip away when he saw a rider withdrawing along the base of the bluff. But only one? Where was the other? Then Riles noticed what he thought was a top hat, but the man and horse were gone. A top hat! He had seen Franz Kurt once in Virginia City and again in Limbo. Kurt had been ordered to deliver the loot to Morton. No doubt he was somewhere in the area. Could he and someone else have seen the fire and investigated? Could the rider really be Franz Kurt? The intriguing thought tasted delicious. If it were Kurt, he would be laden with the money, here, within reaching distance, and Morton didn't know. Riles had the chance of a lifetime. He broke into a flush of sweat. If only he had a horse and a gun. He started for the bay when Morton and his sidekicks rode out of the trees, their animals lathered from forced effort in the thin air. Fang, seeing Beatty's horse, swung wide to grasp its reins, bringing it galloping with him.

They came up, the hooves a cannonading of dust. Morton pulled his horse up tight, twisting it sideways to rear and paw the air, its eyes bugging as it squealed in frustration. Before it came down, Morton rolled from the saddle and caught Riles squarely across the face with a backhand; the inertia knocked the hatless outlaw flat and almost into a back somersault. Riles sat up dazed and made a reflex reach for his empty holster. Morton, his legs parted, a finger pointing, glared, fitfully at him. "You stupid son of a bitch, I knew I shouldn't have left you in charge, not with a girl. How in the hell did she get away?"

Bobbling his head, Riles came to his knees and struggled wearily to his feet. Blood seeped from the side of his mouth and around the soaked sleeve of his upper left arm again. "She got a drop on us after she started the fire."

"How?"

"She threw the lantern into the bed."

"And got both your gun and Beatty's, I see."

Fang and Liddicoat, meanwhile, dragged Beatty away free of the heat. But the effort was too late. The big man's dilated eyes had glazed in death.

Morton looked at the twisting flames, settling slowly now into a steady burn. "Poor dumb bastard, I never thought he'd be done in by a little girl. You maybe, but not him—a little girl with a hell of a lot of guts." He curled his lips contemptuously. "Where is she?"

Reluctantly, his face drawn, Riles started to answer, but warbled his words. He busied himself wiping the blood from his lips with a bandanna.

"God damn it, answer me."

Riles looked foolish as he said, "Up yonder on the mountainside somewhere."

"Somewhere? On your horse?"

Riles looked at his feet, the anger seething but the pride gone. "On my horse."

"We damn well better get ridin', then, and fast. She's one hundred thousand dollars on the loose out there." With a hefty swing, Morton climbed back on his pinto.

Riles added quickly, "Must tell you, just for our safety, there was a stranger here for a time, that's why I couldn't get to Beatty's horse; otherwise, I would have been hell-bent after her."

"Stranger? What do you mean?"

"Guess the fire drew him here. Last I seen him was in them pines back of the cabin."

"A lawman?" Morton's dark eyes flashed as he scanned the area, a hand on the butt of his rifle. Liddicoat and Fang withdrew their firearms, their horses shifting, sensing a sudden nervousness.

"Don't know."

"Did he have a high hat?"

"Nope."

"Just a thought that it might've been Kurt—on a wild chance of finding his girl." Morton's eyes narrowed as he bit his lips. "Was he a big man?"

"Couldn't tell."

"Just by chance, was he riding a chestnut?"

"Might have been."

"Jesus Christ, that could be . . . !"

"Landry, you mean? Couldn't tell."

"Good God. Up there, look," said Liddicoat, pointing. On the spine of the ridge where Kellie had ridden, a horseman crossed a clearing, open to view briefly.

"God damn. God damn," Morton throated.

"Landry!" said Liddicoat in a shocked whisper.

"God damn, how'd he get here?"

"He's trackin' the girl," said Fang.

"We'll bury Beatty later," Morton said, his face poisonous, the eyes crazed. He shrilled, "You, Riles, you got us into this. You take Beatty's horse and rifle and get back to Midas fast as that horse will take you. Contact Jenson, tell him plans have changed. Tell the boys there to be ready. If we don't get the girl, and if we can't kill Landry, tell them the marshal and the female may be coming in with all the money, that they might be able to intercept him."

"How do you figure he's got it?" Riles studied Morton carefully.

" 'Cause I been playin' cat and mouse with him a lot of years. He's the one who was bringing the money, I'll wager, till he saw this fire and got wind of things."

"You don't think Kurt was with him?"

"I don't know." Morton looked quickly at Riles. "Why, you know something I don't?"

"Just trying to figure what the hell's going on. I need a sidearm," said Riles, pulling himself painfully aloft on the big bay.

Morton dug into his saddlebags and produced a revolver. "Time's wasting." Without looking back, he spurred the pinto toward the mountain rise. "And get that arm fixed up when you get there," he shouted over his shoulder.

"You better buy a sombrero when you get to Midas," Fang said, grinning at Riles. " 'Cause the sun's going to burn them pretty curls right off your skull." Guffawing, he and Liddicoat leaped their horses away.

"Go to hell," Riles shouted. He headed the bay around the tempering fire, through a draw where the willows clustered, and along the base of the bluff. The big horse plodded heavily, its hooves clinking on the rocks. Before he reached the terrace, he could see his three partners weaving higher through the grooves of pinyon and juniper. He smiled secretly to himself. He checked the revolver and the rifle; both were loaded, and he found adequate ammunition in the bags. Fortunately his gun arm was not hurt. He worked his bandanna under the split sleeve and over the wound. The arm was stiffening, paining, but at least the bleeding had ebbed. Riles looked once more at Morton, growing smaller with distance. "You smart bastard," he said aloud. "This is going to be one on you." The man who he figured was Franz Kurt could not be far ahead with the money—money that could be his if he shot the horse out from under the old man. And it seemed logical to Riles that a man of Kurt's pride would not relinquish the ransom, even to Landry.

On a rib of the mountain, Kellie Kurt maneuvered the sorrel down a slope gnarled with sage, toward a shady stand of white-barked aspen, their light green leaves fluttering in the late afternoon sun. Although she could no longer see the cabin behind her, she could see the high roils of smoke; however, the intensity had diminished. Satisfied that the man called Riles could not pursue her unless he somehow found Beatty's horse, she breathed easier, although her heart continued pounding. Morton and the others would surely be on her trail, for they could not help but see the fire. Her thighs and side ached, and it seemed as if her whole body was aflame, too. The horror of it all settled heavily. The kidnapping, the nightmare attack of Riles, the killing of Beatty. In all of her eighteen years, she had never seen a man die, until now. A man dead from her bullets. And worse, she was not free yet. Midas was a difficult distance, considering the rugged country ahead. She would descend, and with luck she could reach the stage road before dark, with only a half hour or forty minutes ride from town. But where would Morton and his gang be? Alone on the road, she would be totally at their mercy. But she had no alternative but to try. There might be someone along the way whom she could trust— even a posse out looking.

However, now, between her and the aspen, there lay a shale slide. She knew that volcanic material that had peeled away and had avalanched could be dangerous, but to avoid it meant climbing straight up to a naked top of enfolding domes, a time-consuming and likely fruitless effort where she would be exposed, and it might not lead anywhere. To parallel the funneled rock straight down to its base would be safer, but it would also delay her, and drop her back on the terrace where the Morton gang could ride her down. Her features set, she directed the sorrel onto the slide area. The animal snorted and balked, but she pressed it on. Some flat rocks shifted, the horse tripped but caught its balance, then felt its way slowly as Kellie stifled a held-in scream.

Suddenly from above, some rocks skimmed down noisily, rotating slowly. Below Kellie and the sorrel a sheet of rocks rumbled away. Unsure, the horse pranced and pivoted. Kellie knew she had made a fearful mistake, but as she attempted to dismount, the animal bolted, throwing her. Screaming, she fell heavily, knocking her breath out and smashing her elbow. The sorrel broke toward safety, but the shifting rocks gave way and the animal fell shrieking to its side and came up to scoot down the drop on its haunches like a squatting dog. Kellie felt the rocks crumble and then steady and hold. She lay breathing with difficulty, not daring to move. The sorrel worked free, but it was dragging a rear left leg and limping badly as it cleared the slide.

Determined, Kellie began crawling with the utmost care, fearing that at any minute the whole slide would flush away to carry her tumbling down, to be buried alive. But the broken slabs simply teetered under her weight, shifting some, nothing more. Inch by inch, for what seemed an eternity, she worked across the few feet over which they had ventured. Her right arm dangled numbly to the side. She wondered if a bone was broken. At last she reached safety, to sit collapsed on the soft dirt. She wanted to cry suddenly, but the sight of the animal struggling pitifully to keep upright drew her to her feet; she plunged toward it, half falling and sliding until reaching the sorrel. The horse nosed against her. Kellie knew that the pathetic creature could not carry her farther. She led it, humping and swaying, into a grove of trees. There, she managed to remove the blankets and canteen, the revolver and rifle, and some wrapped jerky. Then, with anguished effort, she uncinched the saddle and unstrapped the bridle with her good hand and arm. She hoped dreamfully, that by some miracle, maybe the horse would survive on its own. She dared not fire a shot to release it from suffering. But now she was alone without transportation. For Morton and his men, it would be only a matter of time until they found her.

The horse suddenly nickered and raised its head. Kellie cupped its nose and listened. Did she hear the clop and jangle of a horse and rider? She crouched in the brush and struggled with her one hand to cock the revolver. She could hear some-one drawing near. The interloper stopped; an agonizing si-lence followed; then the animal advanced, leather creaking, then stopped and started again, determinedly, almost as if its rider were seeking her. She sat down by the sorrel's legs and braced the revolver across her knees, pointing at the approaching sound.

(8)

In Bullion, as the late afternoon shadows lengthened, a
sizable crowd filled the Aurora Saloon to drink and gamble.
In a dim corner under the staircase, his back to the wall,
Willard Dragmire sipped a beer. He watched Schick and
Dade; they had been talking to a dance girl in a short blue-
and-white dress, the frilly hem rising nearly to her knees.
She had bright red hair coiled high under a blue feathered
band. Schick seemed to be boasting about something; often
he would stop and rotate his weasel-shaped head, the hostile
eyes roving around the room like an animal on constant
guard, but he did not see Dragmire, or at least he did not
recollect him. Wiry and gaunt, the man hunched toward the
girl as if intimidating her, a thumb hooked in his gun belt.
Dade stood to the side, his eyes devouring the creamy flesh,
his craggy face sullen as always. Dragmire envisioned putting bullets in both of them, seeing the lead home, preferably
between the eyes or under the heart or simply in the lungs.
He drank deeply and licked the froth from his lips; a dreamy
smile played across his face, his eyes remote and strange.

Then he saw Schick tuck some money in the girl's cleavage
and whisper something. Dragmire guessed that he was promising to return, for the two sauntered out, the little bounty
hunter cocking his hat in a rakish manner. Dragmire rose
and followed, not too closely, but casually. The pair swaggered through a stringy crowd to the telegraph office. He
wondered what possible business they had there; perhaps

they were on the trail of someone. He waited, leaning patiently in the alcove of a dry-goods store that had closed for the day. After twenty minutes he approached the office. Through the window, he saw the telegrapher working over a desk, the back door ajar. Dragmire found his way to the rear of the building, but the two had vanished. Had they seen him and become suspicious?

He walked back to the Aurora. At a hitching rail to the side of the saloon he recognized their animals: the Appaloosa ridden by Dade, and the brown with the stocking feet and white star that Schick had. He sighed with relief. They were in town still. He looked once again inside the saloon, but they were not there. Dangerous business, he knew, shadowing men of their type. He didn't understand his feelings, really. He simply felt a compulsive sense of vindication, of wrongs made right, by knowing that if he killed them, the world would be so much the better. Justice moved slowly and ineptly. He saw nothing wrong with any vigilante act if it served a purpose of ridding the land of scum. All Dragmire's life, because of his thin, freakish appearance, he had been bullied by their likes. Their type had surely accosted his wife. To keep his perspective rational, he took a cooling walk along the edge of the desert, but not so far that he could not maintain surveillance.

In the flush of dusk Dragmire returned to the Aurora. Experiencing a perverse comfort, he saw Schick at a poker table, with Dade standing behind. Apparently they had re-entered through the rear. The gunsmith took a seat in the shadows once more, not far from his prior spot. For nearly an hour, with a half-empty beer before him, he watched the players, grim-faced, as Schick pulled in stacks of chips. The little bounty hunter kept downing shots of whiskey and taking pleasure in his winnings. A few ranchers folded and moved on, while others took their place, including a clean-shaven youth in well-worn chaps. The game grew more serious. A pianist pounded out tinny tunes, and the glasses clinked steadily as tipsy drinkers reveled on, their voices rising. Then Dragmire stiffened. He saw the youth point at Schick and come to his feet in a crouch. A girl shoved her fingers to her mouth and screamed as those around scattered; the table went up and over, the glasses and chips scattering over the floor. The youth backed over his chair, knocking it askew, his hand on the butt of a sidearm. But before he could draw, Dade clubbed him from behind, soundly beside the head with the barrel of his revolver. Schick remained seated, gun in hand but not yet aimed. A grim-faced bartender with a big stick hustled from behind the bar. "It's all under control, bartender," Schick said, smiling thinly. Dade pulled the dazed youth to his feet. "You damn near got yourself killed, sonny." Schick sat back and replaced his Colt. "You don't insinuate no claims unless you can damn well back it up." The wobbly youth, his eyes dilated, might have collapsed except for Dade's firm hold. "Throw him out. And sonny." The youth's face paled at Schick's calculating mannerism. "You walk back in here again, and I'll kill you." Schick pointed a deliberate finger. "I'll gut you first, then I'll blow your brains out."

"I want you two out along with the kid," said the bartender, a big man with muscled forearms.

"It's all under control, bartender; we was havin' an enjoyable time till the smartmouth there sounded off." The youth blanched, his lips trembling. "Sonny has guts, I must say, or he's just a damn young fool."

"Don't want no trouble. This is a respectable place," said the bartender. "I'm sendin' for the constable."

"I know your constable. He's probably stone drunk by now."

The bartender drew back, scowled, and licked his lips with uncertainty.

Schick leered at him with confidence. "That constable of yours couldn't hit a barn door with buckshot by now. I seen him in action before. Besides, it's no use botherin' him, everything's in order now.''

"I don't want no trouble," said the bartender, weakening. "This is a respectable place."

"Throw sonny out," Schick ordered. Dade roughed the boy to the front, where the iron doors had been folded back, and sent the youth sprawling into the mired dust of Front Street. "I'd consider it beholdin' if somebody would assist me in all my chips."

"Help him," the bartender said, motioning to the redhead girl in the short skirt as he returned in defeat to duty behind the bar. The girl, kneeling down, began gathering the scattered pieces, rapidly, as if wishing to get the chore over.

Schick, squatting beside her, said, "Buy you something nice with some of this, but first we're going to dance." He piled the chips into Dade's big hands. "Turn this in for me." He booted the broken glass from the center floor and yelled at the piano player, " 'Buffalo Girl,' and fast. I want it fast." The pianist fingered a rousing rendition. As Schick hooked the girl's waist, he looked back at Dragmire and seemed to sneer. Dragmire could not tell for certain if the bounty hunter was communicating, but he felt uneasy. For fifteen minutes Schick loped up and down, whooped and shrilled, his boots whomping the hard floor. He two-stepped, polkaed, waltzed, and generally improvised. He whirled her, swirled her, chased her as the crowd began clapping and stomping. High on music, and whiskey, and a building excitement, Schick removed his vest and his neckerchief and tossed them aside; he removed his flat, round hat and spun it away, to knock some bottles shattering off a shelf. He pressed close to the girl, chest to chest, bumping and grinding lustily. The girl laughed. Caught up in the spirit, she began twisting and stomping, too, jerking an arm to the right, swinging and jerking an arm to the left, her breasts rolling and swaying.

Schick suddenly ripped at the upper bodice. The redhead slithered away, reached deliberately to her shoulders and pulled the short sleeves down her arms to let the dress slide free, her hips undulating in the white of corset and black garters. The men whistled and catcalled. His eyes blazing queerly, Schick unbuttoned his shirt and groped for the girl, finding her. His frenzied hands pawed at her body. Teasingly, she slipped away. Schick's hands quickly clasped her wrists like the springing of steel traps. The girl's playful smile rounded in pain, her face squinting. But before she could protest, he hurriedly steered her upstairs, their feet beating a rapid tattoo on the boarding until he slammed a door closed, all to the thunderous approval of watchers. Dade picked up Schick's clothes and hat and lumbered after the couple. The circle of viewers stood watching, then laughed knowingly and returned to their diversions.

Dragmire sat stoically, looking down at his beer. He arched a brow in thought and downed the drink in troubled gulps. The pianist offered a medley of Steven Foster favorites, which seemingly eased the patrons, lulling them into a languid mood. Dragmire rose to leave. From upstairs came an anguished scream. The pianist again quit. The crowd froze. The woman whimpered and subsided into prolonged sobs, then screamed once more, pitifully. People turned their eyes toward the second level and waited. They could hear the woman begging and then gagging into silence. But Dragmire thought he detected her groaning still. With his bung stick the bartender headed toward the stairs, when Schick appeared, buttoning his shirt, Dade behind him, still carrying some clothes. "Ain't no real accommodatin' women in this here town," he announced, pushing past the bartender while ignoring the man and his stick as if neither existed; the two swaggered out the front entrance.

The bartender rushed clumping up the stairs. As Dragmire stumbled his way out the rear door, he heard the big man exclaim, "My God, what have they done to you?"

The lights of the saloon flickered dimly in the thick dark of an empty alley. Dragmire found his way around the side.

He pressed against the building to hide under a side stairs until his eyes adjusted. He could barely make out Schick's and Dade's horses, still posted. He would wait for them under cover. Before he could react, two black forms materialized from each side and caught him, wrenching his arms behind him painfully, pinning him. He could smell the raw whiskey on the breath of one, and the acrid odor of old sweat and tobacco on the other.

He struggled to free himself, but the big man behind him twisted harder. Dragmire threw his head back and wailed in pain. The smaller figure to his left hissed, "Who the hell are you and what do you want?" It was Schick. Both forced him to his knees and bent him over to push his face into the turf. "You following me 'cause I slopped whiskey over you the other night? Or you been paid by somebody? Answer me." Schick punched Dragmire's head into the ground again, then let go to stand back while Dade pressed his weight down, immobilizing the gunsmith.

"I ain't followin' you," Dragmire grunted.

"Lyin' bastard." Schick cracked a pointed boot into the man's ribs. The spindly body contorted. "Talk, skinny man, or my friend here will stamp your head in. He breaks necks real good, too. Want to feel how he does it?" Dade emitted a deep, rumbling chuckle, and laid an instep of one boot across Dragmire's neck.

"I ain't done nothin' to you," Dragmire gasped desperately, knowing they would just as soon kill him as not.

"Why'd you follow us? I seen you come in the Nugget after we arrived. Then when we left, so did you; and then after we come back, so did you."

"Just chance."

"The hell it was." Schick kicked fiercely into the lower ribs. Dragmire cried out. Both men looked around them in the dark. The wind willowed through the eaves, and the piano in the Nugget wafted sadly. "Somebody hire you to tail us?"

"No."

"Then you was tryin' to back-shoot one of us when you got the chance?"

"No."

"You was considerin' you'd try to even things up between us. That it?"

"No," Dragmire gurgled, wincing with hurt as Dade increased pressure on both the angled arm and on the neck under his foot.

"Want me to kill him?" Dade asked icily.

"Let him up," said Schick. "We ain't gettin' paid to do him in."

"Just for fun? The job in Midas won't be no fun. That's business. This is pleasurin'."

"I said, let him up," said Schick. "We'll give him a friendly warning this time—make him understand that if he plays games with us again, he's dead."

When Dragmire came to, he realized someone was going through his pockets, searching for coins; his whole body seemed afire with pain searing through him, but he managed not to groan or to struggle. He remained limp as the thief undid his vest watch. Squinting, he could not make out features, only the hunched form above him. Surely the man had found his wallet, his derringer, and probably his knife. The thief rose without hurry and backed away. Dragmire could see him clearly then, silhouetted against the front streetlights that filtered into the alley . . . a grubby fellow, probably one of the ruffians who festered in every town, who subsisted on scraps tossed in the back streets, leeches all of them. Dragmire twisted to his side, his whole body knotting in cramps that numbed him. The thief was carrying the stolen loot in his left hand. Instinctively, Dragmire reached for his firearm. It had been removed. But he felt a stiffness of the sheath at the base of his neck. He reached back and found the bowie knife. The thief apparently had not rolled him over. As Dragmire sat up and pulled his knife, the thief heard him and reeled around. Dragmire threw the big-bladed weapon. He heard the culprit wail and saw him grasp his thigh as he sank to the ground. Angered, Dragmire rose; his belly and back constricting as he attempted to rush the thief, but the man tore the knife free and flung it toward Dragmire, narrowly missing—hobbling hurriedly then into the night while holding his leg. Dragmire found his wallet and money, the watch, and both his revolver and his derringer. But the knife lay lost somewhere in the dark. He figured he would have to retrieve it in the morning, until he detected the glitter of a blade.

Despite his racked body, Dragmire sniggered to himself as he cleaned the knife. He had his belongings back, and the hapless thief would suffer; and if he didn't wash and pack the wound properly, or if he didn't seek professional help, which was doubtful, he would likely succumb to blood poisoning. By morning, Dragmire knew, he himself would have difficulty climbing out of bed. He should try to seek a doctor, if they had one in town, but he didn't want the exposure. He didn't want anyone to identify him later. Now he was more determined than ever to kill Dade and Schick. He could not chance their seeing him ever, for surely they would kill him on sight. He had been too confident, too brazen. Now he would have to be the ghost stalker, the death shadow. But they would pay. He had heard Schick boast to the redhead about taking her to Midas with him. Midas—Cheveny was going there on business. But it didn't matter as long as he, Willard Dragmire, played it smart and kept a low profile. In only a matter of time he would ambush them simply and finally—an act of supreme completion.

Ahead, in front of his hotel, people stirred in the street. He saw men moving in and out of the entrance. Cautiously, he approached. "The constable will be here shortly," a man said, coming up the street. "They're pourin' coffee down his gullet."

"Too damn bad," someone said. "Elect an official, and

he can't hold up under the job. Doctor's up there in the room now, along with the manager. But I guess it's long too late.''

"Somebody best send for Dirk Landry," another commented. "Find out where he is and telegraph him. Somebody's on the loose that's got to be stopped.''

Dragmire stole into the foyer of the hotel. A stumpy clerk with a rim of salt and pepper hair fidgeted with some keys. He kept looking up the stairway that Schick had exited—the one that led directly to Dragmire's room. Dragmire could hear voices in earnest exchange. ''What happened?''

The clerk looked aghast at Dragmire and said plaintively, ''Girl got murdered up there. A prostitute, it looks like.''

"What do you mean?''

"Minnie, one of the girls who sometimes works out of here; a maid found her about twenty minutes ago.'' He leaned forth and said shakily, ''She'd been strangled and laid out proper, like in a coffin.''

"Strangled?''

The little man's eyes rounded. ''And one of her earlobes had been cut off.''

Earlier that day in the high range far from Bullion, Kellie Kurt pointed the readied pistol and waited, her breath held in, her heart chaotic. She had heard the fluttering rattle of a horse blowing air, along with the metallic clack of hooves placed judiciously by an experienced animal picking its way, but sliding here and there in the steep descent. She tightened her grip and braced the Colt on her knees, her right arm throbbing, unable to effectively support the gun. Through the trees she saw a big horse approaching, indistinctly, its rider tall in the saddle, although hunched slightly to study her clear imprints. Damn, she thought, everything was working against her. Suddenly her horse squealed a nervous greeting. "God," Kellie uttered under her breath. Why had she panicked? Why hadn't she muzzled the animal, she who had lived a lifetime training colts and yearlings? She heard the nearing animal draw back and snort. Then came silence, the rider and horse gone in the trees. The afternoon wind swayed and bobbed the sage and the extended branches of gray juniper. She waited, heavyhearted, her eyes filling with apprehension.

"Kellie," came a strangely familiar voice. "Kellie? That you?" The words offered security, assurance. "Kellie—it's me, Dirk Landry. Answer me. You must be able to hear me. I've come for you."

"Oh God. Oh God," Kellie cried in emotional surrender, her body quaking with hope. "That you, Dirk? That really you?" She heard the horse drop easily, directly, with footsuredness down the steepness paralleling the slide. She sat high, her held breath bursting within. Then, through a crack of brush, she saw the muscled chestnut emerge, riderless. Bewildered, she struggled to her feet, her face imploring, pinched with shock and disappointment. She stifled an anguished cry, her knuckles white in fists that clutched the gun.

To her right, under a twisted mahogany, Dirk Landry stepped out, his revolver cocked and pointing from his hip. "I'm sorry, Kellie. I had to be sure you were alone, not under pressure."

"Oh, Dirk," Kellie called. "Thank God." She lifted her cotton dress and plunged toward him, stumbling recklessly over the tumbled rocks, unfeminine and not caring. And he to her, open-armed, until she clutched his waist fiercely, burying her head in the center of his wide chest. "I dreamed and prayed you would come." The tears and convulsive sobs came freely. Landry embraced her shoulders and rocked her slowly. They held each other for some time as sun played shadows along the upper reaches and springwater gurgled tenderly down the wooded break.

"Hurry now," Landry said at last, his voice deep and steady. "We haven't much time."

"My horse, he can't go on." She looked up at Landry's towering frame, her face wet-streaked.

"I know. You will ride with me."

Her eyes strayed to the crippled horse. "Can he survive? Do we have to kill him?"

Landry answered solemnly. "We can't chance a gunshot now, not under any circumstances." He tossed Riles's rifle into the brush, then led Kellie by the arm, tucked her gun, the blanket, and what few supplies she had into his saddlebags, swung himself into the saddle and hoisted her up behind.

"What's in all those bags across your pommel?" she asked, seeing the extra haversacks that her father had given him.

"Your ransom," he said, "one hundred thousand."

She gulped. "One hundred thousand?"

"That was the bargain."

"What are you doing with it?"

"Saving your skin, if need be. Hopefully, we can outrun Morton and save you and the money. Hopefully." He guided the chestnut down to the terrace, pulled across the base of the flow, and drummed the animal's ribs with encouragement, urging it ahead.

Kellie's voice had a hollow ring of despair. "Morton, I'm scared, oh so scared of him, Dirk. I know he's behind us somewhere. Somewhere close. I can feel him. Him and those filthy cutthroats and that Riles." Landry could feel the wrench of shuddering that rolled through her body as she hugged him, her breasts and belly tight against his back.

"They won't hurt you again," he said firmly, realizing that his words betrayed his assumptions.

"I killed a man back there," she confessed angrily. "I had to. But it was terrible."

"I know."

"And the man named Riles. He . . ." She groped for words. "He . . ."

"Never mind."

They rode in silence, the chestnut pacing easily. Then Kellie asked, "My father, how is he holding up?"

"Damn tough old man you got. He demanded that he deliver the money to Morton."

"Where is he?"

"I sent him back. He can do more good in Midas for us than here. Although I know he didn't want to go."

"Poor Pop. All this is my fault. He didn't want me to come home. But I was so sick of school," Kellie lamented. "He can't understand that I belong here in the West, not in all that stuffy world back East." She squirmed around, filled with trepidation at what might be pursuing them.

"Well, your little tantrum of independence is proving costly."

"Look!" Kellie warned, pointing. Landry swung the horse at an angle so that they could see back without twisting farther in the saddle.

"I see." North along the ridge that both he and Kellie had traversed, three riders jockeyed back and forth, following their route. Landry wondered where the rest of the gang was. Had some ventured back to Midas? Were they attempting to cut him and Kellie off somewhere ahead? Had they seen Franz Kurt and ridden in pursuit?

"What are you going to do, Dirk?" Kellie said anxiously.

Landry considered the situation. To continue along the terrace meant he could outdistance them for a time. But the extra weight of the girl would tax the chestnut, despite its superior strength; plus at the lower elevation, the broken country offered little concealment. With a decisive turn, Landry neck-reined the big animal upward, to climb once again in a steady pull through the shallow canyon where the thick of aspen and alder offered a veiled retreat. Morton and his partners would be forced down again by the slide. So far it didn't appear the three had seen them. In the upper reaches he would have a visual and gunning advantage.

"Where are we going?" Her curious words had a sudden, ominous sound. "Will they catch us?"

"Not while I'm alive, because I'm taking you up yonder there." He pointed to the timberline. "To that thick pine ridge where there's good cover. We're going to travel the high country due south until I can drop through a pass, down to Midas, sometime tomorrow."

"Landry's on the girl's tail and making no attempt to cover his tracks," said Morton with satisfaction. Their horse wove around the broken rocks and clumps of downed wood, fine-grained and bone-white. They raised a pale, gritty dust in the crumpled granite. "You can see the girl's route. She's movin' faster than she should; wouldn't be surprised if she didn't get throwed."

"They both headed down toward the flat." Fang motioned.

" 'Cause of that slide ahead, we'll have to go down, too," Liddicoat said.

As they skirted a pinyon grove, Morton called a halt. The horses yanked and danced impatiently as he studied the precipitous slide area. "Got to be careful here. Got to keep to as much cover as possible. Could run into a Landry ambush; a million places he could be waiting out there."

"Well, he ain't," said Liddicoat. "There he is across the way, beyond the slide!" A quarter of a mile away Landry and the girl appeared momentarily, the chestnut fleeting through the trees, then disappearing.

"God damn, he's found the girl," Morton barked.

Liddicoat cocked three rifle shots in rapid fire. They whistled across the space and smacked into the far shrubbery. The three outlaws watched and waited in silence as the wind soughed through the trees. "Ain't going to get 'em from here," said Liddicoat.

"Hell, we're going to have to go down to the flats and then

follow Landry up from there. He'll be miles ahead of us.''
Morton's dish face had bloated with frustration.

"Ain't no other way," said Liddicoat, "considering the
regions above us and ahead of us. Of course, his horse is
carrying two, that'll slow him some.''

"You underestimate Landry; he's got the best of horse-
flesh there, and he knows how much he can push it.''

"Maybe there's some way through up there in them
breaks," said Fang, his eyes narrowing as he assessed the
jagged peaks.

"You're thinkin' my thoughts," said Morton. "I never
been on that crest, but there's a chance a man might get
through up there. Might have to travel on foot leading his
horse. But he might get across better than we can down here,
with all them canyons and rises.''

"But he might not, either," Fang said reluctantly, as if he
was sorry he had mentioned the idea.

"It's a chance we got to take. If you can get through, you
could cut Landry off. With you above him, and me and Liddicoat on his tail, we could cut him off—trap him.''

"Didn't say I wanted to go up there.''

"Somebody's gotta. You're a natural.''

"Me?" Fang squirmed in the saddle.

"You was always good slinkin' around. Besides, Landry
can't take too many chances with the girl. And he's going to
have to stick with any thick timber he can find. All that's
gonna pretty much limit him." Morton smiled craftily.
"We'll get the girl back and I'll bury Landry. It just might
work.''

"And if it doesn't?" Liddicoat said.

"We got the boys waiting in town. Come on, every minute
counts." Morton motioned Fang away and waived to Liddicoat to follow as the threesome separated.

Liddicoat's three bullets winged into the cover above and
behind Landry and Kellie, one slug ricocheting, singing away

with a peculiar humming. Unprepared, Kellie squealed, nearly toppling off as Landry whipped the chestnut to the side, directing it into a protective enclosure of feathery juniper where they floundered ahead, almost recklessly. "Sorry, honey," Landry said, "but we aren't gonna be the victims of a wild, crazy bullet."

"I just about fell." Kellie laughed in relief, sweeping a flop of hair from her face.

Calmly, with almost gentle deliberation, Landry maneuvered the chestnut to the next wooded gorge and rode down the jumbled rockway, the horse stumbling and sloshing where clear water pooled and gathered to crickle loose, musically, over mossy steps. Landry dismounted. "Come on, get down. Quick."

"What are you doing?" Kellie demanded. "This is crazy. We're losing time—they'll be on top of us." Landry lifted her down. "You lost your mind? We'll never make it this way."

"I don't want all our weight on this horse." Without comment, Landry backed the big animal some twenty feet upstream, up the very route they had come down. He turned the chestnut around with the utmost care, then laboriously led the gelding up the waterway past the spot where they had entered, continuing another two hundred feet with Kellie struggling behind. "Try not to overturn any rocks or kick up any mud if you can possibly help it," Landry warned.

After mounting, they clambered another hundred yards to where three sources of trickling water converged; Landry then angled to the south through a long shaft of squat pines toward the next ridge; when safely hidden, he reined the heaving animal to an earned rest. Again he dismounted. "We tried to lose our trail by backtracking—favorite trick of the fox. Let's hope we're as clever in outfoxing Morton." Landry winked.

"Well, Dirk." Kellie sighed. "Your cleverness is making me a wreck."

"Hang tighter, Kellie. We're going to have to perform a few more tricks—some mighty clever tricks before we're out of here and home." Solemnly, he once again took the horse by the halter and stepped gingerly out, his gray eyes judging the rugged landscape ahead, heavily wooded in spots but dangerously open over extensive vistas of sage and rocky outcrops, all serrated and tattered under the bulk of stacked peaks, seemingly impenetrable. "Most of all we need your prayers and a lot of good luck."

(9)

Franz Kurt had left the terrace and was dropping toward the stage road before he noticed the big bay skirting the wooded slope behind him. A rider, attempting to intercept him, now broke toward the section between the Silver Lode Summit and the town of Midas. "Son of a bitch," Kurt spat. Someone was tailing him—someone was attempting to stop him, probably kill him. He had stuffed his vest and a blanket in the saddlebags to puff them more realistically, as if he still carried the ransom money. Whoever—one of Morton's men, he surmised—was convinced that he was alone, an easy mark. Were there others? Instinctively he pulled his revolver and looked around, but the brush and trees hid any other movement. Maybe the rest of the members had taken after Landry. Kurt spurred his mount, gauging the distance to the road. He could see the big bay appearing and disappearing, angling steeply downward. Shortly, the stranger would be able to effectively cut off any chance of his returning to town. Kurt would be an open target on the road, and it would be the same if he headed into the desert. If he remained on the wooded heights, he could at least defend himself, maybe hold off the assailant and any others who might be with him somewhere. Cole and his posse would be leaving Midas soon. The men just might hear an exchange of gunfire.

Kurt had learned, in an aggressive life of financial warfare, that the best defense was an assaultive offense. Hoping to surprise and rattle the stranger, he directed his horse toward

118

where he had last seen the rider, replaced his sidearm, and pulled his rifle from the scabbard to cock it, the sound loud, snapping in the cooling air. Hunching to make himself less of a target, he pushed swiftly through the shrubby trees, around hefty rocks and downed timber. Then he saw the rider appear between a rent of shifted rocks. The man, youngish, bareheaded, held his upper arm as if in pain while allowing the big bay free rein to pick its way where the going had gotten difficult. Not expecting Kurt's approach, he was looking ahead at the ground, at the pitch of an embankment. Now! thought Kurt, rolling from his horse, its reins wrapped around his right arm. He held against the animal's shoulder, aiming, trying to steady the rifle, but the sweating animal shifted impatiently, wrenching his rifle askew. "God damn," Kurt hissed. Again he took aim, unsteadily, the rifle swaying to fire once, twice, a third time blindly.

The bay stumbled in surprise, caught its balance and danced to the side, whinnying as Riles fell free and hit the ground on agile feet, his rifle in hand; shaken momentarily, the outlaw dived into thick sage. He saw Kurt and his horse just above, rifle pointing, spitting lead again. Not believing that Kurt had deliberately changed course to attack, he recoiled and held fire. But after a fourth bullet pelted stinging dirt against his leg, Riles fired back. Kurt attempted to find cover, but his horse balked, then broke away, kicking and tossing down the slope to spin the tycoon aside, dragging him a short ways, until the reins unraveled. For what seemed an eternity the older man lay battered in an enclave of bony roots, his mind fuzzy. Riles took careful aim. His bullet caught Kurt's confused animal behind the shoulder, sliced into a lung and cut deep into the massive chest cavity. The horse rolled in a squealing frenzy and came up partially, its eyes walled and glassy; foamy blood flooded from its mushed side, then sheeted across its shoulder as it rose on its front legs in desperation before collapsing in a twisted heap, the shuddering body sliding brokenly a few feet farther.

Dazed still, Kurt crawled in a blurred confusion to where some prongs of rock offered protection. He waited, his eyes moist, the dirt and dust cloaking his dark clothes in a soft gray. He worked his fingers anxiously to be certain they still functioned, for his back and shoulders tingled numbly. Had he broken some bones? Pulled some muscles? Twisted some ligaments? He raised his head slightly and tried to see. Nothing. He looked behind him and to the sides, half expecting others to appear. Was this how it would end? A lifetime of building an empire, a world of cattle and mines and timber and planned railroads to open the hinterland. Dreams and expectations almost fulfilled. All his. But to die here, on a lonely, godforsaken mountainside by unknown killers while his daughter was still in mortal danger?

Franz Kurt was made of more than flesh and bones. He was the West. For half a lifetime he had struggled against all odds and prevailed—from the primitive world of the California Gold Rush to the heady strikes of the Comstock. Well, he was not now or ever to succumb to some lousy, shiftless gunman who was attempting to do him in and gain a fortune. On his belly, Kurt pulled and wormed himself to the nearest rock slab and twisted sideways to shove his rifle ahead, bracing it in a rock fork. Gradually he could make out the incline, the spots of juniper and the sage clumps that checkered the land. Then he saw the bay partially hidden. And he saw movement, a man low, possibly on his hands and knees. Smiling tautly, Kurt aimed carefully.

The bullet hit too high, but sent shards of granite splintering like shrapnel. Riles howled and the bay pulled away and pranced in a throaty protest. Kurt fired again and heard the bullet whine away. Riles returned a shot that hit above Kurt and burrowed into the crumbled stone. For a time the two exchanged shots in a sporadic, matter-of-fact way, both reloading until Riles called, "You, Kurt, why don't you leave the loot and save your life? You ain't got a chance."

"Go to hell." Kurt plowed two bullets into the earthy parapet in front of Riles.

Riles wiped the dust from his eyes. "I'm closer to the money than you, you damned fool; back off and I won't kill you."

"You don't know that I have it, so why don't you risk your worthless hide and try for it? Come on. Rush me. Take a bullet in the gut, you stupid bastard." Kurt laughed aloud with the pleasurable thought.

Riles could see that the dead horse was closer to him than to Kurt now, the body feet up in a shallow pit, one saddlebag visible, the other somewhere next to the backside. He might be able to reach it if he took care. He tied the bay securely to the limb of a shrunken pinyon and retreated to swing around a rocky outcrop, crawling below it, then up toward the carcass. His arm wound commenced bleeding again. It would be a damn dirty fate if Kurt didn't have the ransom and was forcing him to jeopardize his life for nothing. He could take refuge in the pit behind the body, he figured. He approached the visible saddlebag with caution.

Above, a few hundred feet south, Franz Kurt, his high hat removed, waited and watched, his eyes darting. Nervously, he again looked behind him and to each side, expecting someone to appear with blazing guns. All evidence, however, pointed to only the one man; but now he was nowhere in sight. Kurt could still see a portion of the stiffening horse, its hind legs erect. The outlaw would be attempting to secure the saddlebags, he knew; so he told himself to have patience, to hold the rifle on the area where the man must eventually appear.

Riles thought he saw Kurt in a wedge of rocks, but he couldn't tell for certain. He questioned whether opening fire was worth revealing his position, especially if Kurt focused in with any degree of accuracy. For twenty minutes more they held off in silence, a battle of fraying nerves. A Steller's jay screamed from somewhere above; another answered him from the tall pinyons near the road. The one above left its perch to swoop in long dips, alighting halfway between Kurt and Riles. It jerked with indignation, shrieking its contempt for the noisy invasion of its domain. "Damned bird will give me away," Riles said fretfully, trying hard to see Kurt.

Kurt puckered his face in a droll acceptance of fate. The bird would pinpoint any movement either man made, but it could work in his favor, as the younger outlaw would need to be more active, especially if he was trying to reach the saddlebags. The late afternoon wind rustled the shrubs as shadows stretched in lazy patterns. The jay quieted except for an outburst now and then. Kurt checked his watch. Cole and his men should be on the way, as ordered, if he and Landry had not returned with Kellie. Suddenly, once again, jays set up a quarrelsome racket, this time three or four joining the ruckus. Kurt squirmed higher to see, when a bullet nearly took his head off. He ducked and fell back. The fire-power intensified as Riles slivered a steady barrage.

Again Riles loaded his rifle, to be safe, and began advancing, the jays still squawking. Viewing what he thought to be the form of a man hidden, he snapped a shot in the direction and saw movement flowing away. He leveled a succession of lead-fire in the general direction, and charged toward the dead horse, to flop across the one reachable saddlebag. He tore the flap open and pawed out the contents: a vest, blanket, currycomb, horseshoe, chunked jerky, plate, cup, and utensils. "Hell," he spat, realizing he had been duped. He slid along the down side of the horse, using it for protection as he approached the second bag, lying askew.

Kurt, momentarily blinded by particles of flying dust from the barrage, wiped his watery eyes and fumbled more bullets into the magazine. With difficulty he studied the dead horse and thought he saw something by it. He levered two more shots when he heard the drone of horses approaching. Cole and the posse, he thought.

As the two bullets splotted into the carcass, Riles heard

the rumble of horses, arriving fast, but not before he had learned that the second bag had no money. Cursing, he rolled away into the brush, bolted for his life to the bay, tore the reins free and was on his way before settling into the saddle.

Franz Kurt saw a flash of the big bay through the trees and tried one desperate shot. Before meeting the posse, he moved down the slope as fast as he was capable to his dead horse and gathered the dumped articles, securing them in the saddlebags once again. Cole and Bradly, leading a group of maybe twenty men, came to a halt on the road, all looking up as the horses stomped and milled.

"Heard the shooting; figured you was in trouble," Cole shouted. "What the hell happened, and where's Landry?"

"Landry went after my daughter; she escaped!"

Kurt's riders responded with a rousing cheer.

"Where's Morton?"

"He and his men must be after them both by now; it's a long story. One of them followed me; that's what all the shooting's about."

"What's all the smoke from?"

"From the cabin that was Morton's hideout. Don't rightly know how it got going, except my daughter must have somehow started it." Kurt looked the men over. "Right now I need your help to get my saddlebags and the money free."

"You brought the ransom? You're lucky whoever was after you didn't get it."

"Once in town, we'll get it safe in the bank."

With a few ropes around the upright legs, the riders were able to roll the horse so that Kurt could retrieve his bags and loosen his saddle; he filled the horsemen in with what details he knew. Cole pondered the message from Landry, his handsome features troubled. "This changes things considerably. Did you read it?" Cole asked Kurt.

"Yes," Kurt admitted.

"What is it?" Bradly inquired.

"If Landry's hunch is right, Morton's got men stationed in Midas," Cole announced solemnly.

"Meaning what?"

"I don't know. But I intend to find out. I'm taking some of my deputies back with me," Cole said, motioning nearly a third of those present to him. "You, Johnson. I'm putting you in charge here." A stalwart deputy with muscular arms, his box-shaped face puffy with gray sideburns, nodded. "And Bradly, you will have final say for your men. Get up there where that smoke is. Find out what the hell is going on, and then see what you can do for Landry and the girl. There's enough of you to stop Morton and his gang, but don't underestimate him."

"Landry and my daughter were headed south into the high country," Kurt said, climbing on behind Cole, the saddlebags draped over his shoulder. "He was trying his damnedest to catch her, to try to take her back to Midas." The tycoon looked firmly at those departing. "Be careful, that Morton's not one to fool with."

As the two posses separated, Riles muffled his horse and peered from a brushy glade. Why was the force splitting? Why did they need so many to escort Kurt back to town if he didn't have the ransom? Or hadn't he let on? But again, why was the smaller group returning? He could make out Kurt riding double in his high hat. Perhaps the returning party intended on eventually riding out of Midas and up the mountain, in an effort to intercept and escort Landry back, should he find the girl and attempt to bring her home. It was obvious that the riders climbing the rise were heading toward the burn, doubtless with intentions of tracking Morton and assisting Landry where possible. Whatever, Riles decided he would now continue as planned. Discreetly, he would ride into Midas by nightfall or by early morning, depending. He might still be in on big money.

* * *

Morton and his men followed the chestnut with ease, until they reached the water flow where Landry had executed his fox trick, and there they became confused. "They was headin' down here, but I don't see no trail anywhere," Liddicoat said, bewildered.

"He sure as hell didn't fly away," Morton barked. "I don't think he's gonna head down. There ain't no future in the open. He's going to stay in the timberline, up where them trees are thicker; he may even try to go up into the high country; there's a few passes up there, I hear; if Landry can find them or if he knows about them, he might try 'em."

Liddicoat drove his horse sloshing and clattering beside the gurgling waters, his washed-out eyes riveted on the rocks as he sought to find a broken limb, an upturned stone, a slice of mud, any evidence. In frustration they repeatedly scoured the streamlet, searching to no avail, returning always at Morton's insistence to where they had begun. "Maybe he jumped his horse across here somewhere." Liddicoat took off his hat and rubbed his hair. "Maybe he jumped and took off from there."

"Maybe. Then we'll keep looking," Morton said doggedly. For another thirty minutes they went up and down, each some fifteen feet either side of the flow, but with no success. The afternoon shadows began weaving darkly. Both outlaws began an urgent surveillance of the higher peaks and ridges in a desperate hope they might catch sight of Landry and the girl. But the jumbled panorama held its secrets. Erupting loudly, Morton suddenly exclaimed, "Landry's pulled a trick—an old trick I should have thought of. Bet anything that's what he done." Morton beamed slowly, with growing certainty. He moved his horse rapidly, farther up, its breath coming in deep gulps from the effort. Where several rivulets joined, he gave out a joyous, "Here. God damn it. Here. Landry, that bastard, he backtracked his horse. I see where he took off, due south on the higher reaches there."

"Just what we figured." Liddicoat bobbed his head with disgust. "We should have followed our feelings."

"Don't matter; we know his direction now. Come on, we've got to move, 'cause he's headin' right into Fang's sights."

The confusion had given Landry precious time to set a relatively straight course through protective clots of trees and around blocks of granite. Briefly, he and Kellie dismounted to rest the chestnut, while observing Morton's progress. "What's that white thing like a shield in front of Morton on his horse?" Landry questioned.

"It's a sombrero."

"A sombrero—the disguise he used with the Chevenys."

From between two upflung rocks backed with enclosing arms of juniper, they watched Morton and Liddicoat move tediously up and down the waterway. Landry chuckled deeply, taking a long-needed satisfaction in their plight. Soberly he concluded, "It's only a matter of time until Morton figures out what we did. Best we move."

Kellie pressed against his hulk and stared. "Why only two?"

"I was wondering the same thing." Alert, Landry looked above them, his eyes canvassing the corrugated uplands. "They may have sent someone on another route, higher probably, hoping to catch us in a cross fire." Landry took the girl by the arm. "How many were there in all?"

"There was an old man at the shack, waiting. I think he left shortly, the way they talked."

Landry nodded, taking to the saddle and hoisting Kellie up. "He's harmless, a cook and whatnot; he sets up their getaway camps."

"There was Morton and a man who was supposed to be good with a rifle."

"That's Liddicoat, in dark clothes down there with Morton. He's their best gun."

"The one that just shot at us?"

"Yes." Landry guided the chestnut through a slanted draw between a cleft of washed-out earth, a shortcut to the next saddleback. "That's why we've got to be especially careful. Who else?"

"A mousy little man. I heard Morton mention something to him about Midas."

"Jenson. He's probably in town, up to something by now."

"Then there was a horrible-looking creature. He grinned like a wolf. Made me terribly uncomfortable." Kellie's words came jerkily as the rock and pitch of the horse punched her breath from her.

"They call him Fang. That's the one I'm concerned about."

"Could he be after my father?"

Ignoring her, Landry said simply, "He's probably trying to take us from another angle. He's the one who could be up there. Now, who else?"

Her voice quickened. "The big one I shot."

"That was Beatty."

"And the one they called Riles." Her throat constricted with emotion. "I hope he bleeds to death."

"You certain you hit him?"

"He got out of the fire. He was running after me, but not doing too well. I saw him holding his arm."

"Riles is tough; it'll take more than a flesh wound to stop him, if that's what he took."

"Maybe he'll bleed to death, just crawl off and die," she said bitterly.

"Maybe. If we're lucky." Landry clucked encouragingly to the magnificent animal as it carefully picked its way across a break, tight with sweeping pinyon and belly-high sage, the volcanic rocks tossed heedlessly here and there. Then Landry chose a looping path that carried them swiftly around the next bend, to leave Morton and Liddicoat long out of sight. Landry kept watching above and slightly back of him for one of the gang members who he believed was attempting to intercede. He did not want to be an easy target.

Morton and Liddicoat pushed their mounts harder than normally wise, but not enough to eventually flounder them; although anxious to catch Landry, Morton had succeeded too long in the big country to toy with an animal that was vital to survival.

"Jenson, he always follows orders, but Riles, think you can trust him?" Liddicoat said casually, but his words hit pointedly.

Morton looked questioningly at his man. "Riles is hotheaded, but he knows who butters his bread. He'll come through."

"What of them other two? You may be the boss, but I'm tellin' you, they're trouble. They ain't smart. They bull their way instead of layin' low."

"Dade and Schick? That's why I keep them at a distance, until I need them."

"That why they're comin' into Midas?"

"That, among other things. Apparently someone hired them to do some business. I figured while they was in Midas, I'd use 'em as backup."

Liddicoat studied Morton quizzically. "Don't know what you plan for 'em, but they ain't ones to trust."

"Don't matter. They'll serve their purpose, at least for what I want. But for now we gotta outguess Landry," said Morton. The wind soughing through the trees was welcome, for he had begun sweating heavily. "Landry won't run into the open country with the girl. And he can't run too far south. There's too many big cuts in the mountainside. He's gotta drop down one of them close-by canyons and make a break for Midas. I think I know which one he'll take. Leads right down, almost to town. Lots of brush and trees at the base. That's the one he'll take."

"We gonna ride down and wait? Gun him down there?" Liddicoat looked skeptical.

"Hell no, we got him on the run for the time being. He's movin' higher. He thinks them trees and passes up there is going to lead him out. But he don't know about Fang. We're going to push him right into an ambush. We'll finish it all up there someplace—what we started so long ago, what him and me been tryin' to finish for one hell of a long time." Morton grinned in wicked delight.

Eve stood stiffly in the foyer of the Nugget Hotel, her back to the dining room entrance. She fumbled with her parasol as her face puckered. The frustration and indignity she felt was her fault, she knew, for venturing into town when Uncle Landry had expected her to remain secluded. But she had felt bored and wanted to see a thriving town where life was more than the desert drabness that hung over Broken Bluffs. So she was a prostitute—a whore, if you will; she had not yet found the life degrading. Men ogled her, desired her, looked upon her with lust, which gave her a strangely exhilarating sense of power. As you sow, so shall you reap. Biblical words she had heard from a traveling preacher once. Words that had stayed with her somehow. Men could be tender or matter-of-fact, some beastly. Perhaps she should not have so detested the overbearing, superior attitude of that ass, Nathanael Weldon. But for the time being, she could not help herself. If she gave men company and satisfaction, if she listened to their dreams and to their fears, if she heard about their families and their sweethearts so far away, if she gave them reprieve from the hell of long, brutalizing hours at jobs that could cost them their lives—it was no excuse for them to believe they possessed her, could abuse her, insult, and demean her because she carried on an honest living, even one not acceptable to the social decorum of the established citizenry. However, the number of secret patrons from the mighty, the respectable, and the rich—many cheating on their spouses—had at first appalled her, bringing her to realize that no one was above reproach.

Over her shoulder, she sensed more than saw Nathanael Weldon storm from the dining room into the evening. Eve lifted her shoulders, brushed a straying curl back in place, and composed herself in preparation of returning to the boardinghouse.

The little clerk who had watched her enter and meet with Weldon studied her carefully again. She sensed his eyes dissecting her, judging her. She was aware that of late her whole being was keenly in tune with her surroundings, especially to men who could threaten her in some manner. She had wiped her nose with a hankie, squared her jaw, and started out, when he hurried around the counter. "Miss, miss," he commanded in a high, squeaky voice. She stopped but did not look at him. "Miss, I must warn you. We do not allow unescorted ladies here in the Nugget."

"I was just leaving."

"I mean if you should decide to return." He looked haughtily at her, with an air of contempt. "The Nugget caters only to the select. We must protect our clientele. Do you understand?" As he spoke, his eyes roved over her neck and shoulders and along the cut of her bodice.

Eve envisioned slamming her parasol across the little pipsqueak's head, but she resisted. After all, she had disobeyed Landry's wishes. She had been attracting men; if not brazenly, at least coyly. "I've caused no disturbance."

"I just want you to understand, young lady, that we have strict rules in this hotel. I was merely trying to be considerate before I called the house detective." The shriveled little man relaxed his truculent stance as he became sure and knowing. His eyes darted naughtily, noting anyone who might overhear. "But you, lovely lady, you do grace this place." His pinched mouth arched in careful consideration. "But I can cover for you. I'll tell my boss you're a visiting lady—a dignitary's lady from the East, that he's escorting you. You understand?''

You conniving little ape, Eve thought.

''Afterward, you and me could work it all out, payment for allowin' you to remain here. You understand?''

''The woman is with me,'' Cheveny announced, his arms crossed. He had come from the dining room and had been listening. ''I'm a patron in this hotel, and would suggest you watch how you talk to this lady. If I see you accost her again, I will speak to your manager. Now I suggest you go back to work and mind your business.''

The small men faced each other like two bantam roosters, until the clerk flushed in the face and neck, and expelled his breath slowly. ''Yes, sir. But I remind you, I was only doing my job.'' He returned to his register as Cheveny took Eve by the elbow and escorted her to an alcove of the foyer near a tall tropical fern where the clerk could not observe them.

''You didn't need to do that,'' said Eve. ''But I thank you.'' She felt genuinely touched by the strange little fellow. Freakish-looking or not, he had spunk and character, something that the handsome, suave Nathanael Weldons of the world sorrowfully lacked. ''I must be going now.''

As she lifted her skirt and turned daintily away, Cheveny detained her, a gentle hand to her forearm. ''Please. I couldn't help but overhear your conversation with that man in the dining room.''

''It wasn't pleasant, I'm sorry.''

''No, I'm asking you to accompany me.'' He leaned his head toward the dining room. ''I respect a beautiful woman. A glass of wine and some talk perhaps?''

Eve smiled wearily. ''Go back in there?''

Cheveny twisted a money bill into her palm; in his other hand he rotated the roll of bills, not observable to onlookers, but obvious enough so Eve saw it. ''I've had my meal. But I would like to order the best for you. I'll have a drink while we order you some wine and a meal with all the trimmings.''

Eve was intrigued with his style. She wondered where his wife was and what he did to support such a hunk of money. Besides, she had never eaten in such an establishment, and she was a little hungry. "Why not?" she said with a girlish lilt, squeezing her eyes. The surprised rapture on Cheveny's face melted her momentarily, but not so much as to forget that she was professional.

"All right," he gushed, taking her arm and guiding her toward the dining room. "I'm Noah Cheveny. Business. Guns and gunsmithing through much of the territory, and I'm here to open up another store. You?"

"I'm Eve."

"Eve what?"

"Just Eve."

"Somehow, I feel I've seen you somewhere," he said. "But surely I could place someone as beautiful as you."

"No, I've never been to Midas before. I never saw the place until today." She entered the room confidently, ignoring a few curious glances, for she stood a head taller than he. This was one wealthy little dreamer who she could handle with comparative ease, she told herself.

(10)

"Night's comin' on fast," said Liddicoat. He jetted a stream of tobacco into the shrubs. "Seems like summer ain't got no length no more. Seems like winter is always with us here in this high country."

"We got time enough." Morton judged the landscape ahead and above, then reined his horse ever higher. "Landry will be huggin' the timber belt, and so will we. Wish I knew if Fang got through. If he did, he'll cut Landry off, ambush him before he can make a run for Midas."

"Seems he's moving mighty easy with that girl on behind."

"Don't surprise me none, not with that horse he's got. I told you, Landry knows the land, knows exactly what he can do and what he can't."

Liddicoat grinned evenly, knowingly. "Seems to me you got a heap bit of respect for that lawman. You always did have; ever since I started ridin' with you, I seen it. It was Landry you always saw in a different light from all them other tin stars."

Morton looked back at Liddicoat defensively. But his face softened somewhat as he looked out over the ribs of the mountainside. "A man would be a damned fool not to respect Landry."

The pair pulled higher, the thin air hard on the animals, making them heave, their sides pulsing, forcing the men to stop frequently to steady the horses' balance, Liddicoat, the hunter and marksman, kept his eyes roving across the lay of flats below, toward the upsweep of higher outcrops ahead, where the fingers of watery cuts had made deep grooves in the mountains. But more often he watched behind—a habit he had acquired from years on the trail in flight. "I don't have a good feelin' about any of this. We've overplayed our hand. The girl somehow escaped, and now that marshal's here. Our forces are split and Beatty's dead. We don't even know where the money is for sure. It just ain't no good."

Sullenly, his face set, Morton scoffed at Liddicoat's remarks. "We've put too much into this. I ain't givin' up, not when I know that girl is still within reach; Landry's fightin' against the odds, and I know that money is with him."

"How do you figure?"

"He brung it in for the girl; he's the only one capable. And he wouldn't hide it, 'cause he knows he may still have to bargain for her life, even for his own."

The horses made crunching sounds as they wormed through jumbles of sage and heaped boulders, their hooves grinding the gravelly granite into puffs of fine powder. "Maybe he don't have it. Maybe Riles knows things we don't."

Morton pulled his horse up sharply. "What the hell you saying?"

"I'm saying you was suspicious of him from the start down there, when we come upon him and the fired cabin. You yourself didn't trust him. Maybe there was more men than Landry. We don't know for sure. Seems to me that Franz Kurt is pretty bullheaded. I can't imagine him sittin' home." Liddicoat, staring back, squinted, his features hardening.

Morton nudged his mount ahead, his face introspective. "You're damn smart, Liddicoat. I guess that's why I lean on you most. You're probably right. I keep havin' a gut feelin' that something's wrong, that Riles wasn't levelin' with me."

"Well, we got more problems," Liddicoat said, wrenching around, a hand on his cantle; his face twisted toward the terrace below. "We got a posse. A sizable posse hot on our tracks."

Morton hunched around to see a dozen or so riders tracking them along the flatlands. From behind them the fire continued to funnel smoke. "God damn. They're onto us, armed to the teeth and comin' fast."

"They must have been shadowin' Landry."

"Most likely."

"They've smelled us out for sure."

"Ain't the first posse on my back, and it won't be the last."

"What the hell we do?"

"Just what we're plannin', kill Landry and get the girl back."

With early evening and the rise of a full red moon that whitened in its climb, Landry took refuge in a grove of pines backed by a small amphitheater of granite sides and domes, topped by a gnarled canopy of sage and rabbitbrush that would make human approach impossible without detection. In front of them rose a natural bulwark, with parapets and clear views of any downhill access. "We'll hole up here, for a time," Landry said, assessing the site still. He swung his leg over the horse's arched neck and dropped stiffly to the ground, his old leg wound tightening his left side. He reached to assist the girl down, but she declined, sliding free and landing on her feet with the dip and grace of a ballerina.

"Shouldn't we keep going?" she questioned. "Shouldn't we try to get out of these mountains? I couldn't stand it now to be captive again, not of those animals."

"I understand," Landry whispered tenderly. "But we can't go farther. Dark will be on us in no time. Up here, in the half light of a moon, trying to find our way would be suicide. We can't have any fire, you understand."

"I know."

"So we have just so much time to feed my horse, eat, and

settle in. Keep Beatty's gun with you at all times." Leading
the chestnut off to the side where thick mahogany plumed,
he removed a nose bag of oats, cleared the bit, and secured
the apparatus over the ears and head. "We'll sneak out of
here before dawn." He watched the animal munch with pleasure as he hobbled the front legs. "Usually don't need to do
this," he lamented, patting the gelding's shoulder affection-
ately. "But tonight we can't take any chances." The animal
stopped eating, flicked its ears and rolled its eyes, and backed
up to prance slightly. Landry steadied its head, his hand
dropping to his sidearm.

"What's spooking him?" Kellie's voice quavered.

"I don't know." Landry then circled the stony enclosure,
checking the sweep of alpine rimrock above the chunked
incline where Morton would be advancing. But nothing
moved in the latticed shadows of a fading day. Morton would
be forced to make camp shortly, too. Would the big moon
afford enough light to tempt him to try a search and hit maneuver? Landry doubted it; snug in their temporary fortress,
he and Kellie would have an overwhelming advantage against
anyone floundering noisily about. Even in the bright silver of
a soaring moon, there were unstable rocks, entwining roots,
hidden clefts, and a hundred other dangers that lay waiting
in the night. Only a fool would attempt it, and Morton was
no fool. But nevertheless, Landry would take precautions.
He would hold watch throughout the night. The chestnut
ceased feeding again and shifted, ill at ease. "Keep your gun
with you at all times," Landry said, taking a hunk of wrapped
jerky from his saddlebags. He removed his knife and began
to slice some fat chunks. "Keep your blanket around your
shoulders; without a fire, it's going to get mighty cold up
here, even in summer."

"Up here now, it's really fall," said Kellie, looking at the
bright yellow of the rabbitbrush that bloomed riotously in the
late months. She moved back toward the wall of granite for
protection from a wind sinking off the peaks. The chestnut,

standing high-headed, snorted and wheeled his stern. Landry had secured his knife and reached out to steady the big fellow when a whirring clatter erupted, reverberating in the walled confines. Kellie froze and her lips and cheeks paled as her eyes slid down. Above the thick coil of earthy patterns, a wedge-shaped face with pinched mouth and hard eyes concentrated on the slender leg between her hem and the buttoned shoe tops. From below the two holes of a nose, a tongue flicked red. Beyond the coil, the wide flatness tapered into a blur of movement as the shattering rattle continued.

Landry's sunken eyes seemed cavernous. Instinctively his hand fell to his Colt, withdrawing it. He hesitated, a flash of impressions bombarding him: fear washing through Kellie; his shots announcing their presence and whereabouts to Morton and any other member somewhere in the folds of the mountain; the writhing of deathly filth tensed to strike. Landry's gun barked twice, blowing the rattler away in a twisting frenzy of broken movement; it ended some ten feet away, to flex involuntarily in a pulsing rhythm.

Above, from behind an abutment of lava plugs, Fang heard the shots and crawled to an upthrust of pocked stone, to search out the wooded belt two hundred yards below. The sunset flush pinkened the mountainside as the moon floated high. His narrow face split into a taut grin, the snaggled teeth protruding. Three times in the past hours he had caught sight of the pair, but never long enough to level a shot. Landry was cleverly employing the lay of land and the links of natural cover. But now something had gone wrong. Before dark he needed to lead his mount to where he could gun Landry down. His horse, standing patiently in the compact crater of an ancient volcano, reacted to the echoing blasts—yanking side to side to stretch its neck and shake its head. Fang tried to discern where the gunfire might have come from. Was it from the cirque of rocks? Had Morton closed in? He waited for more shots, but they didn't come.

He had been resting, his arms crossed as he rubbed his shoulders for circulation; already the temperature was dropping rapidly. He hadn't anticipated the long night. If only he had some rags to fill with ash, then tie around the animals' hooves to muffle sound. How easy then to drop into the wooded thickness below, then ahead to where he thought Landry hid. There he'd wait. At the first light Landry would break for it, probably steal forth, keeping the trees as shields. But a fleeing man could not hide indefinitely in the crumpled openness of desert mountain. Somewhere, someplace, Landry and the girl would appear, and he, Fang, would end it.

The outlaw weighed the advantage of staying in his rocky nest or of leaving his horse untethered in the bowl while creeping down into the wooded cover before the moon was too high, its light waning. The venture had its challenges and its dangers. He would be vulnerable in the dark without cover. Landry might see him; rattlers would be slithering from their hideaways in search of prey. They came forth in the cool of the evening, silent death that could strike unexpectedly. Loose, fragmented rocks and pitted landscape could cause a slip and a fall where a man might sprain an ankle or break a leg; all presented formidable obstacles. Doubtless, Landry had learned that Morton's dwindling force had split; but from wherever he hid, how much could he see? Certainly not everything within a 360-degree circle. And would he expect a lone gunman to be hiding on the stark shoulder of a dead peak?

Carefully assessing the situation, Fang decided to use his mount to swing south into the pines, far enough away that Landry would not hear the footfalls. If he hung on to the surefooted animal, giving it direction, it not only would support him, keeping him from tripping, but would be sensitive to any unfriendly critter crawling about. Afterward, he would wrap himself in his blankets and wait. Killing Landry and recapturing the girl would be a coup of coups. Morton would bless him with enough percentage of any take to retire him in comfort for life.

Fang chuckled in satisfaction, a low wheezy sound guttural and cruel. Unconsciously, he withdrew a heavy-bladed knife from his sheath and wiped it along his smoke-soiled pants. He would love to take Landry, find him close enough to gut him, spread his innards steaming and loose on the cold morning rocks; he would have the girl then, all by himself, defenseless, his for the taking and no one to stop him. Women had never been easy for him. Even hardened prostitutes had refused his money, shuddered in his presence. But the pretty girl, the expensive girl, would be his until he took her to Morton. He fantasized deliriously as the moon flowed upward, tinting the earth, silhouetting the dark trees and washing the terrace and valley below.

He thought suddenly of Riles, who couldn't leave women alone. Surely that's how the girl had somehow escaped. Riles had tried something with her that had gone wrong. Fang sobered then, his features contracting, solidifying. His narrow mouth hung open, his tongue wobbling in vexation just back of the lobed teeth. He knew he could never, ever get that close to Landry, not to gut him. Landry was just too damn good. He replaced the knife. He decided it best to ambush the man in the first light as the pair found their way out. He checked his guns, took some tobacco and hard biscuits from his pack, and guided the horse around the lava barrier outward and gradually down toward his rendezvous somewhere below.

Morton and Liddicoat, discussing the encroaching posse, heard the shots and looked up. "Landry!" Morton exploded. "Whereabouts that come from?" He peered into the twilight.

Liddicoat's eyes canvassed the timberline. "I'd say up there." He swayed a finger in the general direction of a frowning crown of granite. "Up there close by, I'd say." His lean features worked slowly, reflectively. "Hard tellin' for sure. Sounds bounce around a lot in country like this."

"But we know he's up there yet," Morton said promptly, his bad-tempered eyes lightened with a touch of mirth. "He's holed up waiting for us."

"Maybe Fang got him."

"Maybe. But it ain't like Landry to walk into an easy trap. But maybe. One or the other. Maybe Fang got his chance."

Unconsciously, Liddicoat cocked his rifle. "We going to look into it?"

Morton wagged a decided no. "It ain't going to be too settlin' waitin' here wonderin', but we don't got any choice until dawn. Too dangerous now with dark closin' in."

"Fang ain't no fool. He could have got a good bead on Landry. He could have got him."

"Tomorrow we'll find out. Landry might be trying to throw us off, like he done back on the trail. He might be trying to draw us into a trap. Or then, he might try to sneak out under dark. But with the girl, that would be crazy. 'Course, you can't ever figure Landry. Then again, it might have been a rattler or the likes. We don't know."

"Least Fang heard them shots, too," Liddicoat said confidently.

"Best to wait him out. If we can catch Landry in a cross fire, we can nail him. If he breaks for it, we shoot for the horse. If you can get that big horse in your sights, I know you can bring it down; then Landry and the girl are finished. They can't outrun us, and they can hide only so long."

"Except for that posse houndin' us. If Landry can hold off, it'll give them time to close in. What about them?" Liddicoat slanted his head toward the terrace. "We could get caught between them and Landry. And that ain't good."

Morton scoffed. "They don't bother me like Landry does. We'll take care of them in due time. We're in good cover here above 'em. They got to find us."

"But there must be a dozen of 'em or more."

"Don't matter. If we get their leader and a couple others, that might shake their spirit some."

"When do we do that?"

"Maybe sooner than expected." The fire from the shack glowed dully in the distance. But now they could see the glitter of a few bonfires in the willows on the terrace. Confident, almost defiantly, the posse members were warming themselves, doubtless indulging in coffee and hot grub, indifferent to Morton and his men, unless they were deliberately trying to signal Landry of their presence.

As if reading Morton's mind, Liddicoat said, "They sure as hell don't give a damn whether we know they're here or not."

"They're cocky and stupid. Being too sure can be a man's downfall." Morton smiled craftily. "We just might visit 'em before morning, or at least take time to welcome 'em. But whatever we do, we can't lose Landry and the girl. It's less than a day's ride to Midas; we can't let them chance making it."

Kellie swayed and almost collapsed in a swoon. Landry was to her, sweeping her in his big arms, cupping her shoulders and then the small of her back; he lowered her. In the lacy flush of twilight, her eyes were fluid above the pale plains of her cheeks; her lips quivered. With a kind of chivalrous gesture, he removed his Stetson and gazed with a fatherly protection at the child he had watched grow into womanhood. She reached a hand to his shoulder. "I'll be all right."

"Rest a moment," he said. He could feel her body tremble, steady, and tremble again. "The skirt and shoes, they might have protected you, but I couldn't chance it." In the softening light she looked doll-like and smooth; not rumpled and harassed from the ordeal, but frail and defenseless, yet somehow willowy and resistant. She would make some man a fine woman, he thought.

"Rattlers, I grew up with them," she said, half laughing. Her dilated eyes looked enormous. "But I'll never get used to such things. The shooting—did it give us away?"

"Probably."

"I'm sorry."

"Can't be helped." His voice was husky. "When you're steady, I'm mounting you on the horse; we'll move out a hundred yards or so, take a different stand until morning."

"In the darkness? Isn't that dangerous?"

"For the time being there's enough moonlight, if we don't delay too long. Besides, we're on an ancient Shoshone trail, originally used by mountain sheep and kept active now by mule deer. It's pretty solid and reliable."

Suddenly Kellie's hands seemed all over his face, his arms, squeezing, touching. "Oh God, I'm so grateful. So grateful for you," she sobbed. Her mouth rounded and held then in a self-incriminating pose. Her fluttering hands withdrew. The two lay for a timeless moment, entwined. "I'm sorry," she said at last, her voice distant. As she made an effort to sit up, Landry disengaged her.

"Don't be ashamed," he said. Quietly, with effort, he rose, went to the chestnut, and prepared the animal to leave. He could see her small, rounded form in the faint light and could feel her eyes upon him. And he didn't know quite what to say now, for he, too, felt disarmed, uneasy, and yet excited, filled with an empathy for her that had lain dormant for many years. He felt a strange tremor quake through his being.

Landry helped Kellie into the saddle and found her slender hand clinging to his, lost in the big cup of his palm. "Trust the animal," he said. Taking the halter with one hand, slipping the other over the chestnut's nose, he edged along a trail that wormed through a covering of pine and juniper. The horse, sound-footed as always, held him up once when he tripped, and again when he twisted his knee slightly as a downed limb rolled crazily. The moon swam across the peaks and into the vault of night while a spice-scented wind made music in the trees. Kellie remained morosely silent, swaying exhausted in the saddle. Momentarily Landry tried to dismiss the girl, tried to dismiss the break of rampant emotions. He struggled to keep his attention on the setting before and around them, but odd little qualms of doubts and disturbing excitements flittered through him. Kellie, an impressionable young girl, was experiencing the worst imaginable: fear, indignity, humiliation, defilement by a human animal, and, always, the threat of death. And the worst might lie ahead if he did not succeed. Understandably, she was reaching for any sense of security, of assurance. To reject her would be callous and cruel. But she was the daughter of a friend, a man of power and persuasion in the territory. And Landry was a professional who could not let what he had felt in the instant interfere with his best judgments and his duty. How he wished he had some whiskey in his saddlebags.

Landry could now see the settling glow of the cabin fire silhouetting a ridge they had traversed earlier. But now he thought he saw something else, something that both pleased and disturbed him—the wink of campfires along the near edge of the terrace, so far down that he could barely make them out. Cole and Bradly, he thought. Kurt had gotten through! They would press Morton. Ahead, as he recalled, the Indian trail diverged, the higher path moving across the upper reaches, the lower into the woods. He would take the latter, not just because of the cover, but because he needed to drop toward Midas; and now with the posse, he might break for it, head hell-bent for them. He might even welcome a brief shooting fray to attract the posse's attention. But Morton was not one to fool with. One never dared take a chance with the likes of him; one never bucked the odds. Come dawn, Landry decided, he would size things up. But he questioned the possemen for being careless or blatant with their campfires. They might be hoping to let him know of their presence, and that was good. But at the same time they laid

themselves open to ambush, even to annihilation, especially
with Liddicoat, a sharpshooter supreme. Even if a score of
them had ridden in pursuit, they were being foolish. Morton,
in his long record, had never been taken by a posse. Landry
wondered if Cole had remembered that.

The chestnut balked and arched its thick neck, tucking its
snout in. Landry waited. He could sense the girl stiffen.
Moving shadows made traceries across the wrinkles of land,
faint in the white light of a drifting moon. Stars now appeared, blinking here and there. Landry thought he saw
something moving upright like a man, hugging the narrow
cleft of a bushy ravine that slanted downward into an island
of trees. He pulled up the rifle he was carrying and squinted
at the swaying branches. Again he thought he saw a hunched
figure, but he could not tell for certain. The chestnut snorted
and rattled its halter. The animal had always had an uncanny
sense for danger.

Landry watched. The wind willowed gustily. Little spirals
of fine dirt funneled spectrally across the wastes. He waited
for what he estimated roughly five minutes, then guided his
charge some thirty feet more into a glade of thick pinyon and
mahogany. He dared not light a match. All he could do was
rely on the infallible instincts of the great horse. Not far away
they could hear the trickle of water and they could smell
summer flowers. The mountain embraced a labyrinth of deep,
hidden canyons and verdant stream-fed meadows that seemed
a universe away from the baked mud and alkali of the outlying plains. If he could work through the forested belt to the
canyon above Midas without being cut off, they had a rea-
sonable chance of making it.

The little glade was circular and plush with pine needles.
Some slate rocks, caught in the natural pocket, arrowed up-
ward between the tree trunks, offering solid protection if
someone tried to shoot recklessly in hopes of hitting them.
Landry laid out the gear and blankets once more. He took
Kellie's hand and placed the Colt she had taken from Beatty

in it. "Keep this near you," he whispered. Next he cut some thick hunks of jerky, handing one to her.

"Don't cut yourself," she said, worried.

He chuckled at her concern. "This knife and me have been friends for a long time," he said. "I could carve my name in this meat with my eyes closed."

"I bet you could. Can we talk?"

Landry could feel her earnest concern. "It's not wise. Best eat. But what do you want?"

"What was it out there?" Her words were barely audible.

"I don't know." He loosened his sidearm, removed the gun concealed in his belt and placed it strategically beside him, his cocked rifle leaning against a rock next to his shoulder. He could hear her eating. They enjoyed the food without hurry, listening to the rise and fall of the wind. "I can tell you one thing," he said, keeping his voice low.

"What?"

"Your father is safe."

"How do you know?" she gasped.

"I saw some campfires far down on the flats. Of course, I can't be one hundred percent certain, but I think it's the lawmen he went after: Sheriff Cole's and your papa's men."

"Could it be Morton or some hunters or some miners?" Fearful, skeptical, her voice went high.

He placed a gentle hand across her arm to contain her. "Not Morton. There's too many fires to be him or some hunters or miners. Whoever, they are separated into groups for their protection."

"Can we get to them, or signal them?"

"It's not that easy yet."

When they had finished their meal, he gave her his canteen. He could see her vaguely and hear her swallow. When she was finished, he tucked her down and covered her, lifting her head and flattening his hat under. "I'll crush it," she protested.

"Doesn't matter." He wished she could have used his saddle as a pillow, but he had to keep the horse in readiness.

"Sure would like to wash my hair," she said to herself. Landry smiled. Feminine pride could not be repressed even in the wilderness amidst reptiles and human reptiles.

"You could be washing your hair." Landry moved closer to her so that he could keep his voice down. The wind now had begun to buffet the trees and to moan balefully around the gabled outcrops. "All of this wouldn't have happened if you'd stayed where you belonged." Both of them had squirmed to a half-sitting position against a boulder.

"The West is my home. I belong here, not in some tea parlor saying proper things and catering to men's egos," she replied quickly, obviously vexed.

"You're too damned headstrong." Landry waited for a retort that didn't come. He thought he saw a smirk on her face. "I might add, just like your old man."

She twisted sleepily, trying to find comfort. "Well, Mr. Marshal, seems you've always been somehow caught between Papa and me. Not that we minded."

"Best we not talk anymore." He glanced around the glade. Then he realized that, exhausted, she had simply dropped off to sleep, her head against his shoulder. He took one revolver in hand and cushioned it across his stomach, a finger on the trigger. He pulled a blanket up and waited for the dawn.

(11)

Late that night as Eve left Noah Cheveny's room, she did
not notice the door ajar midway up the hall, the hazel eyes
watching. Self-consciously, she looked around the empty
passageway and primly adjusted the low-cut top above her
shoulders. She patted her disheveled hair with both hands,
trying to tuck away the mutinous curls. She straightened her
dress and glanced down with finality at her bosom, where
the thick roll of bills wedged tightly between the fitting punc-
tuation of her breasts. Before closing the door, she heard
Cheveny's voice, dreamy and languid. "Good-bye, my beautiful peach. You are exquisite. Tomorrow night I will double
your price. And the night after I will triple. Sweet dreams,
my darling girl."

Eve darted down the nearest stairs, her senses clouded
with a disconcerting mixture of self-disgust and prideful
achievement. She had a tingly feeling of conquest and of
opportunities yet unrealized. Never in her short life had she
earned, had she possessed, so much money. And the little
man, loathsome at first, had revealed a tender, appreciative
disposition. Certainly he was a gentleman, and apparently
quite cultured—an oddity in such a primitive setting. She
realized he was cheating on a wife; but most married men,
she knew, maintained the proper female at home while supporting a mistress, or by indulging in a fun girl at some
bawdyhouse. Besides, it was none of her concern.

For a time after she had disappeared, the eyes between the

door and the jamb caught the light of the smoky kerosene
lanterns that cast a yellow hue along the corridor. The hazel
eyes, like two opals shining from the darkened room, reflected the light and expanded queerly to settle on the stairwell, as if burning into the walls of a mind the image of the
hurrying woman. The door closed slowly. The sputtering
lanterns sent flickers of pallid light across the paneled doors
and over the florid wallpaper, featuring a lecherous old man
peering through massive ferns at a heavy-limbed woman
bathing nude in a water fountain. And then the same door
opened and the slender form of a man emerged, to slip
quickly out the back exit.

Hoisting her skirt, Eve trotted down the long white stairs
into the parquet foyer. New on duty, a skinny young man
with big-boned joints stood behind the clerk's desk. Eve
breathed in relief. The young man regarded her with pleasure. A roar of activity issued from the adjoining bar and
from the gambling palace. A number of coral-faced men in
expensive coats and bright vests talked lively business while
puffing big cigars, the smoke clotting the air. The animated
conversation died swiftly as glassy eyes went out to Eve,
absorbing her totally. She ignored them and flowed into the
street. A blast of night cold hit her. She shivered, wishing
she had brought a jacket, but she had not planned on being
so late. A cacophony of music—pianos, fiddles, harmonicas,
concertinas, and an assortment of odd instruments—clashed
and intermingled from dozens of entertainment houses. A
man on a horse came out of the alley and stopped to watch.
It seemed he was looking at her. Drunks reeled in the street
and lurched in and out of the alleys. She heard a curious
banter of countless nationalities, English, Irish, German,
Swedish, Mexican, and many that she could not distinguish.

A few rowdies, high on liquor, swaggered arm in arm
toward her from the end of the street, intimidating all before
them until some equally rowdy toughs appeared from a dance
hall and defied them. A brawl broke out. Cursing, the young

men fell into a chaos of movement, swinging, kicking, gouging. She heard the grunts of expended effort and the howls and cries of the injured, but she did not look. Trying to avoid notice, she pushed blindly by, through a crowd of jeering spectators, until someone acknowledged her.

"Hey, girlie, how much you want?" a young miner still in work clothes shouted, pointing.

"More than you can afford," an accompanying miner catcalled, laughing loudly, pleased with himself. Several with him guffawed and slapped their legs, while leering at her. Eve's heart jolted. Somebody reached for her. A hand touched her hair. She ducked. Another swiped at her shoulder. She swiveled away, avoiding them. But from another direction someone hooked a finger in her scoop neck and attempted to rip it; she screamed in fear, threw her arms over her bosom, and ran, her torso swinging from side to side in a feminine rhythm as her blond hair tumbled loose and her train whipped over the battered dirt.

Standing in the arch of a saloon entrance was Nathanael Weldon. Chewing voraciously on a cigar, he watched her with amusement, his collar open and askew, his sleek hair flopped carelessly to the side. His eyes had a hollow, purplish look that seemed to bore through her. With an anguished cry of humiliation, Eve hurried on.

It seemed forever until she reached the quiet street with the new homes in progress and with the boardinghouse at the end. Lights still burned in the halls and on the porch. She heard the clip-clop of a horse coming from a darkened street. She looked. The slowly passing rider appeared to be the one who'd been in the alley. Was he following her? It was her imagination, she told herself, easing some as the slow hoofbeats moved on. Still, in a cold sweat, Eve tried to collect herself at the door, tried to compose herself as she grasped the big handle and turned it. Two elderly gentlemen were playing chess at a side table under a rack of sweeping elk horns. Mae sat knitting, rocking slowly next to a rotund lamp in an aura of motherly repose. Eve stiffened defensively, expecting some comment, some attempted retribution. But Mae smiled sweetly and said disarmingly, "I've been very worried about you. This is no town for a girl to be out roaming at night." Mae watched Eve for a response.

"You didn't need to wait up for me. There was a party at the Nugget. Some people asked me to join." Eve plucked her neckline higher.

"How nice." Mae punched her needle into the sweater she was creating. The glow from the lamp flooded her square face. No illusion was there, and Eve knew it. "You must be chilled. This is high desert country; it gets cold here at night."

"I am cold." Eve folded her arms across her chest and clutched her shoulders.

"The kitchen is warmer. The stove in there pushes out decent heat, not like this potbellied one here in the dining room." She rose. "Come. I'll make you some tea; then you should get to bed before you catch your death of cold."

"I'd appreciate it if you could get me some hot water. I'd like to clean up." Eve's tone had mellowed.

"Come on," said Mae. "I'll put a kettle on."

In her room Eve removed the roll of money from her bosom and counted it quickly, her eyes wide with growing astonishment at the amount. She hid it flat under the mattress, below her pillow. Then, in anxious anticipation, she poured a steaming kettle Mae had heated for her into a big basin and cooled it with water from a pitcher. Mae's tea and a few leftovers from dinner had made her feel better. She liked Mae. The woman meant well. Although the braids across her head gave her a severe old-world appearance, she was not that way at all, Eve decided, taking off her dress. Sadly, she noted that the neckline near the left shoulder had been ripped from the grasping kid in the street, and the train and hemline were caked with the dirt and the moisture of the street. She dropped the dress at her feet. Vigorously she soaped the water, and with her eyes closed she luxuriated in washing slowly, deliberately, her face and neck, over her arms and shoulders and underneath, feeling a flush of rejuvenation. She would bathe totally in the morning and rinse her hair once again. Outside, a rising wind rattled the window and belted the siding, moaning on and off through the eaves. Eve didn't like wind, although it was inevitable, as much a part of the West as the awesome sky. She remembered wind as a child, always blowing, it seemed; blowing when her mother died; blowing when her brother lost his leg; blowing away topsoil from their gardens, bringing dust and grit into everything, into clothing, bedding, food, and water.

Eve stopped her sponge bath and instinctively covered her nakedness with the towel. Was it the wind? Had she heard something other than wind? A grating, prying sound? Was something or someone chiseling at her window? But how could it be? She was on the second story, without a balcony outside. Landry had requested such a room, although there were ladders nailed to the building beneath each room, a city fire ordinance for hotels and boardinghouses. But the ladders ended with a fair drop to the ground. A man standing on a horse, however, might reach them. She turned down the lantern so it was just enough to see her way. From the pocket of her discarded dress she removed the derringer and checked it. She could see a cartridge in the dismal light. She stole next to the window and listened. The wind heightened again, rippling along the building. Her breath caught; her throat constricted. She waited. Nothing now. The wind murmured in the eaves and subsided. Silly girl, she thought. Again she had let her imagination, her fears, the killings in Broken Bluffs, build in her. Now she was reacting foolishly. She moved to turn up the lantern and heard the sound come once more. A gradual, careful probing at her window, the sound metallic against wood. Impulsively she almost fled out of the room and downstairs. Instead, her breasts rising and falling,

she steadied the derringer as best she could, and, in her pet-
ticoat, stepped to the window and tore open the curtain.

That same night, Willard Dragmire rested uneasily in his
room, following a brief interrogation by some deputies and
a constable, who was none too sure of himself following
excessive shots of whiskey. For another hour a deputy and a
house detective pored over the room where the girl had been
murdered. Dragmire listened to their droning conversation.
He kept his lantern off and lay in his bed, staring at the
ceiling, at the lights from the street forming distorted patterns, which stretched and shrank, appeared and disappeared
and meshed into one another. Once, he rose to drink from a
brandy bottle and to peer out of the window at the movement
in the streets, at the loud drunks ploughing unsteadily from
saloon to saloon, at the deputies lingering, talking still; most
of the curious had drifted on.

Dragmire considered himself lucky. He might have been
a corpse stretched in the coroner's office now. He hoped the
roustabout who had tried to roll him was in much pain, his
leg swollen and festering, oozing blood, maybe darkening
dangerously. Chances were the no-good would lose his leg,
but more likely die like a rabid dog from blood poisoning.
The thoughts gratified Dragmire for a brief time, until he
soured once again. Dade and Schick. He cursed bitterly.
They'd pay. He would never, ever be intimidated again by
worthless carrion like them—rot, not fit for vultures to de-
vour.

The next hours dragged torturously. Dragmire tried not to
let his thoughts wander, but images bombarded him, of
wanted posters, dozens that papered the law offices in every
town on his route, desperadoes who needed killing; his
thoughts drifted to Noah Cheveny, who seemed to delight in
making people look and feel shorter than he—all except his
wife, Henrietta, of course. He thought of the too many girls
who had been brutally murdered, of the wanton waste; of

precious life that was meaningless to some—those who didn't warrant living; those who should best serve by fertilizing the earth.

And then he thought of his wife. Oh God, his wife! For some reason, he could not remember her face clearly, only the body he had found—ruined, spoiled. A thing used and mutilated. He tried repressing the nightmare that always came to him in bits and pieces—blurred images swimming and writhing. He tried pushing it from his mind, but the scene played before his hazy memory despite his effort; out there in the desert distance somewhere was the person who had done such a thing. Vaguely, in his mind's eye, he saw the killer, but not his face, either. Someday, he told himself, he would see that face in distinct detail. That someone, whom he would then recognize and would kill. Simply, expediently. But for now he would wander and search. He would make the Big Basin safer for the honest, for the innocent, for the good, and for the virtuous. He would do that—a personal and glorious vendetta. But behind his daring, behind his convictions, hung the chances, the taunting possibilities, yes, the likelihoods, that he would find that demon, the one that filled his heart with such hate. And with that man's demise, he at last would be free.

Before dawn Dragmire left his room and lugged his baggage and goods to the livery stable, where a rousted hand grumbled sleepily about patrons who made life difficult for honest-working common folk. Dragmire paid his bill and did not comment, but he smiled inwardly. "I have an appointment," he said, not needing to explain, but wishing to clarify his purpose in case of later inquiries.

The two, Schick and Dade, had some pattern, he was certain. They had come in from the east to Broken Bluffs, north to Bullion and now east toward Midas. Why the roundabout move? Sure, they were drifters, bounty hunters; he understood that. But whom had they searched for so far? What had they found? And why were they headed for Midas now? What ends were they seeking there? They had announced that next stop to the world when soliciting the prostitute. And when Dade threatened his life, the man had talked freely about a job there. Were they biding their time for some rendezvous? Without doubt they had been hired to kill. Dragmire always listened to that part of him, that sixth sense that warned him. Deep in his bones, in his being, he felt that the two were up to something insidious, something violent, and he intended to do them in before they hurt any more people. He didn't relish visiting Midas—site of his and his wife's honeymoon, of their first loving year and then of her murder. But Schick and Dade had to be stopped somewhere.

Lost in his thoughts, Dragmire let the horse set an easy but steady pace in the bracing air as dawn tipped the mountains a steel gray, tinted them a quiet lavender, and exploded riotously into a yellow-pink.

He thought of Cheveny, who'd doubtless be in Midas by now. That fact kept troubling him. But he guessed he didn't give a damn really. So Midas was not on his itinerary. Well, what were the odds of them running into each other? Besides, the place was thriving, bustling with excitement, the queen city in the whole sweep of the Big Basin now. He had a right to a little recreation. He and his wife had lived there when it was barely a promising camp. So, why not see it in all its glory, especially since Schick and Dade would be there? Schick and Dade—they had become a kind of demented obsession, he sensed. But they fulfilled his needs; they symbolized the sin and the diabolical forces that preyed upon mankind, that paralyzed much of the land, that caused so much loss and frustration, pain and anguish, to those innocent, to those crying out, to those despairing. He, Willard Dragmire, could equalize, could rectify, could amend. Schick and Dade would pay. It didn't matter whether they ended in Broken Bluffs, Bullion, Midas, or New York City, he would be there.

Ahead, where the dusty road curled around an embankment, Dragmire could see a man and two boys holding a team and standing beside a flat wagon tipped high on its side, almost to the point of flopping over. As he approached he could see the man, hefty and rawboned, looking perplexed and frustrated. He stood with his hands hanging loosely, his high crowned hat sloping like a tent. The two boys in round hats and bib overalls stood timidly to the side, both grasping the reins of a team that were shaking and tossing their heads; a rangy one-eyed dog sat beside them, its red tongue lolling stupidly. A ruckus of agitated chickens in a half-dozen strewn coops filled the desert morning. Dragmire pulled up. "Accident?" He stared at the hutches, all set upright, packed with reddish and gray hens and a few roosters, which kept up a steady garble of cackling and clucking. Then he noticed several overturned buckets that flushed outwardly with a hardened mix of yellow yolks, clear albumin, and the shattered shells of countless eggs.

"Me and the boys were camping out here last night, right next to the road. We was going to head into town this morning to sell my goods," he said, barely controlling his anger, "when two sons of bitches come riding by hell-bent in the dark, right through our camp—spooked the horses and overturned my wagon. Been all morning trying to get it back up."

"Can I help you somehow?"

"Hardly worth going into town now, except for the chickens. A couple are dead. It took me one devil of a time to calm the horses."

"Got to get your wagon upright."

The man considered the offer. "Yes, maybe you could help."

Dragmire climbed down. The farmer smiled with appreciation and set to harnessing the animals to the front and back wheels, those tilted high. The two boys and Dragmire steadied the wagon as the man coaxed the team ahead; with

Dragmire's additional strength, they and the animals managed on the third try to pull the wagon over and upright.

As the farmer hooked the horses to the tongue and traces and they lifted the coops aboard, Dragmire asked, "Them two last night, was one big in a heavy coat, astride an Appaloosa?"

The man stopped loading to listen.

"And the other small with a flat hat? Was he riding a brown with stocking feet and a star? Could you see at all?"

"It was dark—a little moonlight left. But that sure as hell fits the general description. You know 'em?"

"Yeah, they owe me something."

"The way you sound, you ain't none too friendly with them."

"I ain't."

"Well, when you find them, get a lick in for me, will you?"

Dragmire climbed into the seat and took the reins of his horse. "I'll do that."

"I'm much obliged, mister. Just out of curiosity, what do they owe you?"

"Their lives."

With a heaviness of mixed emotions, Dragmire entered Midas in the flush of early morning enterprise. Boldly, almost defiantly, he drove down the main street, keeping clear of ponderous freight wagons pulling out, many hooped with a canvas covering and piled high with goods and equipment for outlying mines and camps. Merchants with sleeves rolled up were displaying goods or washing front windows or just basking briefly in the first warmth of sun. He was surprised at the town's growth, at its early morning bustle. Already carpenters were pounding in studs on the raised skeletons of a half-dozen new buildings; already the saloons and gambling palaces were in full swing. A long variety of saddled horses lined both sides of the street.

Then he saw the Appaloosa and the brown, switching, their heads down before a restaurant-saloon complex with fancy bold letters across the false front: THE MONMARTE. Dragmire found his way to the livery stable, left his buggy out back, locked his tools and merchandise in it; and with his luggage and a rifle, he chose a cozy hotel built of red brick that caught his eye, the Zephyr. Before registering, he asked for a second-story room overlooking the street and attained one that had been vacated earlier. A chunky maid was just finishing the room as Dragmire took a pair of field glasses from his luggage and set a chair before a front window, which he opened to let a sage-scented breeze billow the white curtain. The street curved slightly downhill toward the desert to the south. From his angle he could see the front of the Monmarte and the big Nugget Hotel across the way where it backed into the mountain stacked high above. The Appaloosa and the brown with the white-of-leg waited patiently. He would remain out of sight, for certain; if Dade and Schick so much as caught a glimpse of him, he knew his life wouldn't be worth a spit in the wind.

That's why he had to kill them shortly, expediently; if not in the night, then at their campfire outside of town, or even in broad daylight, if opportunity afforded itself. He had no qualms about ambushing them. He was fast enough and accurate enough to take them both out nearly simultaneously. What he didn't want was exposure. He didn't want to be seen, or worse, recognized, for he believed deep in his being that he was destined for some noble and heroic purpose. It was he who could move swiftly, secretly, and lethally; a mist, a shadow, anywhere, anytime throughout the territory. Incognito. He who could rid the state of all its filth. He who could make it safe for women and children and for those good men, those citizens who worked and built and dreamed. He could do that. Schick and Dade would be one more step. Killing them would not be so despicable as it had been with the ones before. Truthfully, he knew the act would become easier, more satisfying with time and more executions. In fact, gratifying. In sullen glee he looked forward to the moment he saw the two above his sights, felt the gun explode and saw them collapsing, broken carcasses, their lives expended.

Dade and Schick emerged from the Monmarte. Dragmire focused his field glasses on them. Both were picking their teeth, apparently having finished a meal. They checked their horses, then sauntered up the street toward the Nugget Hotel, but cut across the street to the telegraph office. Why did they always seek out a telegraph office? Dragmire wondered. After some ten minutes they wandered out, headed up the thoroughfare, and disappeared into the Nugget through a side entrance. "They visiting, or they got business there?" Dragmire asked himself. He would wait and watch. If they didn't reappear, he might meander down that way. He realized how dangerous it was to subject himself to detection, but there was a growing number of people filling the street, and he had different clothes in his luggage. He could tug his hat low over his eyes and wrap his neck and throat with a scarf, which would not look suspicious in the cool air—just enough to disguise him. And he would keep his derringer ready and his sidearm cocked if worse came to worst. Before he killed them, he wished he could learn what their purpose was in Midas. Perhaps that was asking too much. If he hid out back where the wooded cliffs came close to the hotel, he could gun them from there and escape, he decided. The two had a tendency to always use a side or rear exit.

That morning, on the third-story veranda of the Nugget, Franz Kurt paced back and forth, stopping frequently to scan the skirt of the mountain through his field glasses, especially the long slope that led to the mouth of a steep canyon. He knew it was premature to expect Landry and his daughter, but he could not help himself. Too much was resting on many unknown factors. Only he, Sheriff Cole, a banker, and his business manager knew that Landry had the ransom. He had included the manager more out of habit than need. Through a reliable banking friend in town, they had concealed the fact that he had not returned the money. Already the rumor had raced through town that a Kurt fortune was in the Midas bank, a fact that did not make either his banking friend or Sheriff Cole comfortable, although they had stationed a number of heavily armed guards. He could understand that Landry did not want any of Morton's cohorts and the world at large to think he was packing that much loot—enough to entice an army of culprits to hunt him down or ambush him and the girl on the way in.

Kurt put down the glasses and lit a cigar, puffing thoughtfully. What mattered was Kellie. But still, it bothered him, all that money floating around out there in the care of one man. All of his liquid assets—everything that meant anything to him—rested with Landry's decisions, capabilities, and luck. He reminded himself that if there was any man he could trust, it was Landry. Yet Kurt had not risen to his position and influence blindly. He knew men, and most men had a price; the most righteous could be tempted. If Landry was so inclined, if somewhere in his heart he felt frustration and disillusionment, if cynicism and callousness or bitterness had twisted him as it did so many lawmen who constantly immersed their lives in the depraved and in the corrupt, then he, too, might be tempted. With one hundred thousand dollars, plus his knowledge of the land and his ability to survive, he could effectively disappear, maybe into Mexico, live the life of a king and never be heard from again. Impulsively Kurt scanned the slopes through the glasses once more.

He assured himself that he had had no other recourse. His and Cole's clumsy incursion into Morton's domain had failed—miserably. Not another man anywhere, only Landry, could outwit Morton and bring Kellie in. He told himself that his edginess was making grotesque phantoms into wild imaginings. Lawmen came in a sizable hierarchy. At the town

level was the marshal or constable, called a chief of police
in the East. He had at his disposal a few assistant marshals.
On the county level, enforcement rested with a sheriff, backed
sometimes by an undersheriff and a number of deputies. Pre-
eminent, at the top of the pecking order, rode the U.S.
Marshal, directly appointed by the President of the United
States, with the advice and consent of the Senate. No doubt
the position had political overtones and could be profitable through personal contacts and private enterprises.
But Marshal Landry had proven to be above reproach—a
growing legend, with a reputation as a lawman among lawmen. So why the concern?

Besides, he had read Landry's message to Sheriff Cole.
Why shouldn't he? His money and daughter were at stake.
After all, he had not achieved his power and status by crum-
bling to the dictates of others. Much of his success rested on
keen awareness and sensing when to act. From Landry's note,
he now realized there was a collusion of Morton people in
Midas. And Landry's one suspect fell right on the mark, now
that Kurt thought about it. Kurt wanted to take his men and
go in and force the man to confess, then tear him apart. But
he knew he would have to live within the law until the man
or men could be proven guilty. For now, he would have to
draw on some inner resources of old and find patience while
keeping faith in Landry and praying for his success. At least
the marshal had suggested how the combined forces of a
Kurt/Cole posse might be able to rescue him and Kellie before dark. Kurt wished the hours would pass.

(12)

In Midas early that morning, Sheriff Brent Cole rolled a cigarette, wet it with his tongue, and lit it earnestly, the spurting flame lighting his handsome features. He tossed the match into a spittoon near his desk and drew deeply, letting the smoke roll out slowly. He looked at his vest pocket watch, smoothed his narrow mustache with a forefinger, and worked Landry's message open once more. He read it with renewed interest and tucked it away next to the watch. The rising sun lanced rosy rays against the steep thrust of the Toiyabes across the solemn valley. A shiver of night still lingered on the dark slopes of Midas. Landry and the girl—they dominated Cole's thoughts. Had the lawman found her, and had he then holed up somewhere? If they had escaped Morton, they would be struggling toward town now, with Morton doubtless trying to stop them. Cole felt frustrated and edgy.

He wondered about the posse he had sent on. Bradly, Kurt's foreman, was reliable according to Kurt, but he seemed a little too anxious for action. And he drank too much. Johnson, his deputy, was certainly seasoned, a good man and a good backup. But he had never led before. The facts suddenly bothered Cole. Like any field general, he had assessed and made a decision. Now he had to live with it. What kept troubling him was the pressing thought that he might have sent them all into an ambush or some trap. He couldn't think about it now, he concluded. They were each experienced and capable men. The decision had been made, and there was nothing he could do now.

He knew it wise that he and Kurt and a few deputies had returned, because they might be able to rescue Landry and the girl by at least making themselves available as he had requested. They might be able to escort them through the open country between the mountain and the town—at least that's what Landry had asked in his message—meet them before nightfall in the wooded canyon back of Midas. But hell, that was a good many hours away. Anything could happen before then. Landry was clever, certainly. But his options were limited, burdened as he was with the responsibility of a teenage girl.

Cole kept mulling why Landry had insisted that the public believe the ransom had been deposited in a Midas bank. Obviously Landry didn't want a number of opportunists heading out after a lone lawman and a young girl to seek the fortune he carried. That he understood. But could Landry be thinking there were those in Midas who might have designs on the money? He had singled out one suspect.

Cole hoisted his gun belt and adjusted his holster out of habit, then tilted his Stetson forward and stepped from the simple but reassuring confines of his office into the street and then to the telegraph office. The wan features of the operator, Joe Hickson, held to the instrument before him. He more sensed than saw Cole. He looked up with tired, puffy eyes, his sagging features tinted under the visor. "Sheriff! What can I do for you?"

"Looks like you've had a long night of it."

"Just about to be replaced by one of the regulars."

"You don't ordinarily work the night shift. Ain't you earned the rights for decent hours?"

Hickson shrugged; his thick throat jiggled. "The kid we hired for the night shift, he ain't workin' out so good."

"Saw you in here on my first morning rounds. Kinda surprised me."

Hickson smiled stiffly. "You know how it is with help these days, Sheriff. Sometimes they just can't be relied on. But me, I'll take time for whatever you need."

"I know you will," said Cole. "Seein' you in here is why I come so early. Got something important. Things are breaking good."

Hickson took a paper and pen and waited in anticipation.

"This is to the city marshal, Hal Sundon of Broken Bluffs, from me." Cole rolled his eyes upward in serious thought. "A posse rescued the Kurt girl. Stop. Her and Marshal Landry are safe. Stop. They'll be coming in after the girl is rested." Cole considered his words.

Hickson's pallid face took a new life; his black eyes had a fire of curiosity. "Did the marshal find the girl?"

"He sure did."

"I'm not doubting you, Sheriff, it's just that so many rumors are flyin'."

"Well, then add this: Morton's gang is broken up. Stop. Didn't get Morton yet." Cole paused and formed his thoughts.

Hickson's pasty features seemed to solidify. He looked questioningly at the sheriff, waiting.

Cole nodded to himself in agreement. "Add this. Say we got proof of members working undercover in Midas and in Broken Bluffs. Stop. Will arrest shortly. Stop. Landry says to keep alert. Stop. He will telegraph you of developments concerning the murders and the stolen guns." Cole took the cigarette dangling from the side of his mouth and flicked the ashes away. "You got that?"

"Yes, sir."

"And Hickson, this is damned important. You best dangwell keep this under your hat."

Hickson looked aghast. "Sheriff, I'm a professional. You know me. You know that I ain't going to spill nothin'. I ain't ever and I ain't now. This is confidential. I know it and I respect it.'' He unruffled some in his indignation. ''I'm a little disappointed in you, Sheriff, even insinuating such.''

''Just caution, Joe. Just caution. No offense meant.'' Outside, Cole created another cigarette. Deftly he poured a length of tobacco from a small sack into the brown paper and curled between practiced fingers as he sauntered into the street, lit his smoke, removed his hat and brushed his hair back. Then he moved on.

From a second-story window opposite the telegraph office, a deputy saw the signal and grew ever more alert. Some fifteen minutes later another deputy on the roof of a big merchandise store waved his hat. Soon, like a furtive cat, Joe Hickson appeared from a side alley to scurry into the Monmarte. Both deputies left their spots.

Noah Cheveny had a steak, eggs, fried potatoes, biscuits with butter, and a side dish of cream and strawberries shipped fresh from California. He felt great—refreshed and ready to meet the world. He anticipated dealing with Mathew Long, the Colt representative. He guessed he would end the day prospectively richer. In fact, he felt fifteen years younger. He quivered at the thought of Eve, her clear green eyes, good-smelling blond hair, porcelain skin, and the long lithe limbs and the soft white of her body. Never before had he seen or experienced one so luscious and beguiling. He would support her, keep her forever if she would agree. She promised to return in the late afternoon again, unless Marshal Landry arrived from his search for the kidnapped girl. Cheveny wished to God the man got delayed, although he didn't wish Franz Kurt and his daughter any more pain than they now suffered. The story had flamed throughout the town and seemed to be on everyone's lips. Cheveny had never met the tycoon, but he certainly knew of him. Well, that was Kurt's problem. Anyone having his money should attract problems; not that he, Cheveny, didn't covet that kind of wealth.

But he had done well; he was successful, and he would do

better. He could buy Eve jewelry and clothes—the best of everything. He went squishy inside at the thought of Eve again. As it was, he had brought plenty of money confiscated from the shop, money that Henrietta, despite her business sense, did not suspect. A nickel here, a gold pinch there. Only he did inventory; and a few unrecorded bullets sold now, an extra derringer sold then, all added up gradually.

He paid his bill, and as he moved out into the foyer, Dade and Schick made their way up the long stairs. Lost in thoughts, he trailed them about a stair length, weaving to the side of businessmen on their way down. When he reached the top floor, he saw the two standing in front of a door. The smaller man was knocking. Then he saw the door open without anyone to greet them, as if someone were taking shelter from behind. The two men quickly entered and the door closed. The act struck him as strange, but then, plenty of people had reason to keep a low profile; it was none of his matter. But the incident hung with him, for the two entrants seemed vaguely familiar, and out of place in a hotel that catered to a more elite clientele, not saddle bums, and certainly that's what they looked like. He dismissed the incident.

Inside his room, he checked his appearance in the mirror. Yes, he looked successful enough, he told himself. Then he unlocked his satchel for the information and contracts he would need with the Colt representative. He thumbed through the papers and noticed that the compartments didn't seem as thick as they should. He checked. The money was gone! A flash of faintness engulfed Cheveny. Frantically he tore at the narrow pockets. Nothing. A few more business papers, some pens and pencils, an ink bottle and blotter, but no currency. No flat packs. "God damn," he uttered shrilly. "God damn. All three of them—gone." Unconsciously, he checked his pockets; then, knowing it futile, but out of dazed reaction, he searched the room, under the bed, the closet, his luggage. But the satchel had not been opened, not since he had put the papers in the night before. The money had been there then. He had made damned certain it was. He thought of the maid and of Eve. But they had no access, no key, and Eve had been in his sight all evening. There were two keys, one on his watch chain, a second in his desk at home. Henrietta! Henrietta had handed him the satchel. But that didn't mean anything, unless she had found a time and place to open it. Had she been snooping at home? Did she suspect? Certainly she knew of the second key. Damn, he said to himself. Why had he not hidden that second key? But to search his personal belongings, that was not like Henrietta; she was always aboveboard and straightforward. My God, that's all she did was bitch and intimidate. But who else could it be? He sat on the bed, bewildered. He had cash in his pocket still, enough to stay on for business and for meals, but not enough to live in the joy that he had planned; not enough to lavish on Eve as he now desired. He felt nauseous suddenly. Henrietta, the damned sneak. It had to be her. It could only be her.

Cheveny saw the grim irony. He had cheated on her, deploying ruse upon ruse for the money; and somehow she knew, and now she had retaliated. But why? Just to let him know she knew? A coldness ran through him. Did she suspect the other women? But how would she know? He had always been discreet, or he thought he had. But there were a lot of worthless vultures in the world who liked to stir up trouble, even if they couldn't witness the consequences. Could someone, somewhere in the past, have seen him? Could that someone have relayed what he saw or thought he saw back to her? His contacts had always been out of town, usually in remote camps, amongst anonymous, mobile people. Only rarely in his early days did he visit a house. His thought of visiting the Monmarte the evening before had been a momentary flirt with nostalgia. He was more careful than that. He always watched, waited, and judged judiciously, picking up on a girl, buying her a drink, and arranging for her to visit him in his room. Enough money guaranteed results. But he had never been so completely titillated, and satisfied especially his ego, as with Eve. She towered above, transcended, the usual tramp: invariably used, worn, doused in perfume, uncouth, with the brains of a flea. Even the very young, whom he liked so much, often couldn't read or talk an intelligible sentence. But Eve, she was a walking dream, beautiful, intelligent.

There was a part of Cheveny that hungered for the best. He read much, liked the popular Longfellow but enjoyed Cooper and Poe more, and even Hawthorne. He liked Hugo and Chekhov for an evening's serious mood. He had tried Plato and some Shakespeare, especially the latter in performance. Most enjoyable, he had purchased a rare book of reprints and sketches from the master painters, and found them most exciting. Art, he had discovered, offered him a world he had never suspected nor dreamed of—a world divorced from Henrietta and from the mass of ignorant drifters who inhabited most of the West. They didn't know a thoroughbred from a coyote, or a Goya from a spittoon.

Eve—God, he thought again, how bright and exquisite; and now he was without the means to have her, to impress her, to be fulfilled through her, by her, with her. His bald little head jerked in spasms on his stringy neck. His eyes grew big and pensive.

If that damned Landry did not return, he would wine and dine her and be with her in the night. And maybe if Landry did return, she would defy him and whatever he had planned for her. She had a mind of her own, for certain. God, the money, he mouthed bitterly. He needed the money. He wondered if Mathew Long, the Colt representative, would be receptive to a short-term loan, hardly an impressive beginning to ask a man financial favors who was judging one's success as a businessman. Perhaps he could borrow at a local bank against his assets or his business. He could say he was robbed or burglarized. Or he could pawn his gold watch. Anything for Eve.

* * *

Earlier that morning, along the wooded edge of the terrace above the stage road, a guard stirred dusky red embers into new life. Both Bradly and Deputy Johnson rolled quickly from their bedrolls to rouse the posse members. They did not lose time by boiling coffee or cooking bacon, but packed their blankets in tarpaulins and gathered their saddles and gear in anticipation of a quick and forceful advance on Morton and his dwindling gang. "We've got to let Marshal Landry know we're close by—that we're here to help him," said Johnson, the rosy firelight flickering across his box-shaped face, highlighting the puffy gray sideburns. "Once we make contact, once we locate one another, we can fight our way toward each other. We'll be hard for Morton to stop."

Bradly nodded and wiped sleep from his eyes. Even in the silver light of dawn, his face had a red hue accentuated by the fire glow. "Landry may have seen our campfires if he's up there. We may have to sound some shots, just to let him hear us."

"I was thinking just that. Of course, Morton is probably aware of us, too."

While the two men walked side by side to check the horses, which were tethered to a rope stretched between two trees, Morton and Liddicoat, one hundred fifty feet up the slope, braced their rifles and aimed. As the lifting sun tipped peaks across the valley to the west, rapid gun bursts shattered the morning calm, sending men and horses into a frenzy. Liddicoat's first bullet caught Johnson in the chest. In shocked disbelief, the deputy looked up into the black of wooded hillside, one of his hands involuntarily grasping his front. He swayed and went limp, tumbling across a bed of sage. Coolly, methodically, Liddicoat levered bullet after bullet, swinging, pointing, dropping two, three, four on their feet. Two still in their blankets struggled to rise as the rifleman stilled them.

Morton, closer and somewhat lower and to the right of

Liddicoat, pumped shots into the horses, sending them into a shrilling, pitching melee as several went down and the others bolted with such force that they snapped the cross rope restraining them. Bradly shouted, tried to force them back as he groped for some halters and was pummeled aside. Morton, his face set and hard like a boxer with his opponent against the ropes, punched two shots at Bradly, the second smashing the man's cranium in a gush of blood that spewed down his front before he toppled backward. Morton dropped another man and tumbled a third to roll loosely. Those few left, shouting and darting, tried vainly to hide in sparse sage or to find protection behind something. One posse member managed to return a couple of wild shots toward the spitting flames before Liddicoat silenced him.

Within a few brief moments, the horses had been stampeded and the searchers defeated, most dead, the wounded moaning piteously, the few escapees hopelessly scattered, running and stumbling to crawl and rise and keep running. The rose-gray of dawn lightened on a carnage of red. Morton and Liddicoat stood up boldly, triumphantly, their rifles hot and smoking. Gratified, Morton motioned to Liddicoat. "Let's get our horses. With all this, Landry will be riding hell-bent for Midas."

Chilled in the frigid air, Kellie wrapped her good arm tightly around Landry as he directed the chestnut through a corridor of pinyon where the pumice softened hoof sounds. Reining the big animal up at the first explosion of gunfire, he and the girl looked questioningly at each other, their faces indistinct in the pearly dark. They heard a continuous volley, the cries of the wounded and the dying, the shrieks of terrified horses. "What's happening?" Kellie's voice was throaty with alarm.

"Morton. Morton and whoever is with him have ambushed the posse looking for us," Landry said, bitterly aghast.

"My father—could my father be with them?" Landry could feel unbridled fear surge through her arms and body.

"No. He's not down there. I gave him strict orders to get to Midas and stay."

"What do we do? Can we help them? Do anything?"

With a morbid finality, Landry replied, "Nothing. There's nothing we can do except to try and get back ourselves." He clucked the horse into movement.

Swaying sickly, Kellie whimpered, "All this because of me."

"You had no way of knowing about Morton."

"But I disobeyed my father."

Fang, lying ahead and below Landry's route, thought he heard the click-scuff of hooves. Aching and cold to the bones, he stirred from cover to readjust himself so he could see through an opening where a rock slide had cleared the trees. He had been listening to the gunfire, and he knew that Morton and Liddicoat had scored. Now if he could only stop Landry, success and the world would be theirs. He crawled stiffly through some low branches and dropped to his belly. Startled, a flock of roosting finches took flight, breaking from cover to dip and dart across the slope, the raspberry pink of the males flashing in the first light. They landed in a conifer and set up a lively warbling. Somewhere higher up, a clark's nutcracker sensed the unrest and commenced a grating caw. Angry, cursing to himself, Fang hunkered down and waited.

Landry was studying the ragged-crowned woodlands on the high slopes, especially the irregular fringes that laced the windswept ridge tops. An idea was forming, when he heard the finches flutter out and saw them depart like bright embers wisping in the wind. He stopped the chestnut. Impatient, it tossed and shuffled, sensing something. "What's the matter?" Kellie asked.

"We're getting down," Landry said tartly.

"We're what?"

"We're dismounting for a spell." Again swinging his good leg over the animal's neck, he slid off and lifted her free. Taking Beatty's revolver from his saddlebags, he gave it to her. "Get off the trail and hide. I'll be back, but, for God's sake, don't shoot me." He unstrapped the ten-gauge shotgun and led the chestnut ahead some fifty feet, clapping it smartly inside the rump to send it reluctantly ahead; then he cut down through the brush, moving stealthily to the right of where the birds had been roosting.

Grinning wolfishly, Fang thought he had caught sight of Landry and the horse once; then for certain he heard the metallic crunch of iron on rock. They were approaching; he readied his rifle and loosened the gun in his holster. The horse was coming on steadily. He poised himself. Within a minute or more it would clomp into the clearing. He aimed. But the chestnut did not appear. Then he heard the animal snort faintly. It was standing in the trees close to the opening. Did Landry suspect something? The golden streaks of first sunlight painted the highest peaks above. Again he heard the animal snort. Still nothing appeared. Had the horse detected him? He thought of pumping bullets into the area where he judged the horse waited, but he knew that could prove fatal.

Against better judgment, he rose and advanced, pushing the pine and juniper branches quietly apart. He paused cautiously. The horse, aware of him, nickered and turned aside. Then he saw the chestnut, riderless. His toothy grin stiffened; his eyes froze. Apprehensive, he pivoted to either side expectantly. When he saw no one, he turned his attention to the chestnut, now plodding back to wherever it had started. He raised his rifle for the kill.

"Looking for me?" Landry growled. Fang swung around, his rifle pointing, to see the marshal at his backside and slightly below him, and the two black-eyed barrels of the shotgun. The double cannonade echoed and reechoed across the slopes. The impact lifted Fang off his feet and flung him loose-armed into a springy wall of branches that tossed him away, spinning so that he landed head down, to tumble in a backward somersault, rolling again over and over until wedging between two small boulders. Landry watched sullenly, his shotgun curling smoke.

He whistled the chestnut to him. When it whinnied a relieved greeting, a horse in the shrubbery down under answered back. Landry reacted. He squatted and whipped his revolver out. Then he saw a dapple gray tied to a small seedling—Fang's horse. He recovered the animal and led it to the waiting chestnut, then continued along the old Indian trail. "Kellie, it's me, we're coming in," he called softly.

"Oh, Dirk," she cried, moving to him, her sore right arm dangling to the side, the little hand clutching the big pistol. "I heard the shotgun."

"One less Morton member—the one called Fang. Morton sent him out to ambush us." Landry steadied the gray as Kellie stiffly pulled herself astride, her body still sore from the horse falling. Tempted to lead the gray, Landry struggled with any fatherly instinct. "Can you handle that Cayuse?"

The girl regarded him with tolerance. "I not only can handle him, but I'll retrain him if necessary."

Landry smiled and looked into Fang's saddlebags. He found coffee, utensils, some skimpy grub, horseshoes, and a cache of ammunition. "We could hold off an army with this," he said, pleased. He reloaded the shotgun and strapped it next to the chestnut's shoulder.

Kellie firmly guided the horse toward Landry and then let it follow casually. Submitting to authority, the horse settled into a nodding step as Landry mounted and kneed the chestnut into long strides; the gray stretched out to keep up. They rode at a steady pace. At last the girl asked, "What do we do?"

"We could race Morton back to Midas. Try to outrun him. Hopefully, Cole and his men will meet us, or seek us out on

the last leg—in the canyon outside of Midas—and escort us
in. But if we go down into the canyon, we're going to have
to lay low until nearly dark, which is dangerous, trying to
hide from the likes of Morton. I think that's what he expects
us to do.''

"Won't Morton try to cut us off?''

"That's my gut fear.''

"Meaning what?''

"Meaning he and Liddicoat won't try to catch us, but will
try to ambush us or trap us on the way down. Most likely try
to kill our horses and leave us stranded. Liddicoat and Morton might split so one could try herding us into the other.''

"Can't we double back the way we came?''

"I thought of that. It's a possibility, except it just puts that
much more distance between us and safety. And I don't know
how many other cutthroats are looking for us and all this
loot.''

"I know you well enough, Dirk, that you won't fall into
any of their tricks.''

Landry grinned broadly, his eyes roving the horizon,
studying the high ridge ahead and down to the dark drop of
spaced trees below, where Morton and Liddicoat climbed in
relentless pursuit. "We're going to try something different—
see beyond?'' He pointed to a distant cleavage of mountain
fold. "Overlooking the head of that canyon that flows into
Midas is a wooded knoll, almost like a fortress. We're going
to hole up there for a time, not down toward the flats where
Morton expects us.''

"What if he finds us?''

"Even if he discovers us up there, we'll have the advantage, 'cause he'll be in the open.''

"Won't Sheriff Cole hear any shooting and come to us?''

"It's too far—too far for him to hear, and too far to reach
us in time. But it's worth a try, because from up there we
might just pull a surprise.'' Landry looked back at Kellie
and winked, then goaded the chestnut faster.

* * *

Below, satisfied with the ambush, Morton and Liddicoat were riding higher up the mountain at a southern angle when they heard the shotgun blasts. Stunned, they pulled back their straining animals and stared at the jumbled gray of mountainside. Feverishly, Morton's eyes remained on the upland, riveting here, there, for some movement. "That was a shotgun. A big shotgun," he said, the words disjointed and brittle.

"And Fang didn't have no shotgun." Uneasy, Liddicoat spat a salvo of tobacco at a currant bush, stirring the branches. He took another quid and irritably tore it free. They waited in silence. Chewing vigorously, the rifleman broke the tense quiet. "Face it, Landry's done Fang in. There ain't been no more shots, no nothin'. You know Fang, he'd be poppin' everything he had at that lawman. He'd make that whole mountain sound like the Fourth of July."

Grim-faced, Morton did not reply. The soft touch of dawn lit his sunken features, revealing them stone-hard, resolute. "We split here."

"Split?"

"Landry's got no choice but to keep to the timber, crossing them ridges until he reaches the canyon that runs down to Midas."

"Well, we figured that. We figured they ain't got no other choice."

"I want you to be waiting just above where the woods quit, you know, just above that long swale between the woods and town." Morton had an inward, crafty look. "They got to cross that. They got to be runnin' right before your sights to get into town. That's where you kill Landry. Best shoot his horse out from under him. Anything. But stop him. He has the money. He has to have it."

"And the girl?"

"She's of no use to us anymore. What happens to her happens."

"And you?"

"I'll push him alone."

"You're crazy. You alone against Landry? He'll kill you. He'll cut you down when and where you don't expect it."

Morton's words had a distant ring. "Me and him been there before."

"Maybe this time he'll luck out."

Morton looked quickly, almost disdainfully, at his partner. "We got no choice. Just you and me now. I got to push him. We can't let him circle back. But I figure with the girl, he ain't going to take foolish chances."

"So you'll drive him toward me, like a couple cows to slaughter."

Morton's eyes narrowed. "It's the only way. He'll take the girl down into the canyon, try to hide until nightfall and then break for town."

"Maybe some more of them lawmen will be out looking for him. We didn't see that Sheriff Cole in that posse we done in."

"Maybe," Morton said morosely, "but how would Cole get wind, unless Riles fouled up or he stumbled onto Jenson or one of the boys? But I doubt it. I suspect Cole's holdin' tight in town, waitin' it out. What concerns me is Riles. Was Riles lyin' about there bein' only Landry? Somebody had to tip that posse that come after us."

"I'll tell you again, I don't trust him."

Morton twisted his face in a smirk. "Riles knows that if he ever double-crosses me, I'll kill him. I'll hunt him down like a no-good varmint. Now if Riles got through, him and Jenson, and Schick and Dade, will put two and two together. Especially Jenson. He ain't dumb. They just could come scouting for us right up that canyon out of Midas."

"That's putting stock in a lot of chance."

"It ain't too farfetched, if Riles got into town. But for now, it's up to you and me to stop Landry."

The side of the mountain, with its chaos of trees and boul-

ders, its gnarled interlacing of downed limbs and exposed
roots, became clearer in the early sunlight. ''Let's go,'' said
Morton, motioning them to separate.

Solemnly, Liddicoat trotted his horse south across the rise
and fall of several sizable clefts to the wooded canyon that
plunged toward Midas. Grimly, Morton eyed the timberlines
above to set his bearings and raked his horse into a raw,
windless morning.

(13)

Upstairs in the back section of the Monmarte, the telegrapher, Joe Hickson, hesitated outside room 22. He looked up and down the dingy hall, his eyes darting nervously. The low light of the kerosene lanterns caught the quiver of jowls, but the green visor hid his fretting face. The place was quiet now in the after hours of work. In addition to catering to a commonplace clientele, the hotel housed the activities of many ladies of the night. He drummed on the door. "Who is it?" a voice intoned.

"Me, Hickson. It's important."

There came some chair shuffling, cautious steps, the click-slide of a bolt, and the door opening slightly to reveal the compressed features of Jenson, gun in hand. His twisted mouth gave him a perpetual sneer; he opened the door enough to permit Hickson to enter. Riles sat at a table near a window that looked up the open incline to the foot of the wooded canyon. They had been playing cards. Riles was clean-shaven and wore a fresh shirt and a new Stetson cocked on the back of his head. "You must have heard something from Morton," Jenson said.

"No. What I learned is bad."

Jenson gave the telegrapher a dissecting look. "What?" The wisp of a man had faded skin, cross-hatched in the forehead, a nondescript individual with a strangely uncanny ability to extract things from people. He had always been Morton's best under cover.

"Heard it directly from the sheriff, from Cole himself. They're onto us." Hickson stared at the door as if expecting someone to break in. "Cole claims one of his posses broke the boys up. They didn't get Morton, but they're onto us." Hickson babbled his words.

Riles sat up stiffly and folded his cards, one hand wobbling a near-empty whiskey bottle. Jenson glowered at Hickson. "What the hell you tryin' to say?"

"I copied the telegram down. Here." He held out a yellowed piece of paper.

"Words are your business; you read it."

"Cole sent a telegram to the city marshal in Broken Bluffs." Blinking, Hickson read swiftly: " 'A posse rescued the Kurt girl. Her and Marshal Landry are safe. They will be coming in after the girl is rested.' "

"It don't make sense," Riles interjected.

"Wait, there's more: 'Morton's gang is broken up. Didn't get Morton yet.' "

Jenson's eyes hunted Riles's, his tortured mouth curved even more. "It ain't like Morton to be taken by no posse. Not him and a posse. Maybe Landry got a few of the boys, but no posse did, not with Morton in charge." He removed his slouch hat and wagged his head.

"There's more. Listen. 'We got proof of gang members working under cover in Midas and Broken Bluffs. Will arrest shortly. Landry says to keep alert. He will telegraph you of developments concerning the murders and the stolen guns.' " Hickson looked at Jenson and Riles expectantly, his face jiggling.

"It just don't make sense to me neither," Jenson lamented. "It just don't fit. According to Riles here, the girl got free from the cabin and took off."

"How'd that happen?" Hickson's mouth went agape.

"The girl started a fire in the back room of the cabin," Riles said defensively.

"You let her escape?"

"Not only escape, but she killed Beatty," Jenson said with disgust. "And there's more."

Riles shifted with discomfort. "Landry and that Franz Kurt arrived after that. Then Morton, Fang, and Liddicoat come ridin' up; that's when we seen Landry hoofin' it up the mountain after the girl. That's when Morton and the others went after them and I come back here under orders to contact you men."

"Well, Morton knows if Landry found the girl, the marshal's going to try and hightail her back here. That's where we can fit in."

"But the money's in the bank," Hickson protested.

"It won't be for long if we can get that girl again," Jenson said.

"It ain't in the bank," Riles interjected. "It ain't in the bank at all."

"What the devil you saying?" Jenson snapped.

"Well, on the way back, I had a little run-in with the girl's old man—would have gotten that Kurt gent, but Cole and his men arrived in time to save his neck. But one thing certain, I learned he wasn't carrying no ransom money. I got to his saddlebags after I killed his horse."

"Why didn't you tell me that before? That changes everything."

"I was going to tell you, but it didn't seem all that important till now."

Jenson stared at Riles. "You holdin' out something more? You harborin' thoughts about that money all to yourself? If Morton ever so much as thought that about you, he'd kill you on the spot." For a long moment the eyes of the two outlaws locked with each other.

"Then why all the ballyhoo about bringing the ransom back?" Hickson asked nervously.

Without taking his eyes from Riles, Jenson answered, "Probably to protect Landry, by keeping anyone with ideas of collecting the loot themselves out of the picture, unless them lawmen are trying to set us or somebody else up.''

"There was about a dozen or more that went on after Morton, not enough to do him any harm," Riles scoffed.

Hickson ran a moist tongue across his lips and dug one finger into his collar as if for relief. ''We got to get the hell out of here. Cole and Landry are somehow onto us.''

"We can't jump to conclusions yet," said Jenson, sitting back down and looking up toward the canyon. ''I can't figure how Cole could finger us, unless he's guessing and hopes we'll tip our hands; and you just might be setting us up by coming here so soon.'' He scowled at Hickson. ''You could have fallen into a trap yourself. Did you see anybody follow you?''

"No."

"Best we expect the worst," said Riles, checking his sidearm. "For your sake, Hickson, I hope you didn't set us up."

"The plans, everything is falling apart," Hickson whined. "I come to warn you, that's all."

"He might be right," said Riles. "Maybe we should clear out."

Jenson gnawed a lip. ''No, not yet. Morton put me in charge of operations here, and we've got to see it through— least until we know the truth. I have a gut feeling that the money is up there with Landry, and he's on his way still, with Morton behind.'' His pinched face grew serious. ''You, Hickson, you get back to work. Morton may try to get through to us. If he got away like Cole claims, he'll keep tryin', you know him.''

Disgruntled, Hickson stared at Jenson. ''How's he going to get to a telegraph out there in the mountains someplace?''

"If Morton needs to get through, he'll get through. Now get back there."

"But we'd be wise to split up," Riles cautioned.

"Yes," said Jenson. "I'll keep watch here for a time." He pulled his watch from his vest. "Schick and Dade will be back here early afternoon. I'd suggest you check by in two hours exactly, unless you see the marshal and the girl coming in. You drift by outside in the back street. I'll wave you up here if something comes to pass. Meanwhile you might wander up to the mine there on the hill. From there you can see anybody approaching from either side of town. Now check your watch with mine.''

After coordinating their watches, Riles stood up and poured a morning drink. He said to Hickson, ''Me and you best go out a side stairs. I'll go first.'' He gulped the drink down, tilted his hat forward, and strolled past them.

Hickson waited five minutes. As he left, Jenson said, ''I know you had to let us know, but I hope your rushing out didn't tip off that lawman.''

Without reply, Hickson eased into the hall, shutting the door. He could hear the laughter of several women, each entertaining in their respective rooms. He found the nearest outside exit, crossed the busy street, hurried to the telegraph office, and entered the rear, where he rented a tidy room and kitchen. He pulled a tattered piece of luggage from his closet and began stuffing it with belongings, pawing recklessly through the drawers of an old bureau. The outside door, left partially closed, swung open to stream morning sunlight into the room. He whirled around to face Sheriff Cole and a lanky, tight-skinned deputy, guns drawn. ''What do you want?'' he gasped.

''We got some talking to do,'' Cole said. He ran a finger along the handsome lines of his mustache.

''You got nothing on me,'' Hickson protested, his face drained.

''We got some talking to do in my office. Maybe a deal, if you don't want to rot in prison.''

''What do you mean?''

''I got proof and I got a witness. Hope you understand that a telegrapher using federal means for criminal offenses ain't taken too kindly.''

* * *

Like a hunter in the field attempting to flush game, Morton threaded his way along the alpine heights, knowing that he could be ambushed by a waiting Landry, but knowing, too, that Landry's best defense was a steady and fast rush down the canyon toward Midas if he was to rescue the girl and save the money. Morton did not track, but chose to keep his eyes aloft, to see and to assess the broad sweep of highland that rippled ahead, checked and patterned with brushy patches and timbered glades, all interlaced with the ruins of shattered rocks and strewn boulders, some uprolled into cathedrallike structures. Unrelenting, he rode on, waiting, half anticipating. He would herd Landry, like some bovine creature, toward a waiting Liddicoat, his rifle unerring. More important, he had to keep Landry from doubling back, past him. But he doubted if the lawman would try such a trick, considering that it would take him and the girl, on tiring horses, farther away from Midas and ultimate safety. He had picked up sign of two animals and surmised that the second was Fang's. Somewhere, he knew, the partner lay dead, done in by Landry. With each mile of progress, Morton grew more pensive and hostile. He half wished that Landry would somehow try to end it all, here and now, in this lonely spot. Morton had killed a number of lawmen. But Landry was something special, a thorn in the side always, someone who had forever dogged him, the only man who had ever arrested him—the force that had led to his imprisonment, until he had masterminded a nationally publicized escape. Eventually, inevitably, he and Landry would face it off. The sooner the better.

Picking their way through the best cover available, Landry and Kellie worked their horses toward the high cirque of rocks and vegetation that Landry sought, hoping to evade Morton. "Up there ahead." He pointed. "See that basin in the trees; see the rocks sticking up? That's part of an old volcanic cone. It's there we'll take cover." Forty minutes later, with the sun already brassy and bright on the peaks, they entered the small bowl, a natural fortress with Limber pines and thick sage, a hollow encircled with parapets of fractured rocks. Landry gave the animals freedom to browse while he and Kellie stretched on their bellies to peek between two slabs in anticipation of Morton.

They saw him coming slowly. "He's not looking for our trail. He's not tracking at all," Landry said, almost gleefully. "He may never realize we're here." Morton came on steadily, his head high, alert, his dark eyes scanning the sweep of mountainside for any signs of human activity. Deliberately, he followed the old Indian route, utilizing the trees and boulders for a maximum of protection while taking care to see if Landry was attempting to double back.

"He doesn't realize we're up here," Kellie said.

"He's figured that we're heading down the canyon there, the one that leads into Midas."

"He's alone. Can we kill him?" Kellie asked tremulously.

"It's tempting, if he comes closer," Landry replied, his voice resonant. Liddicoat, he conjectured, was doubtless somewhere down the canyon, waiting to snipe at them. And Morton, alone, was attempting to push them to him. Landry laughed inwardly, a harsh, scornful laugh. One could not help but respect Morton, an always dangerous but dauntless adversary. The trumpets of ancient rivalry rang in the marshal's being. How he would like to end it once and for all. Landry or Morton here in the high, pure air. But he was a U.S. Marshal, sworn and dedicated to protect. Ego, pride, he had seen their toll. Kellie was his responsibility at all costs. At such distance, should he miss Morton, and Morton return the fire—a stray bullet, a flash shot, and he or she could be splayed dead. "No," he said at last. "We hold tight and hope that he doesn't realize we're here."

"But we can't stay here forever," said Kellie, concerned. "Now he's between us and Midas."

"With luck," said Landry, "we can soon sneak out of

here and proceed south to the next canyon beyond. We can follow it down and hopefully run for it back to town. If we're lucky.''

Franz Kurt, both thumbs dug into his vest, stood on a high rear balcony outside his room, still staring at the highlands and at the deep wooded canyon rising steeply toward the peaks, when an insistent knock pummeled his door. Reluctantly he responded. ''Yeah?''

''It's me.''

''What now?'' Kurt opened the door to admit his business manager, Nathanael Weldon.

''Rumors are all over town about how Landry saved your daughter. You should be out celebrating. The boys are wondering about you.''

''Yeah.'' Kurt returned to the balcony to keep his eyes on the mountain. ''You're probably right, but I'm not an actor. That's why I told you about the ransom. Landry wanted only Cole and me and my banker friend to know, but how could I fake you out, my business manager?''

''You couldn't.'' Weldon accompanied him to study the mountainside. He still wore the gray suit with the gold-flowered vest, his shoes freshly polished again. ''I don't blame you for hiding out here; there's a lot depending on many factors—not only Landry and your daughter, but a lot of money is riding out there.''

''Shortly, Cole and his remaining men are going up that mountain there in hopes of meeting Landry. I'll be with him, and so will my boys. So everybody will learn about the money soon enough.'' Kurt turned to the man. ''You want to join us?''

''You know me, boss. I work with money, not guns. I'll just wait and hope.''

Franz Kurt looked at the handsome face, squarish with the penciled mustache, the straight black hair, and the smoldering eyes. "I'm certain you've found some entertainment here to occupy your time."

Weldon gloated. "Don't I always?"

"You've always had an eye for women. But I don't think you respect them."

"Except maybe for money, I can't think of anything more interesting. I respect them. It's just that women are like good horses—train them right, and they'll do you good."

"Maybe that's where I failed with my daughter."

Weldon grew serious. "No offense, but yes, frankly, she could have used some discipline. That's why you're in this mess."

"I know you're right."

"Well, it's easy to pamper a beautiful girl like that."

"Yes, I've seen you play to her."

"She's an attractive woman," Weldon said warily.

"She's a child," Kurt scoffed. "A rich, spoiled child. And if she lives through this, she will be even richer someday. And, of course, that never entered your mind?"

Weldon stiffened. "I don't think that's fair, Mr. Kurt. I've given you nearly ten years of service. If it hadn't been for me, you still wouldn't have raised the ransom yet."

Kurt puffed his cheeks. "Yes, you're right again. You have been faithful, but at a damned good wage, plus percentages. And you know if I get Kellie and the money back, you'll get a hefty percentage of that for your efforts."

"And I've earned it. I've worked hard for you."

"You have."

"You're much richer because of me," Weldon said smugly. "And you know that, sir."

"And you're much richer because of me."

Weldon shaped a derby he carried and placed it on carefully at a tilt. "No apologies necessary, boss. We need each other. You know it and I know it. We're a fine team. Now I'm going down and buy some good brandy."

"You do that," said Kurt, his eyes steady on the mountain.

* * *

Lying tensely in the little cirque of trees and boulders, Landry and Kellie watched through a screen of brush. Morton rode vigilantly through the pines and juniper, wending carefully while holding closely to cover. He kept his rifle cradled in his arms, his eyes averted, often darting above to the peaks or down over the open woods. Sometimes he would pivot in the saddle and look at his back trail. The white shield over his coiled lariat was a sombrero, Landry saw. Gradually the outlaw came under the cirque; he reined a halt to consider the formation. Landry pushed Kellie's head down, and he too pressed from sight to listen. A morning wind brought the soft clack of hooves and the occasional blowing of air to them as Morton continued, passing slowly below them, but well out of accurate rifle range; finally he took a deliberate pause where the streamlets converged in their cutting plunge down the mountainside. Deliberately, Morton once more assessed the situation before turning his horse into the canyon.

"We may have done it," said Landry, watching, his weary features alive.

"Where now?"

"We wait a while to make sure, then we remain high and ride hard to the south. We'll stick to cover as long as we can. Unfortunately, there's a treeless space right on the hump, which we'll have to chance." His eyes darted to the adjoining ridge. "Hopefully, Morton will be far enough down in the canyon or in the woods that he won't see us run for it. We're going to go down farther on, down the next canyon."

"That's pretty clever, but how do we get into Midas?" she asked with apprehension.

"We ride like the wind," he said flippantly, then smiled reassuringly. "I'm planning—let's say hoping—that Cole and your dad and his men will be on the lookout, although they don't expect us to come in the way we're now going. But maybe they'll be somewhere between Morton and us. Keep your fingers crossed that neither Morton or Liddicoat will be within rifle distance when we go for it. But it's a hell of a lot smarter going in farther south than to have gone down Midas Canyon. Right now, I know that Liddicoat is waiting for us down there with that famed rifle of his.''

''Won't they eventually figure out what's happening?''

''Eventually, although they'll expect us to try and hide until dark. If they do realize what's happened, so much the better. They just might come looking for us up here''—he grinned boyishly—''which will pull them back up here while we're heading down another route.''

''You're pretty smart, aren't you?''

''That remains to be seen.'' Her words had a teasing tone, the first bit of levity that she had expressed since their shared ordeal began. She was feeling good, and for the moment so was he. But he felt compelled to warn her. ''Most likely we'll be on our own, Kellie, all the way. I can only hope what Cole will do and how many men he can spare. I suspect most of his men have taken a bad licking already.''

''What's new? When haven't we been on our own?''

He chuckled deeply. ''You have spunk, kid.''

''But right now, not enough spunk to face Papa, when I think what I've put him through.''

Landry kept a lookout over the area where Morton had vanished. He chewed his lips and said: ''Why couldn't you have stayed, just finished your schooling and made your father happy? You have a whole lifetime to return here.''

''I was wrong, foolish, headstrong, as you said,'' she promptly confessed. ''But I was homesick. You know, homesick for my kind of people. Papa wanted me to have the good life, which meant marry someone proper. But back East, I just found the men so different. Sure, they kiss your hand and fancy-talk you. At first I thought it was exciting. But I soon realized that what most of these so-called proper men wanted was a doll, another possession to always be around when they needed it. You know, to say the right things, to serve tea in the right way. If you're pretty, they wish to display you. They expect you to flatter them and pamper them when they need it. They use you, really. Horses, money, estates, and women are all of equal value. And all my female associates assumed that their husband-to-be would be shared with a mistress. Yes, that's just assumed and accepted.''

''Sounds wonderful.''

''And it didn't seem to upset them, as long as they were fittingly lavished with money and goods. Out here, maybe men do put a woman on a pedestal, but they're honest about it. And they want a partner. They expect us to ride and rope and cook. They respect me for what I am and what I can do. They know I can handle a horse better than most cowpokes can. I love this big, open land. I missed and wanted all that.'' She sat higher. ''Is that wrong?''

''No. It's just the way you went about it—defying your father and jeopardizing your safety.''

''I realize that,'' she said, resigned.

''Come,'' said Landry, helping her up, but crouching low. ''We must go now. We must hurry.'' Morton had long disappeared. The warming sun made the sage pungent and the pinyon spice-scented. Summer flowers were blooming riotously; balsam root, pentstemon, paintbrush, lupine, buckwheat, and mule ears would gradually fill the air with their intoxicating perfume.

''All so beautiful,'' said Kellie. ''Such a beautiful spot. It's man that ruins things.''

Morton left his horse and took refuge in a rocky cleft on a high notch overlooking the canyon, where he could see the naked outcrops and shale slides above him, yet could give him command of the mountain drop that scaled steeply to Midas far below. In time Liddicoat would be settled, waiting, watching. Landry and the girl were somewhere between them in the wooded thick of alder and aspen. Hiding probably, waiting for nightfall, when they could attempt to slip out and ride the last open way to Midas. But were they? He had not seen any sign of their turning down the canyon. Of course, he had not looked much for tracks, hoping to flush Landry and to avoid walking into an ambush. But now he wondered. Morton was practical. He had survived through his life of turmoil and daring by never assuming anything. He took his field glasses and began a systematic surveillance of all that surrounded him. The canyon down to Midas was the natural artery, the only logical approach. But had he misjudged or underestimated the lawman? Had Landry tricked him some-how?

Landry and Kellie rode easily along a dwindling shaft of stunted trees to where an open spine of the south ridge—roughly a hundred thirty feet—led to the next canyon. "We got to chance it," Landry called to the girl. "Let's go." They whipped their mounts into a jerky gallop, scattering loose rock.

Morton more sensed their dash than saw it. He turned around just as Landry and the girl went over the hump, to disappear. The outlaw ran cursing to his pinto. Landry had managed to evade them and was coming down another can-yon. Well, ultimately they would have to ride north across open sage a mile or more to the safety of town. He and Liddicoat could still intercept. It was a race now, and he was closer. He rode the animal as fast as safety permitted down the widening chasm.

By afternoon shadow Sheriff Brent Cole and four deputies, accompanied by Franz Kurt and two of his men, cantered quietly out of town, south along the main road, then swung slowly toward the open incline directly at the yawning mouth of the canyon. A number of citizens watched curiously, won-dering. "Those people back there," Kurt called breathlessly to Cole, "they're sure as the devil questioning."

"It don't matter now," Cole shouted. "If Landry and your

daughter made it through, they'll be comin' down, and none of them back there can interfere now."

"Let's go," Kurt cried, his red-tired eyes absorbing the ascension of winding canyon and the upper mountain bulking huge against the sky.

Riles lay stretched in the shade of a stamp mill, his arms folded, his back against the siding, his new Stetson low over his forehead. But his eyes were aware. He had ridden once into town, only to be waved off by Jenson. Now he saw the small posse emerge slowly, then pick up speed and direction, first south on the main road, then gradually swinging east into the uplands. He knocked his hat straight and sat up, his eyes narrowing. He realized now—Cole's story to Hickson had been a lie, a prefabrication, maybe to shake the telegraph man into a rash action, which it had done. Cole and Kurt were heading toward the canyon, which meant they knew something; somehow there had been communication. They expected Landry and the girl to come in that route, which was logical. Jensen had judged right. Surely, then, Morton and the men were still active; maybe they had stopped Landry; possibly they had the ransom. If not, he and Jenson and those hired drifters could join in. The posse wasn't that big, and the members would not expect someone at their backs.

As Riles rode up to the rear of the Monmarte, he was forced to retreat and hide between some outer buildings, for he saw two deputies leading a manacled Jenson down the outer stairs. Riles knew then that he was on his own.

(14)

Noah Cheveny returned to his room pleased and satisfied. His business record and proposed expansion had impressed Mathew Long, the Colt representative. Now he would be setting up a business in Midas: sales, repairs, and distribution to some of the new camps and stopovers in the hinterland. If things turned out, he and Henrietta might move from the drab and windy town of Broken Bluffs to a new residence in Midas, a city of the future. But who would handle the Broken Bluffs shop? Certainly not Dragmire. He had no business sense. Maybe Henrietta. Maybe she would be willing to stay. They could see each other once a month—a spousal arrangement that looked proper. There certainly would be less bickering between them. Cheveny giggled and congratulated himself on such a thought, although he doubted Henrietta would be very receptive. But anything that separated them for a time was worth a try.

Suddenly he could hardly wait to tell Eve about his coup. She would be impressed. And best of all, Mathew Long had advanced him a sizable amount to commence dickering while in Midas. He needed to find a select site. Hopefully, they would not have to build, and could save capital by renting and commencing business almost immediately. He had set up an account in a local bank, keeping a hefty amount aside to lavish on Eve for as long as she remained in town. He would slip his secret borrowings back into the account as the new business began paying. From his coat pocket he removed the roll of bills and tucked them beneath the papers in his satchel.

He then took a much-needed swig of brandy and felt doubly good. Everything looked rosy and promising. And he greatly anticipated the time with Eve. After Landry was through with her, after all the fears had settled, he would encourage her to return to Midas. He expected the marshal to move her on, at least until the gruesome murders were solved. Afterward, he could set her up in a suite of her own, while keeping her adorned and arrayed in the best of jewelry and clothes. She would be his and no one else's—ever again. He had asked her to come to his room late in the afternoon. He thought it would be pleasant to rent a horse and buggy and drive into the foothills. Midas had such a lovely setting. Then back for dinner and the evening with the beautiful girl and the pleasure of her company. First he needed to clean up, shave and wash, to be presentable and in no way offensive. He looked into an oval mirror above an ornate bureau, saw his little egg-shaped head, pink behind the wire-rimmed glasses, and decided he wasn't half so repulsive as he had always led himself to believe.

There came a gentle, almost feminine knock. It startled him. Again came a light tap at the door. His heart jolted. Was it Eve? She was earlier than expected. A surge of excitement filled him. Perhaps she was in trouble. After all, he had rescued her from that boor the night before. He moved anxiously to the door and hesitated. When coming down the hall, he had noticed the door ajar where the two ruffians had entered earlier. As he had passed, somebody had quickly closed it. His imagination was working too much, he thought. They had no possible connection with him. He had no enemies here, and yet it was never wise to open a door to strangers. "Just a minute," he called. He removed a pearl-handled revolver from his luggage. "Who is it?"

"A message, sir, from a girl named Eve," came the reply. Anxiously, Cheveny unlatched the door and peered out, only

to pale at what he saw. Dade pushed the door wide, knocking
Cheveny back as he and Schick entered.

Landry had not returned. Eve hurried through the busy
street in a new green dress laced with white frills that encircled her wrists, the hemline, and the high neck, a gift to
herself purchased in the late morning with money from
Cheveny. Her washed blond hair flowed in the wind, cascad-
ing from beneath a petite green hat with long white heron
feathers. She would meet with Cheveny, enjoy a meal, and
tolerate him long enough to make the money that she knew
he would lavish on her. But she would not accompany him
for so long this night. She would not incite the problems and
confront the ruffians again, nor chance a brush with whoever
prowled in the darkness. Her white, porcelain skin had puffed
some around the eyes, for she had not slept well after the
scare at her window.

Half expecting a face to be leering at her, she had ripped
the curtains open to see the blurred form of someone—a
man, she assumed—roll over the roof to the fire ladder.
Quaking and frightened, she had informed Mae, who had
promptly dispatched a number of male boarders with lanterns to search around the building. They had found the deep
imprints of some shoes or boots, apparently formed by the
impact of that person dropping from the bottom ladder rung.
But nothing else was seen or uncovered.

Since then Eve had experienced a nauseous, sinking feeling. After arriving in Midas, she had felt reasonably safe.
But the anxiety and the horror of the ordeal in Broken Bluffs
had hung over her, enveloping her like dark storm clouds.
Now she wondered how safe she really was, even in broad
daylight. Who had been outside her window? Was it the man
on horseback? Was it the killer? Had he somehow traced her
to Midas? Certainly whoever had tried to break in had meant
her harm. But the challenge and the money weighed on her.
She was certain that with a little coy coaxing and her femi-

nine wiles, she could fleece Cheveny out of enough to set
her up in a business somewhere, for a new start. Of course,
she might have to promise him the world and a committed
future, but that was not difficult. And Uncle Landry didn't
even have to know. She surprised herself that she could think
so deviously, that she was learning how to survive and profit
in a hostile world. Well, if an unattached girl didn't look out
for herself, who would? She could enjoy care from her uncle
for only so long. And yet the fearful uncertainty of the man
on the roof sent shivers through her still. An emotional part
of her knew that she did, indeed, need Uncle Landry. She
wondered, by going to Cheveny's room, was she pushing
luck too far?

Hastening along the boardwalk, she was jostled and
bumped by a mass of hurried individuals. Ignoring smart
remarks and lustful looks, she nosed ahead, weaving vigilantly toward the Nugget. Suddenly he was before her, ma-
terializing from the crowd as he lurched from the cover of a
brick alcove, his suave face bloated and surly with drink, the
tilt of his derby no longer debonair, but pulled squarely across
his forehead. "Well, if it isn't the queen." Nathanael Weldon, bowing, dipped his arm, palm up in an exaggerated
gesture of chivalry. "Giving favors to rich old men still?"

"Leave me alone," Eve said angrily. "I'm in a hurry."

"To meet some Prince Charming? You better be nicer to
them than you was to me."

"None of your damn business."

His face purpled with seething anger. "Nobody, but nobody, snubs Nathanael Weldon. Especially not some little
snip of a female. You get that, sweetie?" He had a superior,
disdainful look as he impulsively groped for her, his hands
pivoting. "I been watching you, waiting for you like a cat
for a mouse," he bellowed; his eyes had a queer, fierce look.

Alarmed, Eve tried to evade him, tried to run past him,
but he pawed her shoulder. Defensively, she turned into
him, pushing him with all her might. The surprise maneuver

caught Weldon off guard, timbering him backward, his arms flailing for balance. He stumbled against a water trough at the street edge, his body top-heavy. Over he went in a tremendous splash that made people stop and gasp or laugh. Mightily, Weldon sucked in air under the cold, wet shock, his eyes bulging, his hat flying off; he submerged and pulled himself up, bobbing, his feet hanging in the air over one end of the trough. Eve ran but heard him bellow again, ''You'll get yours, sweetie.''

Reeling with exhaustion, Eve reached the top floor of the Nugget, to see two men heading out a back exit—one bulky in a greasy coat, his face whiskered, the other slender, with a peaked face under a round, flat-brimmed hat. The smaller one appeared strangely familiar. She stopped, not only to catch her breath, but to wait for them to disappear—they looked disturbingly thuglike. She could hear the low, even voices of people talking, but luckily for the present, no one entered the passageway.

Quickly, then, she moved to the end of the hall and tapped on Cheveny's door. She heard no movement. A rising flush reddened her neck and face. Again she rapped, harder. Perhaps he was still gone on business, she thought anxiously—disappointed, for she did not want to return the distance to the boardinghouse or to sit alone again in the foyer. On chance, she tried the door. It fell open, almost invitingly. She could wait in his room, she thought. Eve moved in and froze; her hands fluttered to her mouth, stifling a scream. Her knees buckled. She swayed, almost swooning, but somehow managed to contain herself. On the floor, his arms outstretched, his eyes staring sightlessly, the glasses broken to the side, lay Noah Cheveny, a pearl-handled revolver nearby. The room had been ransacked, his satchel left open on the bed. The place showed signs of a struggle. Eve dropped to her knees. Cheveny looked dead, but there were no wounds she could see. No sign of blood. Falteringly she felt for his pulse. Nothing.

Somehow Eve managed to stagger out of the room and close the door. Fortunately no one was yet in the hall, although she heard men's voices drifting up the stairwell. Her heart bursting in her chest, she rushed for the outside entrance where the ruffians had gone. Into mellow sunlight she ran, thumping down the stairs, when the alley three stories below exploded with gunshots. Eve clutched the railing and stared. Dade, in the saddle, was turning the Appaloosa away, about to ride hell-bent when the first bullet caught him between his shoulder blades, jolting him straight, snapping his head back, his high-peaked hat sailing free, spinning to roll loosely, upending and vibrating like a nipped tiddlywink. The second bullet pitched him headlong as his mount wheeled and thundered away. The big man hit hard, rolled over in a spiral of dust, and came up on his hands and knees, blood chuting across his right side as he tried to crawl to safety. Preparing to mount, Schick dropped aside, his instincts alive, defensive. But before he could respond, the third and fourth bullets slammed him into the back siding of the Nugget Hotel. Smiling sickly, he tried to pull his sidearm, but a fifth shot drilled high into his throat, collapsing him in a convulsed heap.

The gunman stepped out of the shadows with a revolver in each hand; but only one smoked. Dade wormed pitifully away in a mush of dirt and blood, face down, his body humping in a bullish shudder before he sprawled flat and stilled. Dragmire, aware suddenly of Eve, looked up at her; she down at him. Their eyes met and mingled, his boring into hers. "You." She shuddered and spun around, racing back to the top floor, he after her, taking two and three steps at a bound.

Nearly panicking, she ran down the fourth-floor hall, her skirt hoisted above her knees. Dizzily she thought of locking herself in Cheveny's room, but the image of his body and being found with it revolted her. Then she bumped into a businessman emerging from a room. She clutched at him. "Please, help me," she begged.

"What's the matter, lady?" He stood stiffly away, his sour-shaped lips clamped.

"Please, he's after me." She glanced behind her. "He's going to kill me. Please," she implored, knowing instantly her effort useless. But she grasped at him desperately, to clasp his lapels, the coat sagging. "Lock me in your room. Or give me a gun! A big gun!" She had replaced the derringer in a toiletry pocket of her new dress. But she knew its effect would be like a peashooter against a cannon.

He saw the wildness in her eyes. His features crumbled with doubt and fear. "No," he wailed, peeling her fingers from him and pushing her away. Like a scampering animal, he dodged into his room, slamming and bolting the door.

Devastated, Eve lunged to the stairwell and fled down, hoping to God that the killer had not made an attempt to cut her off on the third floor. She thought she heard his footsteps, but could not tell for the beating of her heart. She passed more businessmen, some escorting ladies, all regarding her curiously; but now she sought no help, her thoughts instead on the boardinghouse and safety inside her room. Panting, almost delirious, she found her way through the foyer and into the street, busy as always with domestic activity. The strange faces became a squirming sea of indistinct forms. She heard angry words directed at her, which she did not interpret; reeling, she lunged, bumping against people, and in turn was jostled aggressively. One man dug an elbow into her ribs. Vaguely she sensed someone jumping out of her way. She looked back once to see Dragmire, after her, threading his way through the throng of people and wagons.

Descending rapidly, Landry let the big chestnut pick its way, with Kellie behind on the dapple gray. Few words passed between them in the effort, except once Kellie asked, "Do you think Morton suspects our little trick? We did fool him, didn't we?''

"I have no idea," Landry replied. "But we'll know soon enough."

"I think it clever, taking the next canyon down," she called, beaming.

Within another twenty minutes they left the wooded protection of the second canyon and entered an alluvial plain devoid of trees. They could see the block-shaped buildings of Midas, brick red, some wood yellow, high on the lower edge of the mountain a rough mile ahead. ''Are you ready?'' Landry asked.

"Yes."

"Then let's go." He slapped his mount, she hers; they plunged forward; the animals, sensing the urgency, stretched out their legs in long rhythmic thrusts, their manes and tails furling and pluming, their muscles bunching as flecks of foamy sweat sprayed free.

Morton had whistled Liddicoat down from a stone nodule overlooking the mouth of the canyon and the open sageland south of Midas. "Landry and the girl, they're comin' down the next canyon," he called. "But we still got a chance of cutting them off with that rifle of yours. We got a chance at that money." Together, they rode through a meadow of white-barked alder, the tender green leaves shimmering in the soft sunlight. As they made a shortcut, both saw Sheriff Cole, Franz Kurt, and six posse members fanning up the skirt of the mountain.

"What now?" Liddicoat said anxiously; both men stopped their horses. Then from around the mountain bend to the south, far out on the sage, they saw two horses racing like the wind.

Digging his field glasses from a saddlebag, Morton adjusted them. "Landry. It's Landry and the girl. Come on," he ordered. "This is what we've been waiting for."

"What of the posse?"

"We take our chances. They ain't seen us yet." Boldly, he led away, struggling to keep under scant cover. They rode toward the wooded edge, daringly close, while Landry and the girl sped outwardly from their left and the posse advanced steadily to their right.

The possemen heard the cannonade of Dragmire's shots from the backside of town, reverberating against the bluff and echoing up the mountain. Looking around, Kurt saw Landry and his daughter, their horses thromping homeward. Shouting excitedly and pointing, he thrust his field glasses to his eyes. "It's them. It's them," he cried. "It's them riding for their lives."

"Go to them," Cole yelled. "Join 'em. Me and my deputies, we'll cover their flank in case somebody's on their tail."

Splitting, Kurt and his two henchmen spurred their way toward the south of town, where Landry would enter, while Cole and his boys galloped into the foothills.

Meanwhile, in an alder grove, Morton and Liddicoat had dismounted. Morton's round, concave features had hardened, his eyes dark slits as he watched the marshal and the girl, their horses straining to reach town. Liddicoat had braced his rifle across his saddle as he judged the distance, the speed, the needed trajectory. "Get Landry's horse," Morton said intently. "The girl's no use to us anymore. But it's Landry we want. He's carrying the money. Drop that chestnut, and the fall might break that lawman's neck. At least it'll stun him and give us a chance to get to him."

"About two hundred yards, I'd say," Liddicoat said, more to himself than to Morton. He was thinking the bullet home; he inhaled, exhaled slowly, and then squeezed off his first shot, high of the mark, to whine above the riders into the desert. As he fired his second shot, hitting slightly behind, Landry dropped his gelding back beside Kellie to urge the gray faster. Kellie was pumping and whipping the animal. The third shot caught the dapple gray in the neck, splotting it, going through, to rip out the other side. The animal screamed, lost stride, and wheezed, dropping forward, its front legs twisting out from under. Kellie shrieked as Landry swerved the chestnut into her, reached out, and lifted her free with one arm as the gray went down and rolled, hooves high, in a driving plume of dust.

Morton joined with his rifle, both men chancing wild shots as they saw Kurt and his two men heading toward the south of Midas, doubtless to assist Landry and the girl. And then they heard shooting other than their own. They looked to their right to see Sheriff Cole and four deputies bearing down on them, firing at random, the bullets ripping the sage around. "They see us," Liddicoat snarled, pulling back, the horses tossing, trying to break away.

"Let's get the hell up the canyon," Morton shouted, retreating. Both men leaped into their saddles and rode recklessly into the thick of trees.

Sheriff Cole and his men hurtled their horses after the two desperadoes, slowing as they reached the steep-wooded climb. For a hundred yards they wove through thick aspen, until Cole raised his hands. "Ain't no good. We'll never get Morton in this stuff, and we're runnin' too big a risk—too much a risk." He eyed the heights. "Let's get back to town." His men sighed agreeably, then broke into relieved laughter as they swung their horses around.

Overlooking them from a side of the canyon, Morton and Liddicoat watched the posse return. Landry had vanished into town, and Kurt and his two men were nearing. "What now?" Liddicoat looked at his leader. "You figure this beehive is too damn much for us?"

"Morton's thick lips drew taut. "Wait for me here," he said, his narrowing eyes scrutinizing the town. "I ain't beat yet."

"Meaning what?"

"I'm going into town."

"You're what?"

"I'm going in."

"How?"

"Like I done in Broken Bluffs."

"You don't have a chance," Liddicoat said incredulously. "There's an army of gun toters in there."

"They've all been drawn to the south of town."

"But the money—how you going to get that now?"

Morton smiled maliciously. "If I can't have the money, I may just settle for Landry."

Upon seeing Jenson arrested, Riles had retreated to some outbuildings that lined a series of holding pens on the southeast side of town, to think things over. With the sheriff in the field, he judged it not wise to run for freedom just yet. First, he heard the shooting in back of the Nugget Hotel, and then he heard some distant shots from the edge of Midas Canyon. Then he saw riding figures. Gradually he recognized Landry and the girl, and saw her horse go down as Landry lifted her to safety. Then he heard the posse shooting and riding along the forested edge. "Morton. It must be Morton up there," he said aloud. He watched Kurt and his two men returning at a fast pace, and knew then that he had to act quickly. Gun in hand, he mounted and slapped the big bay in an easy run toward where Landry and the girl were entering.

When Landry reined before the boardinghouse, he lowered a quaking Kellie to her feet, sprang from the stirrups with the saddlebags draped over a shoulder, and hurriedly supported her up the steps and inside. Mae, arranging furniture around the dining table, looked up, startled. "Get this girl a room, preferably one upstairs," Landry said. "Maybe she can share Eve's room. And she's going to need a doctor after what she's been through.''

''She can use Eve's room, Marshal,'' Mae said, leading the way up the stairs with a key. ''I'm afraid I've failed you. That girl's hardly been here. She walked out every night. I couldn't stop her. In fact, she's gone now.''

Exhausted and shaken by the long ordeal, Kellie murmured, ''Thank God it's all over,'' and sank, almost in a faint, as Landry caught her and swung her up in his arms.

He carried her to Eve's room, where he laid her gently on the bed. ''She's going to need a woman's attention,'' he said. ''But she'll be all right. Mostly, it's the letdown now.'' He looked at Mae. ''I've got to find Sheriff Cole. I think I saw him and his boys out on the hill riding in. Then I'll get a doctor.'' Landry looked around at Eve's luggage and toiletries and wondered fearfully about her.

''Stay with her for a moment, I'll get some hot water,'' Mae announced, hurrying downstairs toward the kitchen.

Riles hitched his horse in back of the boardinghouse and slipped into the kitchen through the rear door, where he surprised a cook. He dropped the man unconscious with a blow of his barrel across the skull. Hearing somebody approaching, he stepped behind the door as Mae entered to see the cook on the floor; before she could cry out, the outlaw grasped her and brought her to him, pinning her against him with his left arm, his hand across her open mouth. ''You couldn't have arrived at a better time, lady. You're a gift from heaven.'' He grinned cruelly, pushing the wide-eyed woman ahead of him, back into the hallway to the base of the stairs, his revolver against her side but pointing ahead. Two curious patrons seeing the action fled out a side door.

At that moment a terrified Eve, racing up the front steps and across the porch, rushed in, to freeze at the sight of the gunman holding a helpless Mae.

Hearing Eve's anguished gasp, Landry stepped out of the

room, the saddlebags still across his left shoulder. Through the balusters of the balcony, he first saw a stricken Eve, the fingers of both hands thrust against her mouth. Then he saw Riles, his eyes steel-cold, a faint smile creasing his face with keen pleasure. As the marshal's head appeared, the outlaw leveled his cocked revolver at Mae's temple.

Dragmire, pursuing Eve, could not fire at her in full view of everyone. He saw her dash through the gate and up the porch of the boarding house, heard her cry for help, and saw a man, lounging on a bench, stand up, bewildered. Not wishing to confront anyone else, Dragmire veered off and ran to the back of the house, noting the convenience of Riles's horse. He discovered a kitchen door open. Checking the knife in the sheath at the base of his neck, he slid inside to see the cook on the floor. Stealthily, he moved into the hall, where he could see Riles holding Mae while confronting Eve, her face bloodless. Not wishing to be seen, he slipped to the side, into an open coat closet below the staircase, and waited.

"Well, well, Mr. Marshal," Riles said coolly, "looks like you've come full circle." He was eyeing Landry, judging whether to chance a killing shot, but the balustrade stretched between them, offering only a part of the upper torso.

Landry fingered the butt of his revolver; he stood slightly crouched, waiting. "Don't be a fool," he said heartily. "This place will be surrounded. I saw Sheriff Cole and his men riding this way."

"And so did I, but you and them ain't gonna let these here women get shot. Now first, you drop that big gun of yours down the stairs." Landry hesitated. "Now!" Riles barked. Slowly, Landry lifted his gun loose, leaned over, and sent it bumping and sliding heavily down most of the stairs. Watching, Riles had an audacious tilt of his head. The searing anguish in the faces of Mae and Eve was overwhelming. "Now that belt across your shoulder, toss it over the balcony."

Riles's and Landry's eyes held riveted to each other as the marshal removed the ransom bags and sent them crashing below. Behind Landry an unsteady Kellie appeared in the door frame, her face white upon hearing Riles's voice. Sensing her presence, Landry said, "For God's sake, get back."

But Riles heard. "I know the Kurt girl's up there; send her down. Me and her, we've become good friends."

"Oh please, God, not with him," Kellie whimpered.

"She was hurt when her horse got killed," Landry countered. "She can't ride. Take her with you and she'll die on you, and you'll have nothing then. You'll be gunned down like a mad dog. Leave all the women, Riles, take me instead."

Riles blinked, not knowing what to believe. Momentarily disconcerted, he laughed contemptuously. "Not you, Landry, not you. I won't square off with you. I ain't that foolish. I'll take one of the women here. I'll leave her at some ranch along the way, once I'm certain no lawman's dogging me." He scowled at Eve. "You, pretty lady, open one of them saddlebags." His eyes darted from the girl to Mae to the outside windows, up to Landry. Her fingers nervously fumbling, Eve managed to unlatch one and open it to reveal the sacks of gold and the slabs of cash. Her back to Riles, she reached into her dress pocket and felt the derringer, but her icy fingers couldn't quite grasp it. Satisfied, Riles motioned her back near him, his gun remained cocked to Mae's head.

"Give up, Riles," Landry coaxed. "I'll see to it you get a fair trial."

"Sure you will."

Joyfully, Franz Kurt and his two men left their horses beside Landry's chestnut and clomped up the steps. "Look out," Eve cried. Riles sent two shots through the door, nearly winging Kurt. Yelling, the men tumbled from the porch to take cover, guns drawn.

"Get out of here, Kellie," Landry muttered between tight

teeth. "There's a fire ladder outside your window. Get out there."

Motioning Eve past him, Riles suddenly dragged Mae out of Landry's sight, then flung her to the side, where she fell on her knees; like a striking rattlesnake, he grasped Eve's wrist, jerking her to him. "I'm taking you, pretty lady, you're my ticket out."

At that instant Willard Dragmire stepped from the closet and blasted Riles's midsection almost point-blank. Screaming, Eve rolled to the side. A staggering, backpedaling Riles, his face contorted, devastated, swayed his revolver. He racketed a wild shot at Dragmire, who dodged and ran to the kitchen, but Dragmire spun around, off balance, to punch a bullet at Eve, who was clinging to a lower baluster. She dropped, mewing, as the gunsmith disappeared.

Landry, with a small revolver in his left hand, the one he'd hid in his belt, had come down the stairs to pick up his tossed gun when Dragmire's bullets sent Riles stumbling back to crash into the wall near the front door. A picture shattered off the wall. The outlaw held his belly; blood squirmed between his fingers, his shocked features registered dismay. Glazed, he saw Landry and tried to raise his revolver again. Both Landry's guns bucked. The multiple blasts spun Riles to pitch headlong across a lounge chair. Kellie, who had reappeared in the doorway, screeched, "Kill him! Kill him!"

Rushing past a bleeding Eve, Landry hop-skipped down the hall, remarkably agile with his injured leg. He kicked open the kitchen door to see the cook cowering under a table.

Dragmire had stumbled outside, his spindly legs and arms rubbery as he turned one way, then the other, for Brent Cole and his men had arrived in a whirl of dust to join the Kurt clan in surrounding the boardinghouse. "Halt, whoever you are, halt!" Cole ordered. Dragmire saw Riles's frightened horse prancing out of reach. "Throw down your gun," Cole called.

Panicking, shooting blindly toward Cole's voice, Dragmire dodged clumsily back into the kitchen, a hail of bullets splattering the area. As he entered, Landry caught him across the head with a gun barrel, crumpling his hat, which partially cushioned the impact; the freakish body hit the floor, the man's gun flipping away. Landry sank his guns in place, picked up Dragmire, and backhanded him so hard, he sent the man into a slow, top-heavy pitch through the kitchen door and up the hall. He sprawled there, sliding not far from where Mae cradled Eve in her arms. Dazed, Dragmire looked up and pulled the knife from the sheath at the back of his neck.

Kellie, standing at the base of the stairs, cried out incredulously, ''Willard Dragmire!''

A stupefied Dragmire looked up at her, knife in hand, as Landry once again hop-skipped his way, to swing his right foot mightily, knocking the gunsmith senseless.

(15)

Timidly, the cook came out of hiding to stand bleary-eyed and perplexed. Kellie and Franz Kurt embraced emotionally. "Thank God, you're safe," he bubbled. "I'll give you hell later." Then the girl lost her composure and sobbed.

Landry and Mae steadied Eve while opening her back bodice and pulling down the bloodied corset. Dragmire's bullet had grazed her backside, possibly missing a direct hit because the gunsmith had been darting for his life. "You're awful lucky, girl," said Landry. "An inch and a half farther and he would have got you in the lungs." Eve squinted her eyes in pain and in sober realization. Grimacing, she clutched the marshal, held him, and she, too, cried. Landry comforted Eve as a tearful Kellie looked on; and when she had calmed, he said evenly, "This man behind me." He referred to a shackled Dragmire, his head bowed, his eyes averted, as Cole and a deputy stood over him. "He was after you. Could he be connected with what you witnessed that night in the Glacier Palace?"

"That man." She motioned to Dragmire and trembled. "That's him. That's the man I saw coming out of Virginia Sue's room the night she was murdered." Both Kurt and Kellie watched, listening.

"Dragmire! The gunsmith!" Landry said mechanically, as if trying to focus his thoughts. "And he is from Broken Bluffs."

"Haven't had a chance to tell you, Dirk," Cole interjected. "But we've learned that another love dove was murdered, a night ago in Bullion. Same way, garroted, laid out like a corpse and her ear nipped."

Landry looked thoughtfully at the sheriff. "Bullion? Dragmire's a gunsmith and a salesman—that's one of the stopovers on his regular travels."

Eve's whole body quivered. "There's more." She breathed deeply and held her breath, her body rigid in physical and emotional discomfort. "I found a man dead in the Nugget Hotel, room four twenty, top floor, a strange little man named Noah Cheveny." She puckered and fought back another rush of tears. "I don't know how he died, but the place was a mess—all broken up."

"My God, Cheveny is Dragmire's boss! And what were you doing there?"

She looked at him in bewilderment and then continued, ignoring him. "Just before entering, I saw two men leaving. Scary, mean-looking types. After finding the body, I lost my senses and ran out the back entrance. That's when I saw this Dragmire person kill them both. Shot them to pieces." She recoiled. "It was horrible. I couldn't move. It was as if I were paralyzed." She spoke falteringly, her mind distant. "He saw me then. I never thought I could identify him—but when I saw those eyes—oh God, those eyes, and then he recognized me. That's when he started after me. Oh God, I was scared."

"It's all right," Landry said in a warm, fatherly tone; he touched her arm.

"I'll get some more water and cloths," said Mae, rising.

Cole, who had been listening with keen interest, pulled Dragmire to his feet. The gunsmith, rocky still from Landry's blows, almost lost his balance. Steadied, he stared ahead, sullenly, silently. "Take him and lock him up," Cole said to two of the deputies. "We'll get to him later."

"And I want a doctor for this girl," said Landry. "And he should check the Kurt girl, too."

"And get Doc Haden back here." The two lawmen acknowledged Cole, and with one on each side of Dragmire, they escorted him out.

Just as they reached the door, Dragmire broke his silence. He looked around at Kellie and down at Eve, his eyes like those of a tormented animal. "Bitches—tramps, all of you," he spat out.

"Get him out of here," Cole repeated, furious. A crowd was gathering in the street. He looked at his remaining deputies. "And get that carcass of Riles's covered and to the coroner." They responded dutifully.

"Help me lift this girl up to her room," Landry said. He looked at Kellie. "The doc, when he comes, I want him to check you, too." Franz Kurt nodded agreement.

To ease her pain, Cole and Landry coupled their arms to form a human chair and carried Eve upstairs. She bit her lips and dug her nails into their arms but did not say anything. When they sat her on the bed, Cole commented, "You was right, Dirk, it was the telegrapher. We arrested him and a man named Jenson. Riles was in on it, and apparently two bounty hunters named Dade and Schick."

"Jenson was a go-between. And Dade and Schick, I'm not surprised."

Mae returned shortly with steaming water and cloths; a few minutes later Dr. Haden arrived, a dapper man in a pinstripe suit. With twinkling eyes, he assured Eve that she would be doing fine in a few days—that she might carry a scar, but no one would ever know, for it was low on her back. After bathing and bandaging the grazed wound, he met with Kellie downstairs at Landry's insistence. The lawmen and Mae stayed with Eve for a time, until she relaxed and grew drowsy.

"You take it easy," Cole said to Eve as he left. "It's going to be your testimony that puts Dragmire on the gallows."

Landry accompanied the sheriff. Walking down the stairs, he said to Cole, "I'm afraid I have bad news. The posse you sent out after us—Morton and a henchman ambushed them. I don't know how bad it was, but I'm sure whoever survived will be straggling in."

"Damn," said Cole, shaking his head remorsefully. "Something just told me that I should have led them. I shouldn't have relied on a couple of men not all that experienced. And I sacrificed Kurt's men." His face wrinkled in exasperation. "Damn it. Damn it."

"But you were needed here more."

"Didn't do no good. We still didn't get Morton. Him and his partner are up on the mountain someplace scot-free."

"Believe me, you aren't the first one he escaped. It's too damn bad about the men, but we did get the girl and the money back. That may not be that much consolation, but we did what we set out to do. They were all armed volunteers taking a chance."

Cole stared ahead. "Yes, they were professionals, most of them, and all of 'em with a job to do. That's why they was sent out. I'll have to deputize a posse to go after them. Franz Kurt, he doesn't suspect yet. Got to tell him. That's going to be hard."

"You want me to tell him?" Landry offered. "I'll let him know what I think happened."

"No," said Cole, "that's what I get paid for."

Landry picked up the saddlebags with the ransom and handed them to the sheriff. "All over this. It's too bad."

"Like you said, at least Morton didn't get it."

Eventually Dr. Haden and Kellie emerged from the side room, her face tear-streamed. "How is she, Doc?" Landry asked immediately.

The doctor smiled confidently. "Exhausted, suffering from strained emotions and fear. She'll have a lot of bruises and aches and pains, especially that elbow; but with rest, a hot bath, and"—he chuckled—"her hair washed, she'll be fit as ever."

"I'm glad, Kellie."

"Me, too," said Cole. They both shook the doctor's hand as Kellie wiped the moisture from her eyes and sought her father.

"I gave her a bottle of my best liniment. Of course, that won't rub away what she went through in the cabin," the doctor said heavily. "If she told you."

"I learned."

"Sometimes those hurts don't heal so fast. But she's strong and determined, a fighter. She'll be fine."

"If I guessed right about what the doc was sayin' to you, I'd lay odds the culprit was Riles," Cole said to Landry as they turned to the business at hand.

"It was."

"If his no-good carcass was still here, I'd put a few more bullets in it."

Franz Kurt and Kellie were conversing on the porch as Landry and Cole stepped out. A crowd still waited. "It's over. Go on about your business, the show's over," the sheriff told the gawking townsfolk. Then he turned to Kurt. "Landry informs me that Morton ambushed that posse we sent after him. He don't know the details."

"The hell Morton did!" Kurt flushed.

Kellie's face clouded. "It's true. We heard shooting this morning, lots of it, and frightful screams."

"I'm going to organize some men to go after them. Find out just what the hell happened," Cole said.

"I'll have to go with you," said Kurt dolefully.

"No need," said Cole, "no need now. It's all kind of after the fact." His words trailed away.

"But I owe my men at least that." Kurt looked at his daughter, and she lowered her eyes.

An awkward silence followed; they watched the crowd disperse. Kellie suddenly blurted out, "The girl, will she be okay?"

"Eve is strong and healthy. Doc said she'll be fine," Landry assured her.

"I'm glad. I'm so glad. She seems to know you so well."

Landry pursed his lips. "She should, she's my niece."

Kellie's mouth fell open; both Cole and Kurt regarded Landry with astonishment. "I'm sorry," the girl managed.

"Now tell me, how did you know this fellow Dragmire?" Landry said in an interrogative manner.

"I didn't know him. I just knew of him." Kellie considered her words. "He was weird. At least that was my impression." She shivered. "He was a handyman in Limbo City, a drifter from the East somewhere. That was about two years ago. A girl I went to school with befriended him, you know, felt sorry for him. He, of course, was not of her level—she was a daughter of one of the small ranchers there, but that didn't matter to her." Kellie paused. "It was strange."

"Go on."

"They used to see each other, about every day after school, before she rode home. I guess they just talked a lot. She said that he was lonely and lost, that she wanted to help him."

"Anything else?"

"Yes, that he had been in a hospital back East. That he had been very sick. But I never learned the particulars. I knew that he got possessive with Mary Lynn; that's when we all told her to drop him. Of course, Mary Lynn was a flirt, and she was pretty. All the boys found her attractive. She could have had any of the fellows. That's why it surprised me, her friendship with that guy. I do think she was sincere in trying to help him. It's just that he misread it. I don't know what ever happened after that, because I went East about then."

Alert, Landry pounced. "Mary Lynn?" He looked searchingly at Kellie, then at Cole. "One of the witnesses—who was later murdered—told us that she had overhead the killer call one of the victims Mary Lynn."

"Yeah?"

"Interesting, because the prostitute's real name was Virginia Sue."

"Well, it all fits," said Cole, rubbing his chin. "Dragmire and that girl, Mary Lynn, come here to Midas about a year ago, married."

"Mary Lynn married him?" said Kellie, disturbed.

"I never knew much about her while she was alive," Cole said. "But I'll tell you, hers was a strange death, strangled by someone—someone who broke into their room here in town. It had all the details of these killings plaguin' the territory: again, the body all set out like in a coffin. There was a lot of rumors and suspicions, but nothing solid to go on. No one was ever arrested. All our investigation lead nowhere."

"Was Dragmire ever a suspect? I remember the case, but not much about it."

"Sure, but he had a witness that he had been working all day—he was a clerk then in a dry-goods store here. When he went home, he found the body."

"But he could have killed her earlier, before going to work," Landry pursued.

"Of course he could of. I thought of that," said Cole, "but try to prove it."

"What else do you remember about Mary Lynn?" Landry asked Kellie. "You said she was a flirt."

Kellie pondered before replying. Franz Kurt broke in, he was clenching and unclenching his hands. "She had the morals of an alley cat, Marshal. I heard it from my boys. I never wanted Kellie to associate with her. But unfortunately, as you have seen, she's got a mind of her own."

"Meaning?" Kellie asked.

"She wasn't your kind of friend," Kurt said.

"I liked her," Kellie fired back. "She intrigued me. Fascinated me, to tell the truth." Her eyes had a light of disobedience. "Papa, did you ever think that maybe secretly I wished I could venture into her forbidden world?"

Kurt scoffed. "For Christ's sake, child."

Cole interrupted. "I can tell you, Dirk, one of my deputies had some evidence that she may have taken favors while married to Dragmire. I know he was jealous, that he used to follow her when she left their place, and that there was some domestic fights."

"What can you tell us, Kellie?" Landry insisted.

She eyed him reflectively and surrendered in a shrug. "It's true, there was some gossip, mostly from vicious tongue waggers, I think. But what I heard made no difference to me. I liked Mary Lynn for what she was. She had spunk."

"Dragmire left after he buried the girl. He never came back as far as I know, until now," said Cole.

"He took a job as a gunsmith in Broken Bluffs," Landry noted. "And I know he traveled a lot, selling and fixing up all kinds of arms. It's uncanny."

Cole handed Kurt the saddlebags. "You and your boys best get this tucked in the bank."

Kurt took the ransom and looked at his daughter, then Landry, and smiled gratefully. "I don't now how to thank you, Marshal. I've always admired you, but sometimes I thought you were partial to some of my rivals, until now."

"They have as much right to make money as you have," Landry said without expression.

"I'm going to get my daughter back to the suite, let her freshen up and rest, and get something on those scratches. Tomorrow, we'll see about some new clothes." He looked at Cole. "I'll be back shortly, I've got to find out what happened out there to my boys."

Kellie stood on her toes and pulled Landry to her, kissing him heartily on the cheek.

Before Cole could gather volunteers, a stage arrived from the north with three additional passengers who had been picked up staggering along the road, two of them supporting a third with a thigh wound. The latter, one of Kurt's men, and the two deputies told a rapt audience of how they had been caught in a withering cross fire that morning, so unerring as to annihilate the entire posse within a few frantic minutes.

Despondent, Cole organized some townsmen with extra ponies to retrieve the bodies. One of the surviving deputies, although on the edge of collapse, offered to lead them to the site. "I'm going with them," a sobered Franz Kurt told Cole. "Those men died because of me and my daughter. I owe them that much. Besides, there's a chance someone may have survived."

Before leaving, Cole accompanied Landry to the Nugget Hotel. The story of Dragmire's capture had spread like a prairie fire. Disgruntled rumors had already bombarded the lawmen, that a growing number of citizenry wanted the killer's blood. The charged mood of a lynching had ignited the air. A prostitute might not be highly regarded but she was a woman—and any lowdown cuss who hurt or maimed or killed a human female was as intolerable as a tarantula and deserved to be stamped out. "Before long, you best get some more guards on this place," Landry told a worried Cole.

"I know that."

"And someone to watch Dragmire carefully. He just might try suicide."

"Think he's the kind?"

"I wouldn't be surprised."

Behind the Nugget the bodies of the two bounty hunters had been covered by a tarpaulin, with their boots extending. A house detective waited. Landry pulled back the cover to stare into faces gaunt with death. "Dade and Schick," he confirmed in wonderment. "What dealings did Dragmire have with them?"

"Hard telling. But I'm not surprised that they got done in. Those two have long been overdue." In the dead men's pockets they found two equal rolls of money.

"It appears that these two robbed the dead man in room four twenty," said the house detective.

"But apparently Dragmire lay in wait for them. Why?" asked Landry.

"He must have had some prior run-in with these so-called bounty hunters," Cole suggested.

"I wonder," said Landry introspectively. "As you know, there have been a number of mysterious killings around the countryside of late, all unsolved, all men of bad character."

"What are you trying to say?"

"That Dragmire's got a lot of questions to answer."

Upstairs, the lawmen found room 420 roped off, with another house detective standing guard. "I haven't touched a thing," said the man, "except to close his eyes." Cheveny lay waxen, his features frozen in horror. They examined him, then rolled him over. He had been roughed up, but there was no blood or wound. His head rolled loosely, twisting at a peculiar angle. Both lawmen looked at each other. Landry ran professional hands along the stringy vertebrae. "They broke his neck."

"Dade was big enough to do that, certainly," Cole acknowledged.

Landry picked up the pearl-handled pistol, the initials N.C. carved on the grip. "The little fellow must have surprised them and put up a struggle." Afterward, Landry and Cole pawed through his luggage, then tore open his satchel to find papers, but nothing more. They searched Cheveny's body. There was no money anywhere.

"Looks like a simple case of robbery and murder," Cole concluded.

"Maybe it's not that simple," said Landry. "Dade and Schick were mean and worthless, but they were hired guns. They took pride in that. This doesn't seem like them."

"I seen a lot of men stoop lower than a snake's belly when they got desperate or too greedy."

"Maybe so."

"Now, I did get out of the telegrapher, Hickson—the one you was onto—that Dade and Schick was in town on a job. They was to meet somebody here." Cole laughed. "That Hickson come apart, spilled his guts; he's going to be a key witness. Even that tight-mouthed Jenson gave away something to the effect that Dade and Schick had earlier business."

Landry straightened to his full height. All his senses focused on the sheriff and his words. "They were here on a job to meet someone besides the Morton members."

"That's what I gather."

"Get some help and get this body to the coroner," Landry told the detective. "Come on," he said to Cole. Hurriedly, they spiraled their way down a stairwell to the foyer.

"What are you thinkin'?" Cole asked, his features sharp with curiosity.

"Just a hunch. Eve was with Cheveny last night. There were always rumors that he was a lady's man when away from his wife." The little clerk with the squeaky voice who had harassed Eve was now on duty. "I'd like to see your register from the last couple of days," said Landry.

"Yes, Marshal," the little man piped, turning the book around and flipping some pages back. Landry checked the previous two days, and found Noah Cheveny's signature opposite room 420. He ran his finger down the scrolled names and stopped at a Mrs. Henri Smythe, room 436. "Did you register this woman?" Landry asked.

"No, sir, but I was on duty when some rough-looking characters asked for her room. I mention that because you being a marshal, that might be important, I don't know."

Landry grinned broadly, appreciatively. "It certainly does. Is she still registered?"

"No, sir, she just checked out less than an hour ago. She paid one of our boys here, to carry her luggage to Wells Fargo."

"Do you know when the next stage south goes out?"

"Yes," Cole broke in, looking at his watch. "The next one out for Broken Bluffs goes in about an hour."

"Can you describe this lady?" Landry asked the clerk.

"Middle-aged," he replied without hesitation, "with a thin face, and grayish hair pulled back. A no-nonsense kind, if you know what I mean. She could take care of herself, I'm sure."

"Thanks," said Landry, and motioned to Cole. "Let's go."

"To Wells Fargo, I take it?"

"To Wells Fargo."

(16)

Henrietta Cheveny sat waiting calmly in a corner of the station. Her normally dour features had taken on a stoical repose. Then she saw the lawmen entering; her mouth tightened, her body stiffened. Landry walked up to her, his thumbs dug into his belt. "I'm afraid you're going to have to come with us, Mrs. Cheveny."

"Why?" she snapped, thrusting out her pointed jaw. Her hazel eyes regarded him with trepidation.

"A Mr. Dade and a Mr. Schick have implicated you in a little messy doing here in town."

She looked at him straight on, impassively. "I have no idea what you're talking about."

"I think you do, Mrs. Cheveny. The two men, Dade and Schick, who you hired."

"I never heard of them." After she spoke, her lips tightened.

"The clerk remembers them asking for your room."

"That doesn't mean anything."

"The fact that we have a witness who saw them leave your husband's room after they killed him, does."

"You can't prove anything."

"I can see by your saddened shock that you know he's dead. And it's interesting that you are here in town."

Henrietta Cheveny shifted her body. "I came here because I didn't trust my husband. And yes, I found his body. And I panicked. But I hired nobody to kill him."

"Well, it will be their words against yours. Perhaps you have heard there is no honor among thieves. They claim you hired them. And they'll swear to that in court."

"They're lying."

"Why should they? Why should they even bother to mention you, a respectable businesswoman, unless they had a deal with you?"

"I tell you they're lying about my hiring to kill Noah." Landry saw her hand flick involuntarily and her lips tremble.

"We have a very solid case, Mrs. Cheveny. Premeditated, planned murder."

She sighed deeply, her words barely audible. "Already, they have involved me. I heard shooting. You arrested them?"

"Yes."

She sighed deeply in resignation. "I might have gotten away with it, but I doubt it. Everything has gone wrong. Besides, it's all over," she said, almost with relief.

"Your husband was cheating on you?"

She looked at him in mild surprise. "He had cheated for years," she said simply. "With cheap prostitutes. And he squandered our hard-earned money on the likes of them. He thought he was fooling me, but I knew."

"And you hired Dade and Schick to kill him?"

"No. Oh, no, not to kill him. God, no. He was my husband." Her hazel eyes clouded and her mouth puckered. "I wanted to frighten him, believe me, that was all. I hired them just to frighten him."

"We're going to have to ask you to come with us, Mrs. Cheveny," Landry said. "We can talk in privacy along the way." The woman nodded, retaining her composure, and rose. Landry held her elbow and escorted her out while Cole retrieved her luggage. As they sauntered down the street, Landry said gently, "Tell me."

Mrs. Cheveny swallowed dryly and said in a squeaky voice, "I searched his satchel the day before he left. I suspected what I found—a lot of money that he had been cheating me out of. I gave Dade and Schick part of it; the rest I was going to give them tonight in Broken Bluffs.''

"Well, they already helped themselves to whatever your husband had on him, enough to choke a horse, I might add.''

She was taken back. "He had even more money?'' She lowered her head and shook it slowly.

"I'm curious, Mrs. Cheveny,'' Landry said. "Why did you come to Midas? Had you remained in Broken Bluffs, no one could have proven anything against you. Even with the unfortunate end of your husband, you could have played the bereaved wife.''

She said frankly, unguarded, "For once I had to see it with my own eyes. I suffered with rumors for years. This time I had to see, and I did—a beautiful young blonde half his age. She was so beautiful. With all of these horrible murders, I thought I could frighten her—maybe scare some sense into her. I guess, really, I wanted to punish her. She was so beautiful.'' Henrietta Cheveny had a contracted look of inner pain. "Schick and Dade rode in early this morning. Not a half hour later, I saw her leave Noah's room. I had the skinny one, Schick, follow her, to give her a scare. But it didn't work, because she came back. As for the money I owed those two brutes, I didn't dare bring the remaining payment with me. Only in Broken Bluffs, when I was sure it had been done, would they receive it.''

"You were wise there. You say you didn't want to kill your husband, how then did you find his body?''

"This afternoon from my room, I was watching for him to return. The two men were waiting with me.'' She paused and tried to find the words. "At first I was so happy when those two pushed in. I could see fear and shock on Noah's face.'' Her breath came with difficulty from the emotion and the effort of both walking and talking.

Landry, still holding her elbow, stopped her and turned her to face him as Cole came up beside them. "Tell me all of it now, the truth. I can help you at the hearing.''

She nodded. "While Noah took a circular route to see one of his customers, overdue on some payments, I came directly to Midas on a later stage. The plan was to shake my husband up. They were to claim the girl was their exclusive property. I demanded he not be hurt, only roughed up a little and threatened." Her eyes had a begging look. "You must believe that, Marshal. Ours was not the happiest marriage, but I couldn't kill him. I thought if these men could intimidate him, just maybe he might see the folly of his ways."

"What happened then?"

"After the two went in, I could hear noises, like a struggle, and then they came rushing out. I expected them to run, but when that girl appeared . . ."

"Yes?"

"She knocked and waited and then went in. A few moments later she came back out, almost delirious, petrified, like she was about to faint. I knew then that something was desperately wrong. I saw her flee in the direction of the two I hired. Then I heard shooting and a scream. The girl came running back even more terrified. I think she tried to get someone to help her. And behind her, shortly, came a man with two guns. He had a crazed look."

"You saw all this?"

"Yes, I had my door open just a crack and I could see down the whole hallway."

"What about your husband?" The three commenced a casual stroll.

"Below where the shots came from, I heard a crowd gathering. Fortunately, most of the patrons were out of their rooms, it being afternoon. So I stole down to Henry's room." She choked and coughed. "The instant I saw him, I knew he was dead. A terrible, terrible mistake. He must have struggled and fought back. I saw his pistol off to the side. They had somehow killed him."

"They broke his neck, Mrs. Cheveny."

"Oh God."

"Those two you hired. How did you meet their likes?"

"They had been patrons of mine. Also, they sold me guns at reduced prices, taken from their bounty hunts. The little scheme just came quite naturally, with their profession, my frustration, and with Noah being away on his little excursions." The woman's severe features had strangely softened and paled like malleable clay. Her faded eyes stared afar. "Maybe Dade or Schick will confess and I will be cleared."

"Those two were killed by that crazed man you saw running down the hall," Landry said softly. "It's a long story."

"Oh God," she sobbed. "You tricked me, Marshal. That's what you meant, if I had stayed in Broken Bluffs nobody could have proved anything against me."

"Yes, I did. But it all would have come out sooner or later."

"I didn't mean it to end this way. You must understand, I just wanted to teach him a lesson. I wanted to hurt him just a little. He had hurt me for so long." She looked earnestly at Landry. "Revenge is so empty." From an alley across the way a Mexican in a white sombrero watched intently.

At the jail, nine volunteers, including Kurt, were waiting with a dozen extra horses. All the available deputies, those left, had been stationed to guard Dragmire from any crowds with retribution on their mind. Summer nights in Midas grew long and restless, especially after patrons had built bravado with too much whiskey. After locking Mrs. Cheveny up, Cole prepared to lead the men on a grisly mission. "What do you think a judge will do to that lady?" he asked Landry.

"She's guilty, of course, but my guess would be a dismissal, as the sympathy will be with her."

"It was good thinking, Landry." Cole grinned broadly. "Right away, you tricked that woman into confessing."

"She wanted to confess," said Landry. "I did nothing but give her a chance."

Meanwhile, from the Zephyr Hotel, a deputy had brought

in Dragmire's luggage and his rifle. Since juicy rumors were flying about, with everyone talking, a cleanup woman had reported the luggage and the strange man who had been acting suspicious. An alert clerk there put Dragmire's description and the story of the arrest together and notified authorities. A receipt from the livery stable, a key to a wagon box, and the lawmen soon had two trunks before them. Landry unlatched the first, a heavy one with compartments containing various guns, tools, and ammunition. In the second, a suitcase, they uncovered a derringer, a toiletry set, shirts and long johns, another suit and necktie like the one Dragmire had on, plus a bulky coat, a slouch hat, a thick scarf, and a piece of rope. "The garrote," Landry remarked.

Cole shook his head. "Never seen anything like it."

After Cole and the posse left, Landry entered Dragmire's cell. A guard locked the door after him. The marshal talked to the silent prisoner for some fifteen minutes. The gunsmith remained morose, withdrawn, unresponsive, his eyes myopic, unblinking. "We will have to move you out of the territory for your safety and for a fair trial," Landry told him. "You might find a judge more considerate if you wrote out a confession. It would save everybody a lot of time and pain."

For the first time Dragmire looked at Landry with an expression of disbelief, and disgust, almost of contempt. Without reply, he looked back down.

"Eventually, we'll ferret out every little piece of information, every detail about you and the girls. That won't be hard now. What I don't understand is you and the bounty hunters. Did they cheat you somewhere along the way? Did they do you wrong?"

Dragmire's head came slowly up. For a considerable time he looked at Landry. Then he hissed with vitriolic hatred that steamed from somewhere in his being. "Their kind won't hurt no more. They and others like 'em deserve to die."

"And you took it upon yourself to be judge, jury, and executioner."

"If them judges and you lawmen done your work, there wouldn't need to be good citizens out there doing it for you." His eyes blazed.

"You don't mean good citizens, you mean vigilantes."

"Same difference," Dragmire snarled.

"And you've killed their kind before, haven't you?"

Aware suddenly that he was talking too much, Dragmire held in words he had been ready to blurt and turned away.

"There have been a number of strange killings of late, all unaccounted for, all of questionable character. It's interesting, wouldn't you say?"

Dragmire could not contain himself. "Whoever done it saved you and a lot of others their lives."

"Maybe," said Landry, "but you see, the U.S. government and the people didn't grant you that right. You granted that right to yourself."

Dragmire retreated once again into a sullen pose.

Lost in thought, Landry, leading the chestnut, left the law office and headed for the boardinghouse, his strides long and authoritative despite his tired body, which ached from the days of stress and demands. He wanted a shave and a bath and maybe several of Mae's good meals. He would take a room for a couple of days if she had one available. At least until he was certain Kellie was all right and until Eve could travel. He was presently at a loss about what to do with her. Somehow, he had to turn her life around with new, meaningful directions. Except for the Eve problem, he felt generally good, a sense of near completion that he often experienced when a case was closing. It bothered him, certainly, that so many men had been sacrificed. And, of course, Morton was still out there someplace with Cheveny's gun collection. The rare pieces were of little value to the gun dealer now, but at least Morton's major scheme had been foiled. Landry continued south along the main thoroughfare, busy as always. He did not notice or recognize the Mexican wrapped in a blanket at the edge of an alley across the way, his white sombrero tipped low.

Rattlesnake Morton secreted a Colt .45 in his right hand under the serape. He had not been so close to Landry since his trial, which had resulted in a prison term. He both hated and respected the lawman. But the seething wrath of vengeance was not so overwhelming that he could simply kill the man in a rash act of sprayed gunfire. He wanted to see Landry's face, to have Landry know who had played the final hand. Morton, always intuitive and self-possessed, hesitated now. Although adept with a knife, he knew Landry to be too far away for an effective throw. And a gunshot would attract attention. A number of deputies still wandered about town. To gun down Landry could mean his own demise if he could not effectively hide or flee to the mountain. The best way, he decided, was to walk toward Landry, who seemed preoccupied. As he passed, he would merely call the lawman's name, and as the man turned about, he would plunge the knife into his heart. In that shocked instant before death, Landry would see and would know. Quick, deft, silent. And then he, Rattlesnake Morton, would swing astride the chestnut—a fitting booty for a perfect coup.

Morton shifted his revolver to his left hand, in case Landry did not succumb or if someone tried to interfere. He removed the sixteen-inch bowie knife from its sheath and stepped out with determination.

Suddenly, the chestnut balked slightly, snorted, and tossed its head enough to snap Landry from his reverie. "What's the matter, old fellow?" Landry asked, tugging the reins taut as the animal shook its head and pranced, its eyes rolling white. "No snake in this place." And then Landry caught the irony of his comment and stopped, his eyes canvassing the street. The animal had always had an uncanny sense of danger, and Landry had always obeyed. Through habit, the lawman slapped the bottom of his coat behind his holster. Wagons creaked by; people crisscrossed the street. Landry eyed them all, eyed the doorways, the windows in the second stories. A high ore wagon came up from behind and passed them. The chestnut seemed to calm. "What spooked you, old fellow?" For a more commanding view, Landry climbed into the saddle.

Morton, marching toward Landry, welcomed the approaching ore wagon. It would hide his advance, and when it passed, he would appear unexpectedly beside the lawman. But he hesitated again. He had seen the horse react—a remarkable creature, somehow sensing something threatening in his actions or his demeanor. Then Morton saw Landry tense in a defensive stance to look around. And then the marshal mounted. As the ore wagon rumbled by, Morton fell alongside it, keeping it between him and Landry as he moved away. When next to the alley, he veered off and headed swiftly into its protective narrows. At last, certain he was out of the marshal's sight, he straightened up and breathed evenly, replaced his gun and knife, and returned to his waiting horse out back. From his saddle he looked across the backside of the town and said, "Almost, Landry. Almost. But there will be another time and another place." He spurred the animal toward the mountain.

Mae stood in the front doorway of her boardinghouse, watching Landry dismount. "How's Eve?" he inquired anxiously.

"She's fine. She had some soup and is resting."

"She asleep?" He came inside, clomping heavily.

"No, she's been waiting for you to return. If I may say, you're the one that looks tired." Mae's face had a tender, motherly aura. "You best rest up a few days. I got a room available down the way from Kellie, and a big roast in the oven."

"I am tired, very tired, and think I will accept your offer," Landry said gratefully. "But there's much to do still. I must see Kellie before she and her father leave. I must be sure that she's all right. But for now, Eve's my first concern.''

''I apologize that I didn't handle Eve better. You did ask me to look out for her.''

''Doesn't matter. You're not a deputy, and she's awful headstrong.''

Mae looked around to see if anyone were listening, and then said confidentially, ''I've seen her type many times before. It's sad but true that it's impossible for some girls to mend their ways. It's the easy money, and maybe, too, the temptation and excitement of sin. But I'm convinced that most ladies of the night like their work, if you know what I mean.''

Landry smiled wryly. ''I understand,'' he commented, then more to himself added, ''that's probably what Willard Dragmire learned about his wife and hated in others.'' He moved wearily up the stairs as if his bad leg were troubling him.

Eve lay on her stomach, dozing. She opened her eyes. ''I heard you coming.''

''How you feel?'' He stood back so that she could see him with ease.

''Uncomfortable. But that's to be expected.''

''You'll be sore for a time. But you'll be up and around shortly.''

''Then where are you sending me, Uncle?''

He looked pointedly at her. ''It depends. Have you learned anything?''

''Yes, there are dangerous people out there.''

''Very dangerous.''

''That creature named Dragmire, why would he do such things?'' Her eyes had the look of a wounded fawn.

''A twisted mind—two personalities in conflict,'' said Landry somberly. ''The self-imposed do-gooder bent on clearing the world of sin, but who was the most sinful of all.''

''I'll have to testify, won't I?''

''When and wherever they decide to try him.''

''In the meantime?''

''If I set you up in one of the bigger towns—Virginia City, Limbo, one of those—if I look in on you every so often, can you make an honest go of it?''

''Doing what?''

''We'll find something—clerk, maid, waitress, anything to start with, until you can work your way into a solid job. You're pretty, you're bright. You could do it.''

After an extended pause, she replied candidly: ''I'll try, but I don't know. All I can do is try.''

Landry blinked thoughtfully and concluded that at this point he didn't know, either.

About the Author

Kenn Sherwood Roe, a community college instructor at Shasta College in Redding, California, has been an administrator, a rancher, park ranger, navy reservist, public relations man, and the author of several novels and more than two hundred articles and short stories. He once worked at CBS Television City, Hollywood, in production.

He and his wife, Doris, have three children and an apricot toy poodle, Andre Phillipe, who enjoys the seashore as much as does his master, Kenn.